I0732790

THE MALICIOUS MAYOR

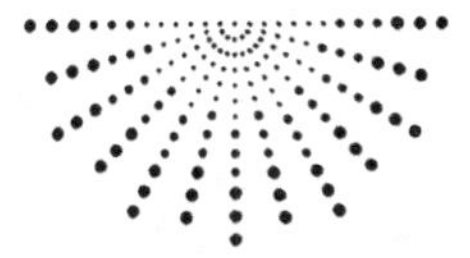

MARTIN BROWN

A BOOK BY

SIGNAL
PRESS

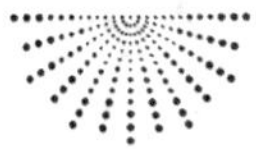

On the morning following a powerful overnight storm, Rob Timmons looked out his bedroom window, anxious to see what debris might have blown onto his deck.

Nothing serious, he quickly concluded—the usual small branches, along with a scattering of leaves. Given how loud the rain was beating against the windows and the roof, he imagined the scene would have been far worse.

The cozy home he shared with his wife, Karin, and two children, Micah and Alice, was passed down from his grandfather to his parents. Rob's family were the third and fourth generations to inhabit a property built for twenty-two thousand dollars and now worth infinitely more.

From his home, constructed on the first of several hills that climb up toward the Marin Headlands, Rob could see the impact of the storm on the Sausalito "flats." The flats consisted of two parallel streets: one called Caledonia Street, the other,

Bridgeway. The latter had been named after the completion of the Golden Gate Bridge in 1938, which connected Marin, Sonoma, and Napa counties to San Francisco.

Rob was pleased to discover that the storm's impact appeared to be minimal throughout the area.

A habitually early riser, Rob grabbed his cellphone when it began to chirp loudly. Not wanting to rouse the family on a Sunday morning, he walked toward the kitchen, the farthest point from the home's three bedrooms. Looking at the phone's display, Rob said softly, "I thought you like to sleep in on Sundays!"

"I do," replied Eddie Austin, a childhood friend of Rob's, who was the lead investigative detective for the Marin County Sheriff's Department. "Sharon and Aaron are sound asleep, and at six-thirty on a Sunday morning I usually would be too. But something's come up."

"I'm all ears." As always, Rob was anxious to hear anything newsworthy in a town that often had too little news to hold the attention of the readers of his weekly community paper.

"I'm getting in the car to head over to Hurricane Gulch; there was a slide overnight that took out a house. I thought you might want to join me."

"Anyone hurt?"

"Don't know yet. The fire department and Sausalito police are there now. More importantly, the house that went down the hill was Mary Anderson's."

"As in, our esteemed mayor?" Rob asked.

"You got it, pal."

"Absolutely I want to go!"

"I thought you'd be interested. I'll swing by your place in a few minutes."

"Great! Let me throw on some clothes. I'll see you in five."

Rob raced back to his bedroom. As quietly as possible he jumped into a pair of pants, he had tossed over a chair the night before. He grabbed an old flannel shirt from his closet and a comfortable gray sweatshirt to go over it. He pushed into his sneakers using his index finger as a shoehorn, not wanting to take the time to unlace and re-lace them before racing out the front door.

Eddie pulled up seconds after Rob quietly closed the front door behind him.

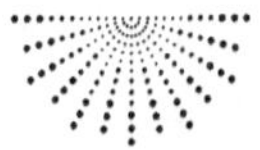

CHAPTER TWO

"Before you called, I was looking out my living room window to see how much damage the downpour and winds did overnight. It didn't look like we got hit too bad. At least that's what I thought until you told me about the slide."

"I was thinking the same thing driving over to pick you up. But Hurricane Gulch has always been prone to slides. It takes the brunt of most of our storms."

"Funny how it's such a short distance south of us, yet storms whip through the gulch like nowhere else in town."

"It gets a bad slide about once every ten years," Eddie reminded Rob. "Some small, some big, and on rare occasions, one that's deadly. Do you remember the slide that happened when we were kids—the house on Crescent Avenue, where what's-her-name died?"

"Yeah, I remember. But what was her name?"

Eddie thought for a moment: "Mrs. Simmons!"

"Yep, you're right, Simmons." Rob nodded. "She had just come home fifteen minutes earlier from a concert she attended with a couple of friends in San Francisco. They dropped her off a little before eleven. They think she must have stepped into her kitchen to make herself a cup of tea."

Eddie nodded. "I remember it was one of those pounding winter rains that came on top of two weeks of steady rainfall. Always a dangerous combination."

"Very much like the weather we've had this rain season," Rob added. "Long soaking rains. Get enough without a break of several days so the moisture has a chance to soak in, and the hill can give way."

"I remember people talking about how sad it was. Three-quarters of her house was nearly untouched by the slide. But the kitchen and utility room were smashed like a freight train had slammed into them." Eddie noted with a shutter. "What a terrible way to go.

"Just a case of being in the wrong place at the wrong time. I'm sure you see a lot of that in your line of work."

Eddie nodded as Rob's mind went into overdrive imagining the shock waves that would quickly passthrough Sausalito if the city's long-serving mayor had met the same fate as the widow Simmons. "Wow...*Mary Anderson*! If this slide took her out? That, Eddie, would be one hell of a story!"

"Don't get too excited, Newsboy. I know how you must be dreaming up headlines right now, but perhaps Madam Mayor had the good fortune to spend the night at a friend's house."

"I can't help but get excited. Sausalito's a town where the closure of a downtown burger joint could be my lead story."

"What do you mean, 'could be?'" Eddie asked with a snort. "Bridgeway Burgers closed up because of two consecutive years of slow summer tourist seasons, that was your lead story just a few weeks ago."

"In my defense, that place was not only popular with tourists, but a lot of locals went there as well."

"I suppose you get a pass then. With local editions of *The Standard* coming out every week in Sausalito, Mill Valley, the Tiburon/Belvedere Peninsula, and Ross Valley, that's a lot of ink chasing too few stories," Eddie said with a shrug. "Let's just say for you and your weekly, the closing of a burger joint wasn't one of your finest moments."

"I won't argue the point. But listen, Eddie, if Mary Anderson, the mean queen of Sausalito politics for twenty-five plus years, is lying dead under tons of mud…there's a story that will stop people in their tracks."

"Going for The Pulitzer Prize on this one, Rob?"

"I wouldn't go that far. But increasing readership and advertising revenue never hurts the cause of a free press."

Eddie parked his car on Main Street. "We better walk up from here, Rob. Between the fire trucks and the heavy equipment, they'll be looking to bring in, I don't need to throw another obstacle in their path by parking too close to the action."

The downpours of the previous night had given way to scattered rays of sunshine and the first pleasant morning the town had enjoyed in over a week. Sausalito, which might go six or more months with barely a drop of rain, can have two, three, or more months of nearly relentless winter rains. This is particularly true on the south end of this small city.

Many of these rainy days bring little more than a persistent cold mist. But occasionally days of pelting rains can cause the soft soils along the ragged edges of the 101 Freeway, which sits atop a ridge of the Marin Headlands, to crumble. Most often, these slides are merely a scattering of some loose rocks and soil that do little harm to the homes below the ridge. But once every ten or twenty years, a large chunk tears free along the relatively short distance between the Robin Williams Rainbow Tunnel and the entrance to the Golden Gate Bridge. Soil, rocks, and vegetation then plunge past the homes of Sausalito Boulevard, Crescent Avenue, and Lower Crescent, bringing with it an avalanche of mud, rocks, and trees that gains significant force as it increases in speed. When this happens no person, car, or house in its path is safe.

As Eddie and Rob walked steadily up the hill, it became increasingly apparent that this had not been one of the fortunate times when a slide passed without causing significant damage. From a higher vantage point, the two longtime friends got their first glimpse of the horrifying scene.

"Wow, Eddie. If Mary Anderson was home when this hit, it's hard to imagine she survived!"

"You're right, Rob. The queen bee of Sausalito politics might have met her maker. Feel free to use that line in your story if that turns out to be the case. Just don't quote me."

"I wouldn't worry about that," Rob chuckled.

A short time later, Rob and Eddie were talking to Bill Vogel, who'd succeeded Rob's dad as Sausalito's fire chief over a decade earlier. They stood on a parking deck just above Crescent Avenue, just one house over from the gaping hole in the hillside that the slide had created.

"It's remarkable to see the force of one of these slides, and the damage they can do," Eddie said, awestruck by what he was seeing.

"Thank God they happen rarely," Vogel replied. "Just look at this! Mature trees toppled like saplings, and a home cut in two. Two-thirds of the home lying upside down in the backyard of a house on Crescent Avenue, the other third about sixty feet uphill, still clinging to its foundation. It looks like something a tornado could do."

"That's Mayor Anderson's house, although it's hardly recognizable," Rob said. "Over the years, I've been to several receptions at her home. This is just unbelievable."

"You're right, Rob. It's her house, alright." Vogel replied. "It was built by her father. Both of them lived there until he went into an assisted living facility many years ago."

"I'm guessing he's been gone over ten years now," Rob added.

"That sounds about right," Vogel added with a nod. "Nasty old fellow as I remember."

"That was certainly the consensus of those who knew Gus Anderson," Rob replied with a smile.

Eddie listened without comment, looking down on the wreckage of the house lying on its roof, partially swallowed by mud that looked to be six feet deep. "Has there been any attempt to get into the half of the house that got sheared off?"

"Not yet Eddie. Too dangerous at this point. The remaining portion of the structure is not at all stable. Two fire and rescue units are coming over from the city. SFFD has got some rescue and recovery apparatus we don't have."

"I imagine someone has reached out to Mary Anderson?" Rob asked.

"We called the home and cell numbers we have for her.

Nothing," Vogel said with a shrug. "If she's in that wreckage, I don't like her chances. Perhaps the most hopeful sign is that the half of the house that escaped relatively unscathed includes Mayor Anderson's bedroom, so perhaps she had a late night and is sleeping through our attempts to reach her, or her phone is out of reach, or turned off."

"That's a glimmer of hope, I suppose," Eddie said.

"On the other hand, she would not be the first person to fall asleep in a recliner on a Saturday night while watching television," Rob added.

"You're right, Rob. I've done that once or twice myself," Vogel replied as he patted Rob's shoulder. "We'll just have to wait and see."

"Whatever happens, you and your team are in for a long day and possibly a long night as well," Eddie said. "We should get out of the chief's way, Rob, and let him do his work."

"Nothing we're facing at the moment is going to be easy, or quickly resolved. I'm happy we're getting backup from San Francisco. Just surveying the wreckage of the house down below, the recovery effort is going to be a long haul. That much seems certain."

"I assume you also requested a location search of her cellphone?" Eddie asked.

"We did. The last call was made from the mayor's home shortly before seven o'clock last night, approximately nine hours before the hill gave way."

"That's not good," Rob said, instantly regretting his blurting out the obvious.

"Rob, when your dad was fire chief, I often heard him say we have to resist the temptation to get ahead of ourselves. This is going to be one of those times. We'll just have to be patient and take this one step at a time."

Eddie and Rob walked back down the hill in silence. Both were turning up their collars as a chilled wind started to stir and a light rain began to fall. They watched as they stepped to avoid small rocks and other debris that might cause them to slip and at best embarrass themselves, or at worst sustain an injury.

As soon as they shut the car's doors and Eddie turned the key in the ignition, Rob asked, "I suppose it's possible that Queen Mary's time in power has come to an end?"

"Funny you should say that. Looking down on the ruined half of Anderson's house, I kept thinking what a dramatic end this would be to her long reign if indeed she's buried under a ton of mud. Either way, you're going to have a big story for this week's edition."

"I've got to tell Holly about this."

"Rob, it's seven forty-five! She might shoot you for banging on her door before eight on a Sunday morning."

"After all the nasty things she has said about Mary Anderson over the years, she might shoot me if she finds out I knew about this and *didn't* come tell her."

"The old damned-if-you-do and damned-if-you-don't conundrum," Eddie said with a half-smile.

"Exactly! But if there's one thing Holly hates more than an early wake-up call on a Sunday, it's not being one of the first to know about a big story. And at this moment, I don't know if we've ever had a bigger story than this."

CHAPTER THREE

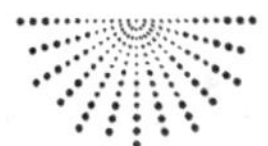

olly came to the door with one eye open and muttering a string of obscenities under her breath. "If this is some school kid selling magazine subscriptions, they're never going to make it out of high school!"

When Holly opened the door and saw it was Rob, she frowned and asked, "Do you have any idea what time it is? Someone better be dead. Or you might be, pal."

"Holly, if I didn't come and tell you where I've been and what I just saw, you would never forgive me."

"That sounds like a stretch, but I'm up now, so try me," she muttered in a low growl as she opened the door wider and beckoned her longtime friend to enter.

"There's been a significant slide over in Hurricane Gulch. One house got split in half and took a tumble down the hill."

"Big story, no doubt, but not worth a seven-fifty-five wake-up call on a Sunday morning."

"You're right. But I haven't told you the other piece of news: the wrecked home is the residence of our esteemed mayor, Mary Anderson."

"Queen Mary!" Holly said with a stunned expression. "I better make us some coffee and get myself something to eat. This is too much to process on an empty stomach. Do you want any coffee?"

"I'd love a cup! Eddie picked me up nearly an hour ago and we didn't stop to grab a couple of coffees. We were both too anxious to see the slide for ourselves."

"Wow! This is unbelievable. Coffee coming right up. Normally I hate getting up early on Sundays, but this is the biggest story we've had since…gosh, I don't know when!"

"Absolutely, Holly!"

"How long has that insufferable woman been Sausalito's mayor?"

"She was mayor long before I took over *The Standard* from George Benton. I was in elementary school when she first ran for a seat on the city council."

"She knew how to take control and never let go. You have to give her that!"

"I can't even imagine Sausalito without Mary Anderson," Rob added as he followed Holly into the cozy kitchen of her one-bedroom apartment.

"Frankly, Rob, I can't either. I suppose I was too young when Anderson was elected to pay any attention to such grown-up issues. I know she's had her hand in everything that's happened in Sausalito for a quarter of a century."

"I wasn't sure I'd find you here. How come you're not up at Scott's?" Rob asked as he sat down in one of two chairs kept tucked under a small table in one corner of Holly's kitchen.

"He's an early riser. He tries to sleep in late on a Sunday, but for him that means getting up after eight. You beat that, Rob, showing up before eight. But to be honest, I would have done the same thing if I were you. Mary Anderson getting crushed by tons of mud and rocks is certainly worthy of an all-points bulletin!"

"You know, I can't remember when the other members of the city council did anything without first checking with her."

"Neither can I, Rob."

"If she did die, we're going to be pressed to come up with a few nice things to write about her. She was probably my least favorite Sausalito politician, and we've certainly had our share of clunkers."

"You're right! Digging up fond memories of Queen Mary is not going to be an easy task," Holly added as she filled her coffee maker with water.

"I'm convinced, and I have been for a long time, that Anderson had her hands in more pockets than the two of us could imagine. And we've tracked some pretty unsavory characters."

"True. When it comes to slick politicians, Mary Anderson is, more likely was, in a league of her own."

"When I was doing freelance writing for George Benton, after I got the boot from *The Independent*, I stumbled across my first case of Anderson shaking down a property owner."

"I remember that case. James Armstrong, the guy who was the publisher of *The Independent*. He wanted to build a mega mansion up near Cloudview Park. Right?"

"Yep! He was a slick operator."

"A little too slick! That's how he became the victim in Eddie's first homicide case!"

"That was also the first time you and I got to help Eddie by snooping around at Armstrong's funeral."

"Rob, I remember that service at St. Dominic's in San Francisco. I was so excited. My first involvement in a murder investigation. I was hooked on the news business from that day on!"

"Anderson was also involved in shaking down Willie James. And he was the complete opposite of Armstrong. A really great guy."

"I remember James. You're right; he was a great guy," Holly smiled as she took milk from her refrigerator and handed it to Rob.

"The three of us would run into him at Smitty's on Friday afternoons after work. He was friends with the two guys who own the place. Actually, I think he might have invested with them when they first bought Smitty's."

"I remember how Willie always had a smile on his face. I never see him around town anymore. Did he pass?"

"Eddie told me that Willie moved to San Diego and died on the golf course of a heart attack. It was just a couple of years after he retired."

"That's too bad. He really was a nice guy."

"Eddie and I thought the world of him. Jokingly we used to call him Uncle Willie because when we were teens, he was always hiring us to do yard cleanup jobs. He owned three properties in town. Sold them all before he moved south. The biggest was the undeveloped lot off of Bridgeway. You know the one. It's two blocks down from the firehouse. Eddie got me in on that job. We were both in high school at the time. Twice-a-year cleanup jobs. We got fifty bucks each for about five hours of work. Back then, that was some serious cash for a couple of sixteen-year-olds."

"Pretty sweet, Rob." Holly took two bagels out of the freezer and popped them in the toaster oven.

"Helluva lot better than Mary Anderson's dad," Rob replied.

"That old skinflint!" Holly laughed.

"Wow, the coffee smells great." Rob was grateful to ease into the comfort of something warm after a day that began like no Sunday should. "Anderson's dad, Gus, was a miserable old coot. Few who knew him would debate that."

"I suppose with Queen Mary, the nut didn't fall far from the tree."

"Let's just say whatever money went into the old man's pocket never rarely came out again." Rob smiled. "When Eddie and I did cleanup work for him, we considered ourselves lucky if we got paid half of what we made working for Willie James."

"Do you think it's true that Gus Anderson made his money running drugs out of Canada?" Holly asked. "I heard he worked the old smuggling routes the rum runners used back in the prohibition days."

"That wouldn't surprise me in the least. He's what my pop likes to call 'a real piece of work!' Running drugs was a lucrative business. Still is, I assume. They'd rendezvous in the San Juan Islands with boats coming from the coast of Washington State and the Olympic Peninsula. It was all to avoid US Border Patrol. Stopping drug traffic is like plugging a hole in a dam. Patch one hole, and another one pops open. That's particularly true when you're talking about smuggling done at sea."

"Rob, how long has it been since you first wanted to do an exposé on Mary Anderson?"

"Can't say for certain, but I know it's been years."

"I never asked you what happened. I mean, you're not one to shy away from a fight. So why not do the story?"

"I was taught that shying away from a fight and knowing when to come out swinging are two different things. We've snapped at her heels on more than one occasion, but I wish we could have done more. Bottom line, I knew if I really went after Mary Anderson, she would turn right around and come after us. Knowing Anderson's approach, I knew that meant with both barrels."

"You mean go after our advertisers?"

"Absolutely! And anything and everything else she could do to put us out of business."

"Such as?"

"Well, let's start with pulling our office out from under us."

"How could she do that?"

"Think about where we're located: the top floor of an old Victorian on Princess Street. It's a little too noisy for residential tenants considering all the tourists that go up and down the block, but it's perfect for a small office like ours, and we have it for a very affordable rate, just as George Benton did before he handed the paper over to me. If we really started digging and went after her consistently, I think there is an excellent chance she would lean on our landlord to give us the old heave-ho."

Holly's eyes opened wide. "You mean Anderson would go after Mister Simons to get us thrown out?"

"Yep, that she would. I guarantee it!"

"But how?"

"As you know, Holly, Sausalito has a huge inventory of surviving Victorian structures. That's particularly true in the historic commercial district. Buildings that are pretty to look at and charming for tourists to snap photos of, but they are not easily maintained. And when you're talking about building codes, there's always something you can throw at an owner to make their lives more difficult." Rob shrugged. "We've been Ezra Simons' tenant for going on a decade, and he's never once raised our rent. He likes having a local paper in town. Keeping our rent low is his way of encouraging us to keep doing what we're doing. But if Mary Anderson wanted to rattle his cage, she simply has to start leaning on the town's building department to check that everything in all of his buildings in the downtown district is up to par. He's got a half-dozen buildings and given their age it's unlikely that all of them are up to code in every conceivable fashion."

"So, she tightens down on various property owners to keep their tenants in line?" Holly asked as she poured both herself and Rob a second cup of coffee.

"Yes. And she used those tactics on a whole host of different tenants, like merchants who play music too loud, or sell products Queen Mary considered tacky. Even, possibly, a newspaper that asks too many questions and digs a little too deep."

"Wow," Holly murmured.

"And if Queen Mary wanted to put *The Standard* out of business, she would not have stopped at putting the heat on our landlord," Rob added. "She could have gone after our advertisers as well."

"What if one of them resented that kind of bullying and blew the whistle?" Holly asked.

"That's possible. Leaning on people in what is an obviously improper, or perhaps downright illegal fashion, carries a risk. But people who like to play the kind of hardball Mary Anderson thrives on are willing to take risks. Plus, there's a good chance that if you're a merchant, or a landlord, or perhaps both, and you go after her and miss, she would have done everything she could to make your life miserable. If all else fails, there's always the 'you misinterpreted my sentiments' defense. People like Anderson are never shy about justifying their behavior and-or denying culpability."

"I suppose they get called on frequently to do that, so they get a lot of practice in the art of justification," Holly nodded.

"Other people wouldn't dare attempt many of the things someone like Anderson would do without a second thought."

"What if you had taped your conversation with her when she's telling you to shape up or else? Hopefully, that would have allowed you to prove that what she was saying was not casual banter, but a-not-so-subtle threat to take down *The Standard*."

"If you want to tape a conversation in California, the state requires two-party consent. It was done to avoid malicious entrapment. In a lot of states where you have one-party consent, people are being recorded without their knowledge. That can lead to blackmail, extortion, etcetera. But beyond that issue is the simple truth, that most of these folks live by the rule of 'go along to get along.' They didn't acquire properties or open a store or restaurant in the city's business and visitor areas to get into a losing battle with the city's most powerful politician."

"Too bad," Holly grumbled. "I guess she is, or maybe *was*, comfortable turning the screws on people."

"Absolutely! And Anderson was very good at it. You can't do what she did and be shy about pushing people around."

"And how is it, Rob, that she was able to keep herself in the mayor's seat for so long?"

"That's also pretty simple. Like in many of California's small cities, no one runs for mayor; they run for one of five seats on the city council. Our city council appoints one of its members as mayor. The council's selection is renewed annually. After that one-year term, another member is chosen to serve as mayor the following year. Or they can keep the same person as mayor for as many one-year terms as they wish, provided she or he is an elected member of the city council."

"But in all five-member council cities, there is a city council election every two years," Holly pointed out.

"Yes, in one of those elections, three seats on the council are up, two years later the other two seats are up. That allows for continuity in leadership—something you could lose if all five seats were up at the same time and current councilmembers chose not to run or failed to be re-elected."

"But Mary Anderson could have been defeated by three or four council members voting against her and for someone else to serve as mayor," Holly countered.

"Absolutely. But in a city where you have a five-member council, the reality is if you want to win support for any item you have to be able to count to three. Since you support yourself, you only need two others to win the majority."

"Rob, to be honest, I hadn't paid much attention to any of this until I started working with you. So, all these years Anderson has held the mayor's seat on the council?"

"Going back to when I first started writing articles for *The Standard,* back when George Benton was owner and publisher of the paper, she's been mayor. I can tell you with certainty that over that period of time she's held the council with an iron grip. A retiring council member who had shown consistent loyalty might have been elevated to vice-mayor, so the honor of having been second in command is something they can take with them into retirement. Play your cards right and you may even get a framed photo hung on a wall outside the city council's chambers with your name and years of service listed below. But cross Madam Mayor, and most likely your name will not again be mentioned in polite society," Rob added with a raised eyebrow and a lopsided smile.

"Rob, that's a bit of an exaggeration, don't you think?"

"I don't think it is. Queen Mary has left a trail of shady deals and questionable transactions. If she's gone, we can dig deeper into her past. Not all at once, but in the weeks that follow, perhaps even sooner, we can begin peeling back the layers of her misdeeds. I'll be interested to see where that trail leads. I'm guessing she has more than one skeleton in her closet."

"That should win us some readers and lose others who'll complain that we're nothing more than a scandal sheet!"

"As you well know, Holly, in the news business, you've got to take the good with the bad. You're always going to have supporters and detractors no matter what you put in print. Or at times, equally controversial, the stories you *don't* print. Our goal is to stay true to our core values and keep doing our best work. Even if our forward movement at times feels glacially slow, if you have a defined goal and you're convinced there is more to uncover, then by all means, keep digging." Rob took a long sip of his coffee. Then, putting down his mug, he added, "If Mary Anderson is lying beneath a ton of mud and rubble, we're going to find ourselves doing as much digging, figuratively, as the search and rescue teams will being doing literally."

"So, what does your gut tell you, Rob? Should we start the process of pulling together an obit for Mary Anderson? With the number of years, she has spent at the center of Sausalito politics, it's going to be a long story."

"It's Sunday. When I go home, after I tell Karin what I've been up to for the last couple of hours, I'm going to sit myself down and write a page or two regarding the high points of Anderson's long tenure as mayor. That file I've kept on her record these past years is going to make that job a lot easier."

"I suppose whatever you write about her, you're going to have to tiptoe around her more-questionable decisions."

"As bad as Anderson was, it's not going to do us any good to tear into her before she's eulogized and buried," Rob shrugged. "If Sausalito's queen bee is under tons of mud and debris, our lead story this week writes itself."

CHAPTER FOUR

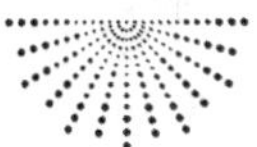

It was past nightfall when Mary Anderson's body was removed from the entryway of her wrecked home.

Sausalito's fire department rarely had news of any kind to report. But Chief Vogel knew this was one story Rob was certainly following.

"Just on my way home, Rob. I wanted to give you an update. Mayor Anderson's body was recovered less than an hour ago and has been taken to the county morgue."

Rob tried not to choke as he swallowed a bite of the roasted chicken Karin had prepared for the family's Sunday dinner. "Kind of you to call, Bill; I'm sure it's been a very long day for you and your crew."

"One of the worst I can remember. But as your dad always reminded me, in this job, you learn to expect the unexpected."

"I'm sorry to hear she's been lost," Rob said softly.

Vogel knew that Rob had just told one of those little white lies required by polite society. Through the years of Rob's ownership of *The Standard,* it was clear to readers that Rob was not a fan of the politician who dominated Sausalito's daily life in countless ways.

"It will be interesting to see the political fallout her death brings," Vogel prodded.

Rob was determined to avoid this topic, knowing any comments he made about Mary Anderson were bound to be repeated. "After a long run as Sausalito's most powerful elected official, the political realignment will be significant," Rob noted and left it at that.

When the call ended, Rob immediately called Eddie, who answered by saying, "I just heard, Newsboy."

"Who told you?"

"Not everyone in the Sausalito PD tries to avoid me."

"Yeah, why is that?"

"Simple! For the most part, cops don't like cops that outrank them or have a better job. You know, sitting in a squad car for most of the day waiting for some hapless driver to run a stop sign, or do thirty-four in a twenty-five-mile an hour zone, isn't as exciting as you might think. And don't forget ticketing drivers for a rolling stop."

"Huh?"

"That's when you almost stop at a stop sign, but not quite. So, your wheels are still rolling."

"Wow! That's silly even by Sausalito's standards. Well, what do you think?"

"About our recently-deceased mayor?" Eddie teased.

"Duh!"

"I think she was in the wrong place at the wrong time. It's as simple as that."

"Duh, times two," Rob retorted.

"You and I both know that you want me to give you a call after Max Brownstein has examined the corpse," Eddie replied.

"You read my mind. My readers are going to want details. That's particularly true of the forty percent of our population who referred to Mary Anderson as the 'Queen of Mean.'"

"She did have a legion of fans *and* a sizable number of detractors. Max should have something by tomorrow afternoon, if not sooner. I suppose blunt force trauma will be his call. But we'll see. I heard they found her body near the entryway to her home. Perhaps she bolted out of bed and was trying to get to the front door when the home got torn in two. I suppose if she had stayed put in her bedroom, she'd still be alive."

"She didn't know what was happening. More than likely she was probably in a panic. That's a natural reaction. No one wants to be inside a home that's about to be washed away by a wall of mud and debris. Not that running outside is likely to improve your odds of survival. But very few of us are going to behave rationally at a moment like that."

"True that, Robbie boy. Same thing happens in earthquakes. A lot of people instinctively bolt for the front door only to get banged over the head when they get outside. Could be falling bricks as their chimney comes tumbling down, popping windows, or sliding roof shingles—no good choices. Whatever happened to our late mayor, I'm sure it wasn't pleasant. We all have to go sometime, but buried by a mudslide? No thanks. I'll take a hospital bed and a slow fade to black!"

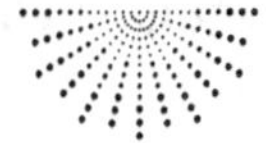

The following morning, just after eleven, Eddie got a call from Max Brownstein.

"Where are you?" Max asked, sounding unusually agitated.

"About ten minutes from your examination room."

"Get over here as soon as you can. I've got something to show you regarding your town's esteemed mayor."

Moments later Eddie left the Sheriff Department's headquarters in San Rafael off the 101 Freeway for the short drive to the Medical Examiner's office. He tried, but failed, to ignore Max's obviously urgent tone. Perhaps Max found drugs in the late mayor's system or something equally unexpected. Nevertheless, when Eddie met a short traffic snarl in Terra Linda, he opted for his light and siren.

Max was in his examination room, still studying the corpse of Mary Anderson, when Eddie pushed through one of two doors and said, "What's up, Max? Sounds like someone or something threw you a curveball."

"I would say you're the one who's been pitched the curveball."

"How so?"

"Mayor Anderson was dead before that slide tore away half her house. Including, most importantly, the part in which her body was found."

"Heart attack?"

"No. The poor dear died of head injury. A subdural hematoma to be precise. Here, let me show you." Max reached for one corner of the sheet draped over the late mayor's shoulder. Before he could pull the sheet down, Eddie grabbed Max's arm.

"Is it essential to show me her entire body?"

"What do you mean?"

"Born and raised in Sausalito, I can close my eyes and see this woman's face. She's been on the city council nearly my entire life. If you don't mind, I'd rather not see any more of her than I absolutely have to!"

"Alright, Mr. Sensitive. What's important, I can show you with the sheet tucked just below her shoulders."

"Thanks, Max, you're a prince."

"My mother already told me that. But thank you for confirming her opinion."

"So, how did Madam Mayor take her leave?"

"The first thing we needed to do was wash the entire body. While I'm sure a lot of the mud that encased her fell off between her being pulled from the wreckage and her being placed in a body bag and transported here, we still needed to take a hose to the corpse. Washing it down removed bits of mud, small pebbles, and a countless number of wood splinters —and of course, plaster dust particles, which were everywhere on the body. As you would expect of anyone, dead or alive, pulled out from under a landslide, the body itself took a real beating."

"The only thing worse, I suppose, would be working on a bomb victim," Eddie offered.

"That would depend on the size of the bomb, and the victim's proximity to it," Max responded with a Dr. Frankenstein expression on his face that never failed to unnerve Eddie.

"Given all this body was subjected to, how did it become apparent that she was killed before the slide?"

"That was quite simple. Once I had a clean body to examine, I noticed immediately the classic signs of blunt force trauma were missing. Whether a victim is dropped from a height onto a hillside, or a hillside falls on top of him or her, there will still be multiple signs of bruising over most of the body. That's not the case with the mayor. You know enough about my work, Eddie, to know why this would draw my attention."

Eddie nodded. "Being dead before the slide, blood movement through the body had ceased. Therefore bruising, which is a form of internal bleeding, would not have occurred."

"Correct. There is another obvious sign that this individual was deceased at the time of the slide. When our airways are blocked, both nostrils and throat, our effort to breath remains a matter of automatic reflex. The brain becomes increasingly desperate to take in oxygen. Slide victims will have mud and debris in their nostrils and mouths. It's not by choice that they do this; it's a result of our basic instinct to survive. The airways of this corpse reveal no evidence that any attempt was made to inhale a single breath. Explaining why we find no evidence of inhalation of water, mud, or debris. "

"All pretty clear, Max. So, was this a heart attack or stroke prior to the slide?"

"That would have been a possibility. But Eddie, I think you must have been looking at her body with just one eye open. You're being far too shy. Take a closer look. This time focus on the face of the deceased."

Hesitantly, Eddie came closer to the corpse.

"For God's sake Eddie, she's not going to bite! Get in there and take a good look."

"Geez Max, you're right. I missed a pretty big clue. There's bruising along the cheek and the jawline. You're suggesting Queen Mary was murdered?"

"'Queen Mary?' How did you come up with that?"

"It was the nickname given to our honorable mayor by many of her detractors. I was a kid the first time I heard it. I thought they were talking about the pirate's bride on the ride down in Disneyland."

"Hah! I'm sure you had a good imagination. An important ingredient in the making of a good detective."

"Guilty as charged. I really did have an active imagination!"

"I spoke with Chief Vogel this morning and asked if he could give me a description of the area of the house from where her body was removed."

"And?"

"Apparently the house had a marble entryway with a step up into the living room. Given the bruising to the side of the face, the likeliest scenario is she argued with someone, an individual likely several inches taller than the victim. This person struck her against the jawline, explaining the bruising here, here, and here." Max pointed to the line of discoloration along the left side of Mary Anderson's jaw. "It's a near certainty she was knocked down, and the impact that occurred when she hit the base of her skull on that step caused a subdural hematoma. A result that could have occurred simply by her head striking a marble floor, but it's reasonable to conclude that the edge of that step likely added to the severity of her injury. I checked to see if she was taking any blood thinning drugs, which of course adds to the likelihood of internal bleeding. But no such drugs were found in her system. She ingested, however, an avocado salad and a fruit cup including cherries and blueberries approximately two hours prior to her death. All three of those foods thin the blood and likely exacerbated the brain bleed she suffered when she struck the back of her head."

"Good work, Max. Sounds like she and her visitor had one whale of an argument."

"Angry enough for the perpetrator's arm to cause significant bruising along the jaw line."

"From the angle of the injury, was the assailant left or right-handed?"

"Almost certainly her assailant was right-handed."

"This is a classic case of a dead man—I mean dead woman—telling tales. Providing us with a pretty clear picture of how she died. Considering the mess this body was extracted from, I'm grateful you were able to garner this much information. So, the cause of death was a subdural hematoma?"

"Absolutely. You need to talk with our illustrious county sheriff. I'm sure he would be happier if Madam Mayor died as a result of that slide. I can't sit on issuing the autopsy report for more than twenty-four hours. By midday tomorrow we're going to have to come clean about the manner in which she died. I assume the media will have a field day with this story, so you better give Jack Canning a head's up."

"Geez! Mayor Mary Anderson killed as a result of a violent argument in sleepy Sausalito! I'm going to have to talk Jack in off the ledge when he hears about this."

"I suppose it doesn't sound good when a long-serving elected official is killed in a violent altercation in her home," Max commented with a shrug. "Tarnishes the image Jack likes to pedal of an always-peaceful Marin County."

"It doesn't sound good, that's for sure, along with the fact that Anderson was in her late sixties. The average citizen reasons that if a well-known, long-serving mayor is killed in her home, then how safe is this county for people who have no friends in high places?"

"Poor Jack Canning," Max said. "He never stops campaigning, even when he's just been re-elected sheriff months earlier. Maybe he'll pass on running next time?"

"Canning? Pass on running? No way! Jack's a lifer, Max. Being thrown out by the voters, or poor health, are the only two ways he'll leave office."

"Just like this woman. How long was she Sausalito's mayor?"

"She's been a member of the city council for nearly twenty-seven years. And most of those years, she's occupied the mayor's chair. But, in or out of the mayor's seat, she's been the town's principal powerbroker for a long time. If you wanted to get something done in Sausalito, you started by going hat in hand to Miss Anderson."

"Eddie, go tell your peeps the queen has fallen."

"Let the palace intrigue begin."

CHAPTER SIX

For Eddie, sitting on what he had just learned from Max without informing Rob and Holly was all but impossible. But proper protocol required he meet first with Jack Canning. Reaching out to his secretary, Carla Vitale—known at headquarters as "the guardian of the gate"—was the first thing he did.

"What's up, handsome?" Carla's Midwestern twang had diminished only slightly during the twenty-plus years she had lived in Marin County.

"I have to meet with Jack and bring him up to speed on the death of Sausalito's mayor."

"Sorry, hon. I can't get you in to see him until tomorrow morning."

"Nothing sooner?"

"He's in San Francisco with Judge Peter Botherton, playing at the Presidio Golf Course. Unless it's super urgent, I wouldn't bug him while he has his hands wrapped around a golf club."

"Okay. But just so you know, this is something the press will be looking for Jack to comment on. The news won't be released by the coroner's office until early tomorrow afternoon. I'll send him a memo detailing the particulars, and he and I can meet at his convenience tomorrow morning. Just be certain he knows this is happening. Neither you nor I want Jack to start getting calls from the media without his having been briefed on the status of the case."

"Okay, doll. I hear you loud and clear. I'll be sure to give him the message, and I'm putting you on his calendar for tomorrow morning at nine."

"Thanks, Carla. You're a sweetheart!"

"That's what my dad always told me."

Eddie pushed end call on his phone's display, then tapped Rob's number.

"We have to talk."

"When?"

"Now."

"Lunch, here?" Rob asked.

"You got it. I'll be there in thirty or less. You pick up the sandwiches, I'll bring coffee and pastries. You're going to flip when you hear what I just learned regarding Sausalito's late mayor."

"Any chance you want to give me a sneak preview?"

"And miss that dopey expression you get when a big story drops into your lap? Not a chance, pal. Trust me, this is too incredible to blab about over the phone. See you in thirty or less."

Before Rob could plead once more, Eddie ended the call.

Putting out four weekly editions in the towns of Sausalito, Tiburon-Belvedere, Mill Valley, and Ross Valley was more than a full week's work for a two-person operation. Ninety percent of *The Standard*'s reporting followed mostly routine stories. Dog park openings, playground improvements, new road paving projects, new tax bond measures, and storm damage repairs. But every now and then a story came along that was irresistible and had to be followed to its logical conclusion. It was working these stories that pushed Rob and Holly forward. Not editing the society news, reprinting the agendas for city council and local commission meetings, or juggling the ever-changing flow of advertisers, which provided the financial fuel to pay their salaries, put the paper on press, and deliver it to mailboxes.

The demand of having to put out a quality product four times a week felt less burdensome during those rare occasions when a big story came their way. It could be a shocking crime like the murder of Sausalito's premier chef, an odd character forever known as the "Gossiping Gourmet." Or the shocking revelations revealed by the murder of Mill Valley's "Phantom Photographer." Plus, the scandal surrounding the infamous "Wicked Wife" of Belvedere philanthropist William Adams. Each of these and other stories were a welcome relief from the ninety-plus percent of their weekly work that was performed by rote.

Sunday's slide, which had taken Mayor Anderson's life, was

big news. But it was also a story that the county daily, *The Independent*, would cover prior to Wednesday's in-home delivery of *The Standard*'s Sausalito edition. Neither Rob nor Holly could have imagined how much more interesting that story was about to become.

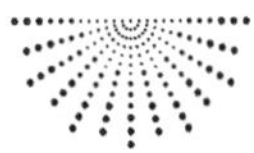

CHAPTER SEVEN

Eddie, tall, lean, muscular, and always starving, stepped into the coffee shop directly across from the Princess Street offices of *The Standard* and picked up a few pastries and three coffees to go.

Minutes later he was sitting with Holly and Rob who, as usual, had started work more than four hours earlier at eight o'clock.

"What's up, copper?" Holly said, curious as always to know the latest news.

"More than you could possibly imagine," Eddie said, sitting down to a roast beef sandwich purchased minutes earlier at one of his favorite shops, Venice Gourmet.

"Thanks for grabbing me a sandwich. You wouldn't think that spending time in Max Brownstein's examination room would leave me with much of an appetite, but for some reason I'm starved."

"Eddie, we've hung out together since middle school. When are you not starving?" Rob asked.

"True, pal," Eddie conceded with a shrug.

"Did Max have a chance to examine Mary Anderson?" Holly asked. "I know she wasn't my favorite person. Far from it. Still, I would think being buried alive by a landslide would be a terrible way to die."

"I wouldn't want to go that way either," Rob opined. "But I imagine it was at least over quickly. I mean, wow, buried by a tidal wave of mud and debris. It's hard to imagine!"

"Fellow travelers, I can assure you that based on Max's examination of her body, Queen Mary never felt a thing."

"Huh? How does he know that from an autopsy?" Holly asked. "I would think in her last few moments Mary Anderson must have realized her house was being destroyed and her life was in great danger. I never liked the woman, but I wouldn't wish that on anyone!"

"Then you'll be happy to know that Max estimates her time of death was approximately four to five hours before the slide occurred."

Rob and Holly each barked out their amazement:

"What!"

"How could that be?"

Eddie smiled and said, "The what and the how of her death is what we're here to discuss."

"And I thought it was just to spend time with your old pals," Rob said.

"Give, Eddie!" Holly slapped the detective's shoulder. "Don't tell me she was murdered!"

"Yep. However, Max and I agree that from the results of the autopsy her slaying is unlikely to be prosecuted as first-degree homicide. More probable, her killer will be charged with voluntary manslaughter."

"I've heard the term used, but I'm not exactly sure what it means," Holly said. "And while you're at it, Eddie, explain the difference between voluntary and involuntary manslaughter. I'm uncertain about that as well."

"A first-degree homicide is when you plan to kill someone. You acted with forethought. Voluntary manslaughter is when, for example, you argue and struggle with someone. The victim is killed, but the prosecution is unable to prove that the victim's death was the killer's intent." Eddie waited until that sunk in, and then continued: "Involuntary manslaughter is when, for example, a robber drives away from the scene of a crime and in his or her haste, they kill a pedestrian or the driver of another car. The killing occurred because of a felony, but the victim was not someone even known to the killer. You could call it collateral damage. Involuntary manslaughter can also be an act of negligence, such as operating a vehicle at a high rate of speed that causes a fatality, but there is no evidence of intent to kill."

"I just don't believe Queen Mary was murdered regardless of the charge," Rob said, shaking his head in disbelief.

"Neither do I," Holly nodded. "You've got to be pulling our legs."

"Okay, don't believe me. But you may change your mind tomorrow afternoon when Jack Canning releases the medical examiner's report on Anderson's autopsy."

"Tomorrow afternoon?" Rob said with obvious excitement. "That's terrific!"

"How so, paperboy?" Eddie asked with a bemused expression.

"Canning's news will be too late for *The Independent* to report the story in their Tuesday afternoon edition, which goes on press shortly before noon each day. Obviously, the story will get out through television, radio, and the Internet, but starting Wednesday morning we'll hit every mailbox in Sausalito, so we'll be the first to get the full story out in print in a community where Mary Anderson's death has the most impact. Thanks for that, pal."

"As much as I enjoy supporting your ever-struggling group of community newspapers, don't thank me on this score. The credit goes to our illustrious sheriff, who went into San Francisco for the day to play golf with Judge Botherton and left a 'do not disturb' order with his gatekeeper, the lovely Carla Vitale."

"Well then, I'm indebted to Botherton and the game of golf. Bottom line: for us, this is going to be a huge story! Murder or manslaughter, Anderson was killed! How great is that?... Hold on, I don't mean that like it must have sounded..."

"That's alright, pal. I think we get your meaning," Eddie said with a laugh.

"In sleepy Sausalito, murder stories are rare enough, and the killing of the town's most admired and most disliked citizen is an unbelievable bit of good luck!" Holly announced with a smile.

"Not for the victim," Eddie declared, flashing a smile of his own.

"You know what I mean," Holly responded quickly.

"Back up," Rob said, waving the pickle that came with his sandwich in Eddie's direction. "You mean, after all these years and all the people she undoubtedly bullied, cheated, and lied to —not to mention the shady deals she made—the people she leaned on every couple of years for campaign contributions, and God only knows what else, she was killed hours before a hillside came tumbling down on top of her? Wow! That's simply incredible. It's like something out of a James Bond movie."

"Agreed! It certainly is crazy," Holly added.

"But, on second thought, it is no more unbelievable than a major earthquake hitting the Bay Area minutes before the start of game three of the World Series between the Oakland Athletics and the San Francisco Giants. On the scale of unlikely events that's up near the top," Eddie shrugged. "Don't think I wasn't stunned when Max told me how she died. Although, minus the coincidental timing, I don't think the fact that she was killed is all that surprising. Given Anderson's penchant for bullying and manipulating people, I think there are a fair number of individuals in our little town who'd probably be delighted to see her out of the picture permanently."

"I can't disagree about that," Holly noted with a smile.

"As Eddie just pointed out, God's been known now and then to have an odd sense of timing," Rob said while still reeling from the news. "Can you imagine what her attacker must be thinking?"

"Let's back up a bit. I haven't yet told both of you how she died." Eddie proceeded to share the sequence of events that led to Anderson's death, as described to him by Max just an hour earlier.

"Wow" was the only word that came from both Rob and Holly when Eddie finished relaying the sequence of events that likely occurred in the entryway of the late mayor's home on Saturday night. "I'm guessing Madam Mayor's killer attacked her in a fit of rage," Eddie suggested. "The way in which she died strengthens the case for manslaughter as opposed to homicide."

"Can you imagine what the killer thought when he heard the news that over half of her home had been crushed in a landslide?" Rob said, shaking his head.

"You say 'he,' Rob, but the killer could have been a 'she,'" Holly suggested.

"Absolutely, Holly! But in my line of work," Eddie explained, "it's unwise to ignore statistical averages. Of all homicides committed every year, approximately eighty-five percent are committed by men. In cases of voluntary or involuntary manslaughter, murder as a result of physical violence, that number is over ninety percent. So, until we have a solid reason to think otherwise, I'll happily bet the odds that her attacker will turn out to be a male."

"What about finding the killer's skin under the nails of the victim? Did they find any?"

"You do like those crime shows, Holly," Eddie smiled.

"Guilty, copper. I love them."

"Anderson's body was encased in everything you could possibly imagine having been inside a structure destroyed by a wall of mud, rocks, sheetrock, splinters of wood, tree branches, and God only knows what else. Two of Max's assistants hosed the body down prior to Max beginning his examination. You can't blame them for thinking this was not a crime victim as they were washing away potentially important evidence. Perhaps some of the assailant's skin under her fingernails as you suggested, Holly. The whole sequence of events is pretty wild stuff!"

"You know...we're all forgetting something," Rob murmured.

"What's that?" Holly asked.

"The back part of the house was spared in the slide. And that's where the bedrooms are located. Minus being attacked in her home's entryway, there's a good chance she would have been sleeping in her bed at the time the slide tore away the front part of the house."

"Good point," Holly said shaking her head. "Even if that had been the case, I still think that out there, somewhere, is a perpetrator kicking himself for acting too soon."

"There's a chance that one of our nosy fellow citizens who lives a house or two away from Anderson heard something, saw something, or both," Rob suggested.

"I'll go knock on the doors of Mary Anderson's neighbors over the next couple of days. By then everyone in town will be buzzing about her slaying, meaning they'll be happy to contribute their two cents. Maybe I'll get lucky."

"Sausalito has no shortage of nosy neighbors, so that's certainly worth a shot," Holly said.

"Fingers crossed that one or more heard something." Eddie said as he lifted his coffee cup.

"Killed, then swept downhill in a landslide," Rob announced with a faraway look. "That's some pretty wild stuff. So, taking this at face value, Madam Mayor was struck and left, presumably unconscious, and then sometime between when she was struck and the house was destroyed by the slide, she died from the bang she received falling back and striking the base of her skull on a step."

"Max's best guesstimate is she expired between ten and midnight. Her death could have been relatively fast or slow. Anderson was dead at the time of the slide, that much is certain. It's proven by the simple fact that she inhaled none of the mud or debris she was extracted from late the following day, and she had no internal bleeding, despite having a hillside fall down on her. The fact that this was a killing, intentional or unintentional, is likely to be the only easy part of this investigation. Figuring out her killer's motive, that's likely to be considerably harder."

"With Mary Anderson's penchant for putting the squeeze on people to do her bidding, you might have an address book's worth of potential suspects," Rob cautioned.

"I was wondering on the drive down here if this case will make up for the lucky break I got on the Bent case," Eddie responded with a disappointed shake of his head. "I was hoping my luck might hold awhile longer."

"You're right! You could be facing an uphill climb with this case," Rob suggested.

"Let's just say you're going to need something bigger than that little notebook you keep in your inside jacket pocket," Holly offered with a mischievous grin. "For all the charm of Queen Mary, I would imagine there's at least a baker's dozen worth of credible suspects."

"There's a good chance Holly is right about needing a bigger notebook," Rob added.

"Eddie, my guess is a third of Sausalito thought Mary Anderson was a saint," Holly continued. "Another third thought she should be locked up and the key thrown away. The final third probably paid no attention at all. That third is only interested in the opening of a new restaurant, the schedule for Jazz by the Bay, or the weekend sailing report."

"Holly, you and Rob have been tracking Anderson for a number of years; between her backroom deals, arm twisting, and God only knows what else, she must have created quite an impressive list of enemies."

"Eddie, I can't begin to imagine how many people Anderson bullied, leaned on, or generally ticked off," Rob grimaced.

"I wouldn't venture a guess either. What I can say with a high degree of confidence is that Queen Mary had quite the track record," Holly added. "Her arm twisting was little known to the public, but I'd suspect with some digging you're going to start compiling a list of enemies that will stretch from the south end of Sausalito to the north end."

"Really?" Eddie asked with a grimace.

"Yes Eddie, really. In fact, I'll bet the bank on it!" Holly nodded confidently.

"Just out of curiosity: at this point, can either of you give me any examples?"

"Not with all the deadlines facing us at the moment. Not to mention we need to get busy pulling together bio information on Sausalito's recently deceased mayor," Rob said. "But come our regular Friday cocktail hour at Smitty's, we'll happily give you a full breakdown on our reliably unpleasant mayor."

"Speaking of reliably unpleasant characters, who said, 'Fasten your seatbelts, it's going to be a bumpy night?'" Eddie asked.

"Bette Davis in *All About Eve*, 1950," Holly announced.

"Gee, you're good at film trivia," Rob said with a smile.

"Not really. Scott and I watched it Saturday night. Great movie. But what made you think of that line, Eddie?"

"Just something about this case. My gut is telling me to buckle up because Mary Anderson had a lot of secrets. I'm guessing this is going to be a bumpy ride."

CHAPTER EIGHT

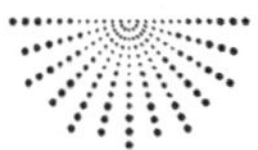

The prospect of unexpected twists and turns in the investigation of Mary Anderson's death caused Eddie to have a restless night. The mayor's death was still on his mind when he awoke to an alarm that was set for seven. Just how deep would he need to go before learning why Anderson's life ended in what was most likely a violent argument?

Eddie dragged himself into the shower, hoping it would revive him before the start of another long day, beginning with breaking some unwelcome news to Jack Canning.

While Sharon got their son, Aaron, ready for school, Eddie made pancakes and sausage patties for the family. It seemed no matter how hard they tried, invariably the Austin family managed to be a little late every day of the school and work week.

In a rush all three of them ate in silence, then it was off to St. Hillary's School across Richardson Bay in the town of

Tiburon, where Aaron attended second grade and Sharon had reluctantly accepted the role of organizing the school's annual fundraising event. Right behind them was Eddie, whom Sharon stopped for a moment in order to straighten his tie, just as she had done with Aaron's tie moments before.

"The Austin boys might be sleepy and grumpy in the morning," Eddie said, "but thanks to you we at least look our best."

Thirty minutes later Eddie greeted Carla Vitale, perched at her usual spot a few feet from her boss's door. He handed her a small bunch of wildflowers picked from his backyard the night before.

"What are these for, doll?"

"For you being you."

"Well, thanks handsome. Before you walk into the lion's den let me give you a word of caution."

What now? Eddie thought.

"Judge Botherton apparently crushed Jack out on the golf course yesterday afternoon. Next to hearing bad news, losing a bet on his golf game is Jack's least favorite thing."

"Well, I'm not bearing *good* news."

Carla shrugged. "Better you than me."

When Eddie walked into Jack's office, he was determined to be upbeat and so he began with, "Beautiful day, isn't it?"

"Really? I hadn't noticed," Jack responded in a tone that confirmed Carla's words of caution. "What have you got for me?"

"Nothing you're going to like."

"Not surprising, Eddie. It just means my streak of bad luck

continues. You should have seen me out at the Presidio yesterday afternoon. I was playing with Pete Botherton, and I'm telling you, my short game was my worst in memory! I couldn't sink a putt to save my life. I was okay on the fairway, but once I got near or onto the putting green I just fell apart. I hit one chip shot that sailed over the hole and into a sand trap on the opposite side. Golf can be a lot like marriage. Great one day, lousy the next," Jack shrugged and tried to put a bad round of golf behind him while Eddie chose not to comment.

"So, what's up? Oh, and wasn't that something about Mary Anderson being buried by a landslide? I've attended a few events with her. Between you and me, I found her to be a bit creepy and not at all shy about pushing people around. I guess the word 'annoying' best described her, at least from my perspective."

"How so?"

"It's hard to explain. There was always this sense of entitlement about her. Perhaps she got it from her father who, from what I understand, was also a real piece of work."

"Really?" Eddie said, realizing for the first time that the list of Mary Anderson's detractors extended beyond Sausalito's city limits.

"She was one of those politicians whose entire life revolves around getting re-elected."

Eddie did his best not to laugh, considering there was never a time in Jack Canning's long tenure as county sheriff that he didn't appear to be thinking about re-election.

"So, what's up?"

"Max had some surprising news yesterday after he performed what he thought was going to be a routine autopsy on Mary Anderson. Not that examining the body of a supposed landslide victim is part of his usual routine."

"What do you mean, 'supposed' landslide victim?"

"Mary Anderson was killed hours before that slide slammed into her house."

"Back up, pal! You're telling me that the queen of Sausalito politics was dead before she and her home got slammed?"

"Yes, Jack. The bruising along her jawline indicated that she was struck near the entryway of her home and died approximately five hours before the slide occurred."

"DAMN IT!" Jack shouted loudly enough to make Carla, outside her boss's closed door, jump in her seat.

Jack got up from his desk and stared at Eddie. Determined not to speak before his boss spoke, Eddie was even more stunned when Jack fell back in his chair and started to laugh. "Oh my God, I know this isn't funny, but it sure feels that way to me."

"Huh?" Eddie muttered surprised by Canning's reaction.

"You live in Sausalito so maybe you don't know this, but Madam Mayor was disliked by nearly every elected official in Marin County, with the notable exception of the four other individuals who serve alongside her on Sausalito's city council. Apparently, they all think she's terrific. So wonderful that they continue to support her remaining in the position of mayor. I'm not sure they're actual fans, but they fell into line whenever she snapped her fingers."

"You're right about Sausalito being a small town where politicians and wealthy insiders have created their own little fiefdom," Eddie explained. "Personally, I have very little interest in politics."

"That's too bad. I've been thinking you might be a good candidate for sheriff when I decide to retire."

"Really?" Eddie was shocked—by Jack uttering the word "retirement." And then shocked again by the suggestion that he might be Canning's hand-picked successor.

"Sure, why not? Your mug has been out there a lot, particularly on high profile cases when we do our dog and pony shows for the media. The women think you're easy on the eye. Trust me, that never hurts."

Determined not to allow Canning to take his attention off the matter at hand, Eddie pushed forward.

"Max wants to release his autopsy report on Mary Anderson today by one o'clock. I thought it would be good for us to get out ahead of this story by holding a press conference ninety minutes later—say, at two-thirty?"

"Works for me. You and Max take the lead. I'll bat cleanup. And if I digress and say something like, 'This is likely to be a long investigation because Mary Anderson was not well-liked and we're expecting a long list of possible suspects,' feel free to cut me off."

Back at his desk, Eddie called Max to say a news conference on Mary Anderson was set for two-thirty, and that a press release regarding the cause of death should indicate that the county's medical examiner, lead investigator, and Sheriff Canning will be in attendance and available for questions.

Max groaned. "Here we go again. If Jack keeps putting me on TV, it won't be long before people start coming up to me in restaurants asking how their ninety-seven-year-old mother could die in a nursing home when she appeared to have been in such good health."

"Really, Max? People ask you that?"

"Absolutely. In most places in the world, death is viewed as sad, but inevitable. In California, the land of sunshine, yoga, spa treatments, and body cleanses, people prefer to think of death as optional."

Eddie's second call was to Rob and Holly.

"We're holding a press conference at two-thirty to discuss Mary Anderson's cause of death," Eddie began.

"Great. We're buried in deadlines over here, but we'll listen on the radio. How did Canning take the news?"

"Better than I could have imagined. And here was the real shocker: he was no fan of Mary Anderson."

"Wow! I suppose her reputation as the Queen of Mean reached beyond the boundaries of our little town."

"It's amazing how voters can see a politician in one light, and elected officials outside their orbit can see a completely different person."

"Honestly, Eddie, that doesn't surprise me. Politicians are like entertainers. In front of an audience, they're one person. Backstage, they can be completely different."

"I'm starting to think that was particularly true about Mary Anderson."

"It's a safe bet," Rob said. "I'll see you Friday at Smitty's, if not sooner."

CHAPTER NINE

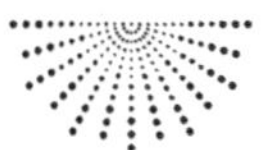

Wednesday morning Rob came into the office floating on a cloud. It was one of those rare days when, as publisher of a community weekly, he was first in print with a major story that would generate front page coverage across the San Francisco Bay Area. Mary Anderson's death in a Sunday morning landslide evolved over a period of forty-eight hours from an unexpected tragedy to an unanticipated mystery.

The San Francisco Chronicle, San Jose Mercury News, and *Oakland Tribune* all had small front-page items noting that the death of Mayor Mary Anderson had been the likely result of a violent argument. It was being classified as an act of unintentional homicide by Marin County's medical examiner. But Rob and Holly were the only reporters to provide their readers first-hand, detailed information on how these dramatic events unfolded.

By noon, when nearly all of Sausalito had opened their

mailbox to find their weekly edition of *The Standard*, phone and text messages began pouring in. Facing the balance of this week's editions, Rob and Holly pushed hard to keep at least half of their focus on other stories making news around the county.

While the two of them happily juggled the demands of a particularly busy day, their thoughts drifted back to what Eddie might learn that day, if anything, regarding the slaying of Sausalito's powerful and longest-serving politician.

During their rushed thirty-minute lunch break, Holly asked Rob, "Any thoughts about Thursday's funeral for Mary Anderson?"

"My first thought is I'd rather not go. Unfortunately, I think I can't avoid it. She was simply too dominant a figure in this city's history for me not to put in an appearance. I won't be there for the purpose of snooping, but I suppose there's always a chance I could get lucky and overhear something interesting. I doubt I'll pick up anything of value to pass along to Eddie; I know with the week we're having we can barely afford the ninety minutes or longer that it will take out of my workday."

"But you're right to go, Rob. I'll get in here tomorrow at seven and get an early start."

"I'll do the same."

"Marin Academy is on break this week, so I'll see if I can get Scott interested in going as well. It never hurts to have an extra set of eyes and ears. Not to mention it will likely be too big a crowd for you to cover on your own. He and I met at the reception following the service for his mom. He knows better than most that interesting things can happen when you least expect them."

"I'm with you on that, Holly."

"I suppose they're doing Anderson's service at Star of the Sea Church. She was Catholic, as I recall."

"Yep, she was. Out of curiosity I looked this morning. The service is posted on the church's website starting at eleven."

"Probably won't be more than a lot of moaning over the late great Madam Mayor. But what the heck, Rob, you never know when someone will say something of value. Plus, yesterday's news conference and the coverage in today's *Standard* has got to have chins wagging. One or two of the mayor's fan club might actually have something of value to say."

"It would be wonderful to hear anything we or Eddie can use in the days or weeks to come."

"From your lips to God's ears. I think what you'll hear repeatedly is the question: How could something so terrible happen to someone so wonderful?"

"You're probably right. But I'm certain a fair number of our fellow citizens had a healthy disdain for Anderson or were at least suspicious regarding her motives for holding on to power," Rob responded.

"You would think it would be hard to put the squeeze on as many people as we think Anderson did without attracting some, if not many, detractors," Holly smiled.

"Perhaps it's just part of that old story about people living in glass houses being hesitant to throw stones."

Holly chuckled. "My guess is that when the first couple of questions arise regarding Mary Anderson's supposedly unblemished record, all the stones will start flying."

The most logical place for Eddie to begin his investigation were the homes closest to Mary Anderson's Sausalito Boulevard address. The house across the narrow roadway, and one door up from the late mayor's home, was owned by a widower whom Eddie remembered as his sailing instructor in the youth program held for two weeks every summer at the Sausalito Yacht Club.

When he opened the door, Eddie could see in an instant how much the once healthy, hard-living sailing enthusiast had aged. Sean O'Hara's face carried the scars of a fifty-year love affair with cigars and aged Kentucky bourbon.

"Eddie Austin! How long has it been since I last saw you?" The old sailor's welcoming smile enhanced the deep creases on the permanent tan he had after forty-plus years of weekend outings on the bay.

"Good question." Eddie flashed a smile while extending his hand to shake. "Not as far back as when you were my sailing coach, and not as recent as to be easily recalled."

"Sounds about right," O'Hara said with a laugh that soon turned into a cough. "Can I buy you a drink? I'm friends with the bartender," he added, chuckling at his own joke.

"You certainly could, if I wasn't on duty."

"When you're a cop and you carry a gun, I suppose they're pretty strict about the rules. That's okay, my doc said I'm not supposed to touch booze, but that's not easy for an old sailor to do."

"I can drink, I just have to be off-duty. Shooting someone accidentally while under the influence, that will end a career faster than you can say, 'Oops!' Not to mention the criminal and civil penalties that you would be buried under."

"Wow! File that under not worth the risk," O'Hara exclaimed. "I'm glad to see you haven't lost that sense of humor you had as a kid. I never had a nicer, more thoughtful junior sailor than you. Do you miss those afternoons out on the bay?"

"Partially. Learning to handle a skiff was great, but I could have done without the bay's cold summer winds."

"My late wife hated that as well. She'd say it was too cold to be out on the boat, which in her estimation was true for all but a handful of days each year. I'd say it was bracing. Of course, I always wore a thermal shirt underneath my windbreaker. It hardly matters what month of the year it is; when that cold mist pushes its way through the Golden Gate and into the bay, it's time to zip up."

"...And bundle up! I don't even try getting my wife out there. She's more of the sun, sand, and beach type. And now our little boy, Aaron, seems to be the same way."

"I hope you have a picture you can show me of both of them."

Eddie opened the photos app on his phone and proudly shared a few pictures with his old sailing instructor.

"Wonderful!" O'Hara announced with a toothy smile. "Are you still tight with Rob Timmons?"

"Just had lunch with him two days ago. He's busy working the Mary Anderson story."

"I'm glad he found something he's good at. It certainly wasn't sailing. If I remember correctly, he went overboard on more than one occasion. Good thing those bright orange life vests are mandatory for all junior sailors. We had to fish him out several times."

"You're right about that," Eddie said with a chuckle. "Lucky for Rob he went into a profession that doesn't require sailing skills."

"I'll say. He was all thumbs when it came time to set the sails. Not to mention he couldn't tie a decent knot to save his life. But I think with *The Standard* he found his true calling. George Benton did some good work with the paper, but Rob's taken it to a whole other level. That was one hell of a story he had on the front page of this week's edition. I knew Anderson would be dead when she was pulled out of the wreckage of her house; nobody could have survived something like that. But slain earlier that night? Holy guacamole!" O'Hara's toothy grin came with a shake of his head.

"Holy guacamole pretty well covers it. It certainly threw me for a loop when the county coroner told me how she died."

"I didn't see or listen to any of the evening news, but I read Rob's story in *The Standard*. I saw you're the lead investigator on the case. So, by now, I'm guessing you'd like to know if I heard or saw anything in the hours before the slide?"

Eddie nodded. "Anything you recall from that night?"

O'Hara smiled. "I do, and the funny thing is that I didn't give it a thought until I learned she died late Saturday night. A car pulled out from her parking deck while I was watching an old Hitchcock film. Whenever it's been raining for a day, or in this case nearly a week, there's always a screech from the sound of the tires going into reverse over the wood planking of a parking deck. Terrible sound! What you rarely hear, however, is a second screech when the car goes into drive. Whoever was driving certainly was in a big hurry to get out of there."

"Did you take a look to see who was out that late?"

"I did, but the car was already two houses down the road

and going too fast for me to see anything other than the glow of red taillights. I had two thoughts: One, somebody is late for something; or two, someone is not a happy camper. It was not a good night to go speeding off like that. Particularly along the narrow winding streets we have up here."

"Any chance you happened to notice the time?"

"I did. It was ten forty-five. I've got one of those TVs that when you put the picture on pause, it goes to black, and a time display scrolls across the screen. Pretty cool. I love these new big screen sets! Perfect for someone like me who loves old movies."

"We think there's a good chance Mary Anderson argued with her assailant. I don't suppose you heard any raised voices?"

"Nope. Between the rain and the sound of the TV I heard only the screech of those wheels on the wood parking deck and then on the wet pavement."

"You ever hear anything like that before? I mean, a car taking off like that relatively late at night?"

"Not that I recall. As you can imagine, it's generally pretty quiet up here. I would think other neighbors heard that screech as well. I wish I could be of more help, Eddie."

"You've given me a lot of help, Sean. The medical examiner's best guesstimate was that Anderson died between ten and midnight. What you heard leads me to think that timeframe was spot-on."

"That's great! I'm glad I could be of some help, and even more glad that you came by. I was thinking of giving you a call. Cars speeding off like that is a rare event in this part of town. Particularly in the middle of a downpour like that. Everyone who lives up in these hills knows that slow and cautious is the only way to go on narrow steep streets that have a handful of blind curves. It's not the best place to drive, particularly when you reach a certain age, but then there are those views of the bay! On a clear day, you really can see forever. Well, at least as far as Mount Diablo."

"Sean, I appreciate your time and help. By the way, did you see Mary Anderson in the days before the slide?"

O'Hara gave a short laugh and said, "I rarely saw her, even though there is just a patch of paved roadway separating our two properties. Still, she did her best to avoid me, and I did the same."

"Not on the best of terms?"

"You know, Eddie, as a teen you were nowhere near this diplomatic."

"I know! Marriage, fatherhood, and a decade on the force have smoothed over what my bride likes to call my rough edges."

"Hah! I went to a couple of fund-raising parties held for Anderson when she was campaigning. Not a rare occurrence in her life. She certainly knew how to pour on the charm. But one-on-one—*ugh*! She could be one nasty piece of work."

"I've heard."

"She could get her nose out of joint over just about anything. 'You're playing your music too loud.' Or telling me that if I painted my deck more often it would improve the look of my house and extend the life of the wood. She wasn't wrong. Just bossy. Shakespeare said all the world is a stage. Mary Anderson apparently thought she owned the theater and wrote the show as well."

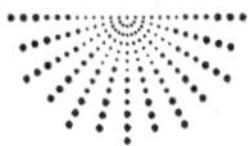

CHAPTER TEN

That night Holly asked Scott if he would attempt to snoop around during the reception following Anderson's funeral service.

"Gee, I suppose I should feel complimented," Scott shrugged. "You, Rob, and Eddie have turned snooping at funerals into a cottage industry. I'm surprised you're not going."

"I would, but I can't, for two reasons. First, it's really been an over-the-top week at the paper. I don't think this is going to settle down until a suspect is identified in Mary Anderson's slaying. Second, I could not stand the woman! She could put on a smile and glad-hand people from dawn to dusk. But on a scale of deceitful politicians, she deserved a perfect ten."

"Do you think it will be a long time before the police identify and arrest a suspect?"

"I don't think it will be all that long. One person, or more, knows something that should crack this case wide open.

Maybe that's wishful thinking on my part, but this is a small town with a big reputation. I'm certain that Anderson had a lot of secrets. With all that's happened, some of those secrets are bound to come tumbling out."

"Why do you say that?"

"Two reasons. First, Eddie's leading the investigation. Let's just say if I killed that malicious old woman, I wouldn't want a bloodhound like Eddie Austin on my trail. Second, Sausalito is one big fishbowl. It's hard to do almost anything, good or bad, in this town and not attract notice."

"You suggested last night that Mary Anderson has made enough enemies to likely create a long list of suspects."

"I still say that. And in a town where gossips and blabber-mouths are as abundant as migrating monarch butterflies in spring, there's a reasonable chance someone knows something significant. It might be a secret, but secrets have a short shelf life in this town."

"Okay, I'll go! In fact, I'm happy to be able to help. So, what should I be listening for, and whom should I be standing near at the reception after the service?"

"Mary Anderson had her own little clique. Mostly aged spinsters, widows, and gossips, many of whom are members of the town's leading social club, the Ladies of Liberty."

"My mom was in that group. Probably gave them a good amount of money, knowing her."

"Yes, that sounds like something Henrietta would have done. There wasn't a crackpot in this town who didn't come knocking on her door hat in hand at one time or another."

"Poor old thing, she was a bit of a whack-a-doodle, but she kept up with the in-crowd."

"You mean Sausalito's collection of aging widows," Holly said with a smile.

"Exactly!"

"Be on the lookout for Ethel Landau, Marilyn Williams, Beatrice Snyder, Robin Mitchell, and their queen bee, Alma Samuels."

"Alma Samuels, she can't still be alive. She must be a hundred by now."

"Not quite, but you're right. That old sourpuss is closing in on a century of disapproving stares."

"Huh?"

"Just teasing, Scott. In truth, all those old gossips make me laugh. Cool summers and mild winters no doubt have helped to preserve the old girl and the rest of her coven."

"You're right. All this fresh air must be conducive to a long life. At least for someone like Samuels."

"Rob claims it's not the fresh air. He insists Samuels, and most of her posse, run on battery acid."

"Yikes! That's not a plausible explanation. So, what should I be hoping to overhear or, perhaps, coax out of someone?"

"Anderson was careful to stay on the right side of people like Samuels and Williams. And, you probably don't know this, but before retiring, Robin Mitchell served on the city council alongside Anderson for many years. Plus, she supported her for mayor every time she wanted another one-year term. She might have some thoughts as to who had a particularly strong disdain for Madam Mayor. And like the rest of those magpies, she has a hard time keeping her mouth shut about other people's affairs."

"Are any of these people you're talking about discreet enough to keep their thoughts to themselves?"

"You would think, but when you've held power for as long as this clique has, you tend to make certain assumptions that others would be very hesitant to make. Call it the arrogance of incumbency," Holly explained with a shrug.

"What do you think someone like Mitchell might say?"

"Could be most anything. For example, she might say to her gal pals, 'I wouldn't trust mister so-and-so as far as I could throw him.'"

"Got a name of this mister so-and-so that I should be listening for?"

"Yes. Mike Nelson. He's a local architect; I think he and Anderson scratched each other's backs for years. Another local architect you might hear mentioned is Andrew Dexter. Rob and I believe that Nelson and Dexter are two heads of the same snake."

Scott grimaced. "That sounds like an unpleasant duo."

"There's certainly good reason to think they are."

"Any others?" Scott asked.

"Bob Stanley. He's a contractor in town. And Steve Brooks. He's another builder who does a lot of work in Sausalito. Those aren't all, but they're just the first names that come to mind."

"No women?"

"Nope. Eddie says the odds that Anderson was killed by a woman are very small."

"From what you've told me, there could be a long list of male suspects."

Holly nodded. She then explained Eddie's reasons to think that Anderson's death was the result of a bitter dispute: "The killer might have been furious with her over any number of things. Still, Eddie does not believe he arrived at her house that night with the intention of harming her. He probably came to discuss one grievance, or several. But if it was the killer's original intent to harm her—commit a premeditated act of murder—he almost certainly would have taken more overtly lethal actions."

"Interesting. I never thought about it from that perspective, but Eddie's theory makes sense."

"Anderson's body might have had traces of skin from the person who assaulted her, but none of that evidence was left after the mud and debris were washed away at the coroner's office prior to the corpse being examined."

"That was a pretty big oops on the part of the coroner's office."

Holly sat up straight. "Just think, Scott! Of all the mudslide victims in the history of the world, Mary Anderson might be the first to have been killed hours before she was swept away. I can't really see blaming the medical examiner's staff for washing the muck off of her before she was examined."

"Agreed. But you have to admit, that's some pretty whacky stuff."

"What can I tell you, it's Sausalito, Marin County, in the San Francisco Bay Area. In this part of the world, whacky stuff is one of our specialties!"

CHAPTER ELEVEN

Other than history and tradition, there's little to recommend St. Mary Star of the Sea Catholic Church. Standing on a hill surrounded by multi-million-dollar residential properties emblematic of Sausalito's modern era, the church is an unimpressive structure that relies greatly on the loving support of a tight-knit community of devoted parishioners.

Rob and Eddie gathered with their families here during Christmas and Easter celebrations, but at other times of the year, like so many others, they found their attention drifting away from weekly services at the aging church.

Unsurprisingly, the ground floor was filled to capacity for Mary Anderson's service. Rob and Scott, who arrived separately just minutes before the scheduled start of the funeral mass, headed upstairs and squeezed into two of the unoccupied spots remaining on the church's top floor.

After the service, which felt like an eternity to Rob, but

actually lasted less than an hour, both men passed each other and nodded, but made no overt show of greeting, having agreed by phone earlier in the day not to call attention to their acquaintance.

The basement of the old church hosted countless receptions over the years, including the annual Lion's Club crab feed and St. Patrick's Day fundraisers. Nearly all the attendees stayed after the service. Coffee, tea, sandwiches, and desserts were hosted by the Ladies of Liberty, stalwart supporters of the late mayor since her earliest days in office.

Mourners searched their memories for when, if ever, they had seen a funeral service so well attended. Most could not recall seeing the second-floor pews fully occupied other than at Easter and Christmas: proof, to those seeking reassurance, that Mary Anderson was beloved and would likely be remembered favorably for years to come.

Julie Phillips, Vice Mayor and now acting mayor, approached Scott before he summoned the courage to strike up a conversation with any of the attendees.

Although he spoke to students on a daily basis and was frequently called upon to address the student body of Marin Academy, Scott continued to feel uncomfortable in his adopted home of Sausalito. Pasadena was where he had lived from age five until his late thirties. He missed the milder, dryer weather of Southern California. But he was ever thankful for the presence of Holly in his life: a relationship that would not have been possible had he not attended the funeral of the woman he'd always thought was his aunt. Holly had unraveled that mystery and in doing so, changed Scott's life forever.

Uncertain whether to address her as Mrs. Phillips or

Madam Mayor, Scott settled for flashing a smile, extending his hand, and saying, "Julie, it's nice to see you again."

"It's nice to see you Scott, although I wish it was under happier circumstances."

It would have been unusual for Phillips to recall the name of a citizen she rarely encountered unless it was one who, if he wished, could make a generous contribution to a pet project of hers—or to her next re-election campaign. Scott Silva's name and face she would never allow herself to forget.

Naturally shy, Scott did what he'd done at numerous parent faculty mixers and allowed himself to simply relax and float with the tide. "I could not have been more shocked when I heard the news; you must have been as well," Scott exclaimed.

"I certainly was," Phillips replied in her tight-lipped, cautious manner of speaking that had made her a reliable number two for Mary Anderson. "Mary was an incredibly gifted public servant. This town has suffered a loss that will require all of us to come together and share in the struggle to regain our equilibrium and move forward."

Scott wasn't exactly sure what all that meant. Still, he wasn't about to ask. He assumed, like most politicians, the sentiment expressed was meant to sound significant while meaning little if anything.

"I know we'll bounce back, but it will not be quick, nor easy," Phillips added.

Wondering how to respond, Scott chastised himself for not being better at what his aunt Ruth called "the art of small talk." In the meantime, Mike Nelson walked over and turned their twosome into a threesome.

"I'm not sure if we've ever met," Nelson said, thrusting his open hand forward toward Scott while flashing a relaxed, confident smile. Given the cause of the gathering, Scott was taken aback by Nelson's jovial manner and tone. He recalled, as Holly had shared with him, that this was Sausalito's premier architect. In appearance and manner, however, he seemed more like a polished entertainer, or politician.

After introducing Scott, Phillips added, "You must have heard of Scott Silva, Mike. When the wealthy heiress, Henrietta Hammer, died, Sausalito learned the surprising news—along with Scott—that this handsome gentleman was not her nephew, but actually her *son*."

"I never met Scott, but his fame certainly precedes him. That must have been like winning the lottery!" Nelson smiled slyly. "One day you're a math teacher struggling, I imagine, to pay the monthly bills, on what I assume is too small a salary, and the next day you're a multi-millionaire. That's a dizzying series of events."

Scott needed a moment to adjust. He was an intensely private individual and was instantly put off by Nelson's casual familiarity. The topic of his windfall inheritance was one that came up often in Sausalito. Although Scott found it somewhat demeaning, he had learned to accept it as an inescapable reality. One evening while they were curled up in bed together, Holly said, "Better to be known as the guy who had a fortune drop into his lap than to be the hapless soul who lost a fortune." As usual, Scott found it difficult to argue with her logic.

Julie, turning to Scott, nonchalantly added, "As one of our community's most distinguished citizens, I hope you'll allow me to call upon you to join one of the city's boards or commissions. In fact, right now there's an opening on the Parks and Recreation Commission. I'm certain you'd make a good addition. Everyone still tells me how impressed they were when you contributed the funds to create the Elijah and Henrietta Hammer Playground on part of the green space in front of city hall."

Scott knew he was supposed to feel pleased, honored, or both, by the acting mayor's suggestion and praise. But he was neither. Scott, with good reason, was certain that what made him distinguished in the acting mayor's estimation was rooted in the estate he had inherited. Although he felt trapped in the moment, he kept his smile and expressed his desire to learn more about the city's parks and recreation programs.

Scott's truest desire was to not be on the radar of people like Julie Phillips.

On the opposite side of the room, Rob was working with the confidence of an experienced journalist. He was well practiced in the art of interviewing people who were not inclined to speak, on or off the record. Unfortunately, however, most of the attendees kept their distance from Rob, hoping not to see their names in his newspaper.

Fire Chief Bill Vogel walked up and put his arm around Rob's shoulder, an action that was viewed unfavorably by a few careful observers who thought Rob had been far less supportive of the town's longtime mayor than he should have been.

"You're probably not the most popular guy in this room," Vogel said teasingly. "I suspect a number of these people might have a framed photo of you in their garage."

"If they do, it probably has circles drawn on it and several dart holes."

"Sounds about right," Vogel said with a chuckle. "What is it that you've done that so irks these people? Anytime I mention how great a job your dad did as the town's fire chief and how much I learned from him, they inevitably agree with me. But then they add something like, 'that son of his is one seed that fell far from the tree.'"

"Yeah, I know, Bill. I wasn't a favorite with Mary Anderson and her crowd. I think they distrusted anyone who wasn't a sycophant, let alone someone who keeps a close eye on them."

"So now that the queen has fallen, who will the council settle on to fill the balance of her term?"

"I think they'll stay with Julie Phillips for now, at least until the next council election, which is less than a year away. From what I can tell she was liked by Anderson. She didn't become vice mayor by accident. Unless there is someone in their inner circle, they find more desirable and better deserving, they'll probably hold onto her."

"I'm always amazed by the amount of intrigue a town of fewer than eight thousand residents can have. It makes you wonder what the chances are for real change."

"Not much, would be my guess, Bill."

"I'm sorry to hear that. Some of our equipment is aging out. The fire house is a real architectural show piece, and I have no doubt that Mike Nelson was well rewarded for his design and oversight of that project. But if we get hit with a major fire up in the hills or, God forbid, a serious earthquake, having a fire station featured in a half-dozen magazines is not going to help save lives. Bottom line: I'd like to see either an increase in our budget or some onetime special items approved so we can get some of the equipment updates we badly need."

"As you probably know, in his time, my dad said much the same. Anderson always had a list of pet projects, and fire safety was never high on that list. Inadequate police coverage can get a politician in trouble a lot faster. Voters coming home to find they've been robbed will get a politician tossed out of office a lot faster than concerns over future fire and earthquake risks."

"No doubt, Rob. I live with that reality every day."

"We haven't spoken since Sunday. Any thoughts about the surprise—or I should say, shock—regarding the coroner's findings?"

Bill thought for a moment. "Sunday, I was on the scene for ten-plus hours, so I wasn't the least bit surprised when Anderson was found unresponsive. In an event like this, there's always a chance debris will fall in such a way that an air pocket will form and save a life. Given the nature of that particular slide, and surveying the wreckage, none of the rescue team thought this was anything other than a search and recovery mission. As for the fact that she was dead hours before the slide—now, *that* was a shocker. I saw some of the press conference Eddie did with Max Brownstein and Jack Canning. I certainly didn't expect to hear that Anderson died hours before the slide! I watched a clip on the early evening news at the firehouse with some of the recovery team; all of us were stunned," Bill shook his head. "I suppose Eddie's got his hands full with this case. Just between us, I think Anderson was both the town's most liked, and most *disliked*, individual all rolled into one. I suppose that's what people in your business would call a polarizing figure."

Rob nodded. "That was my impression as well. I suppose Mary Anderson was the perfect example of that."

"I try to keep my nose out of politics, but from what I know, it seems that our long-serving mayor was not universally beloved," Vogel shrugged.

"Far from it! She seemed to have a talent for pleasing all the right people, while ticking off the ones she saw as politically expendable. Most of the people who voted for her didn't really know her. They knew her positions on maybe two or three issues. Like other talented politicians, she knew how to sound like she was saying a lot when she wasn't saying much at all. Most importantly, she had a real talent for recognizing those issues that truly mattered to the occasionally interested, but rarely engaged. That's a category which covers a majority of Sausalito's voters."

"She also did a good job of saying the right thing at the right time, even if she had no intention of actually using her power to effect change," the fire chief added. "No one can say she wasn't a talented politician."

"A political figure of the first order, Bill."

"Do you think she had much to hide, and will some of those secrets spill out in the coming weeks?"

"It's possible that they will."

"Why is that?"

"If I've learned anything from hanging out with Eddie all these years, it's that when someone is killed, secrets come tumbling out like candy from a piñata."

"I'd say that's right," Bill smiled. "But why is that?"

"Because the only way any investigator can reverse engineer a crime is to keep digging into the victim's past. Did she have any enemies? I think in Anderson's case you and I would guess she had many. Also, what was the full scope of her professional and personal life? Financial transactions, business dealings, and so on. If you want your past to remain a secret, die a routine death. That would be my advice. And if there is one thing you can say about the death of Mary Anderson, it was anything but routine."

With the reception winding down, Scott knew he had little of value to report. He hoped to change that if for no other reason than to impress Holly. But how might that happen?

At that moment, an older woman tapped Scott on the shoulder. She wore a simple black dress with a black sweater that hung from her shoulders.

"Aren't you Scott Silva?" she said in a soft voice, as if hoping to keep his name secret.

"Yes I am."

"My name is Kayla Fox; I knew your mother. She was a very nice woman. All the local children saying she was a terrifying teacher was just so much silliness. She cared deeply about her students being fully prepared to move on to their next grade. Henrietta was right to think that their success was more important than her popularity."

"Thank you for telling me that. I know she had her admirers and detractors."

"I understand, Scott, that you're also a teacher."

"Yes. At Marin Academy. I'm a math teacher. I enjoy being there: good students, and an environment conducive to learning."

"I was born and raised here in Sausalito."

Scott thought that must have been quite a long time ago, given Kayla's advanced age.

"And where did you grow up, Scott?"

"First in the town of Fort Bragg up in Mendocino County. When I was five, my parents moved to Pasadena. I lived there until I relocated to Sausalito."

"I love Pasadena! Such a lovely place with a great history. You must have gone to the big parade on New Year's Day."

"I did on several occasions, and sometimes to the Rose Bowl game as well. It's certainly an exciting time of year to be in Pasadena. The crowds, however, can be a bit much. The locals are always anxious to get their town back once the holidays are over. Did you know Mayor Anderson well?"

"I was her neighbor for a very long time. I live on the opposite side of the street from where Mary's house stood. My other neighbor, Sean O'Hara, was once the commodore of the Sausalito Yacht Club. It's a lovely street: very nice neighbors, and normally very peaceful."

"You must have been shocked by the news of the mayor's death?"

"I can tell you this, the sound of that slide was simply terrifying. After that, I was certainly not going back to sleep. The power was out, so I took the flashlight I keep on my nightstand just in case of an outage. I walked out to my living room window. I could see the mud and debris between my home and Sean's. Then, when I looked closely through the rain and the darkness, I could see a sizeable part of Mary's house had vanished! At first, I couldn't believe my eyes. I thought of running out into the street. But between the rain, the wind, the mud, and my age, I thought that was probably a very foolish thing to do. One fall when you're my age and there's a good chance your walking days are over. So, I dialed the emergency number and they told me that fire and rescue vehicles had already been dispatched. I was so worried for poor Mary. I had been to several parties at her house, so I knew that the part of the house that was still standing was where the bedrooms were located. I told myself that Mary had been asleep, and she was probably okay."

"It must have been very difficult being alone at a time like that!" Instinctively, Scott took Kayla's hand. The memory of his mother and his aunt's fragility as they neared the end of their lives came to mind.

"I've had several years to adjust to the loss of my husband, but I missed him terribly that night."

"I can't even imagine how upsetting it must have been for you." For a moment, Scott wondered how frightening it would have been for both Holly and him, no less an elderly widow living by herself. "I suppose that was one night you'll never forget," he added.

"You're right. It was a very strange night, even before the slide."

"How so?"

"I went to bed before ten. I always try to read a little when I get into bed. Unfortunately, I rarely last more than ten or fifteen minutes. I dozed off. But I woke up thinking I heard shouting. It sounded like two voices, a man and a woman."

"Did you think one of the voices was Mary's?"

"I was not certain of that. But I'm sure that one of the voices was that of a man; I even thought that the man's voice sounded familiar, but now I'm not sure why I thought that. I knew I had fallen asleep reading, but I was surprised to see that it was only ten-fifteen. Perhaps Mary had her television's volume up too loud. You know, she was in good health for a seventy-something. But her hearing was less than perfect."

"Did you hear anything else?"

"I must have drifted back asleep for a short time. But then I heard the screech of a car's wheels. 'My goodness,' I thought, 'this is one crazy night.'"

"When was that?"

"I know exactly. I looked at my clock's display again; it was ten forty-five, thirty minutes after I first heard that shouting."

"Quite a night for a normally quiet part of town," Scott said reassuringly.

"And then in the middle of the night the slide came and cleared away more than half of Mary's house! I can't say for certain what time that was since, when I woke to the roar, all the power was already out."

"Terrible night," Scott said with a sympathetic shake of his head.

"I can't remember one stranger or sadder."

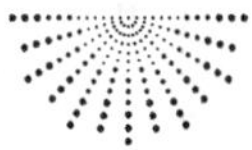

After an exceptionally busy week, Rob, Holly, and Eddie were more than ready for the start of their weekend. But, instead of gathering, as they always do, at Smitty's late on a Friday afternoon, Rob suggested to Eddie that they meet at his office.

"I know Smitty's is usually quiet until seven on a Friday night. Still, at least for now, the information we have regarding Mary Anderson is too sensitive to discuss anywhere it could be overheard. One day we might publish some or all of what we have on her, but this is not the time to detail any of that material in public," Rob explained in a phone call to Eddie.

"That's fine, Rob. I've got some news for the two of you as well: stuff that I'm keeping quiet—at least, for now."

"Good! Bring what you've got, and we'll do the same. I'll get a four-pack of Guinness for us to share, and I'll tell Holly to bring her martini shaker. We'll grab some ice and chips from Venice Gourmet and meet you here tomorrow at five."

If Rob and Holly had not suggested meeting at their office, Eddie would have. All three had previously been involved in two potentially explosive murder investigations involving Sausalito, but neither of those victims, Warren Bradley, *The Standard*'s gossip columnist, nor Henrietta Hammer, Scott's mom, were as well-known as the late mayor.

Mary Anderson was the undisputed boss of Sausalito's insular political world. Just the mention of her name in Smitty's, or most other places in this gossip-fueled small town, would have awakened the attention of even the most inattentive and uninvolved of citizens.

At this point meeting anywhere outside Rob and Holly's offices was taking an unnecessary risk.

I t was a few minutes past five on Friday when Eddie came up the stairs of the aging Victorian in which *The Standard*'s two offices had been comfortably settled since the paper's earliest days.

In addition to putting out cocktails and nibbles, Rob and Holly had gathered information from previous stories and research on Anderson that they planned to share with Eddie. After beers were opened and Holly's martini was stirred and poured, Eddie began.

"You and Rob have been tracking Anderson for years. Between her backroom deals, arm twisting, and God knows what other shenanigans, it's a safe bet she had a long list of enemies. Would you agree?"

Rob shrugged. "We have no idea how many people Anderson bullied, leaned on, disappointed, or just generally ticked off over a long career. I'd guess two dozen, but there's a real chance the number is far higher than that. It's hard to say without getting into the weeds—something we rarely have the time to do with a total of four community editions to put out every week. What we can do, however, is shine a light on some of Anderson's more questionable dealings. Both Holly and I believe that many of her transgressions have remained well hidden, at least until now."

"In my experience, if we succeed in opening any part of Anderson's web of secrets, a lot more surprises will come tumbling out," Eddie suggested. "The trail leading to my suspect might go off in a variety of directions. Possibly more than any other case I've worked. Regardless, all I can do is stay on task, keep my balance, and not allow myself to become frustrated by chasing down one or more blind alleys."

"Very true, Eddie." Holly nodded confidently.

"Whatever you share with me," Eddie continued, "might or might not be linked to her death. But as both of you know, you have to begin the process somewhere and hope that it places you on an undiscovered path as opposed to a dead end. Keep your balance, ignore your frustration, and take it one day at a time. That's what I've learned in my line of work, and I suspect it's what you've learned as well."

"Spot on, pal," Rob nodded. "In my opinion, nearly all of Anderson's dealings are unknown to the public. I suspect with some digging you're going to start compiling an impressive list of enemies."

"Really?" Eddie asked, somewhat surprised.

"I'd bet the bank on that!" Holly added. "She was a vote-getting machine, but she leaned on people with seemingly little, if any, concern regarding future repercussions."

"Sounds like she wasn't shy about ruffling a few feathers," Eddie grinned.

"Not in the least," Rob added.

"Just out of curiosity, can either of you give me some examples?"

Rob smiled and rolled his eyes. "Holly, do you want to start, or should I?"

"Age before beauty, Rob. You go first."

"Mary Anderson was many things to many people. To residents of Sausalito's senior housing complex, she was a steady and reliable booster. The city has distinguished itself county-wide for having the best and most affordable senior housing.

"In the political realm we all know she has broken all records for years of service, and the number of years she has held on to the mayor's seat is without precedent." Rob continued. "The innocent spin regarding her length of service as mayor is that she has, I mean *had*, great affection for the city in which she was raised and therefore became a tireless advocate for all of its citizens, from the wealthiest to the poorest. But Holly and I have long thought there was a darker side to the passion she showed for serving her hometown. Obviously, we're not the FBI. We're just two journalists trying to keep a day ahead of a heavy workload. But, during those rare moments when we have a bit of spare time, we've been tracking Anderson's relationship with the architect, Mike Nelson. For starters, he and his firm, Nelson and Associates, get over two-thirds of their building and renovation projects inside of Sausalito. The only other Sausalito firm, Andrew Dexter and Associates, is also successful, apparently because many of their projects are jobbed out to them by Nelson's firm."

"In other words," Eddie said, "Dexter is not competition at all. More like an offshoot of the same relationship Anderson has cultivated with Nelson."

"That's correct," Rob nodded.

"The amount of work Nelson and Dexter get is information readily available through the minutes of Sausalito's planning commission, and to a lesser extent, the design review board," Holly explained. "No magic involved in learning this, just an investment of time and a little shoe leather on our part. The project plans both Nelson and Dexter submit are not posted online. Still, by city law, they have to be made available for public inspection during the city's normal business hours."

"Nearly all of the major home construction and renovation plans that are filed with the city are submitted by these two firms," Rob added. "In turn, Mike Nelson, and Andrew Dexter, have been feathering Madam Mayor's nest for many years. This is an educated guess, but as you'll see when we take you through this, we have ample reason to believe our assumptions are correct."

"You mean Nelson and this other fellow, Dexter, paid her to get these projects? Work they'll be planning, designing, and overseeing through construction?"

"I doubt you'd find any direct payments from either of them to Anderson, just a variety of what polite society would call 'other considerations,'" Rob smiled.

"Considerations such as?"

"We can name two ways to start," Holly chimed in. "Queen Mary had the use of Nelson's Stinson Beach vacation home for two weeks every year, going back for at least the past five years. Supposedly, she uses it for an annual Anderson family gathering. Rob and I checked up on the property through the county assessor's office. It has four bedrooms and can accommodate twelve guests. It's located on Seadrift Road, which are the beachside homes of the Seadrift complex, along the north end of Stinson Beach."

"Would you care to venture a guess as to what a similar-sized vacation home goes for during the months of June, July, and August?" Rob asked.

"I have no idea." Eddie shrugged. "During the summer I blow up the little pool for Aaron to splash around in while Sharon and I are cooking out in the backyard. I think we paid thirty-nine bucks for that pool at Walmart."

"Similar properties to Nelson's Seadrift home rent for 1,200 bucks per day. Let's say you knock two hundred off for each night of a two-week prepaid rental; that would still be fourteen thousand for two weeks," Rob said, causing Eddie to give a long low whistle.

"That's a nice fringe benefit! How do you know she, the family, or both are not paying for it?"

"Not a chance, Eddie!" Rob snickered. "First, Anderson was well known for being just as tight with a buck as her dad. We learned that when we were teens running our yard cleanup service. Second, there's no way all this work is being sent to Mike Nelson's firm without his jumping through a few hoops in exchange. And by that I don't mean sending her the occasional box of chocolates," Rob laughed.

"I can't disagree, pal. Old man Anderson was more likely to lift ten bucks off the church collection plate than lay ten bucks down. Anything else Madam Mayor received for helping her favorite architects?" Eddie asked.

"She also enjoyed a two-week Lake Tahoe getaway every year at the home of Andrew Dexter," Holly added.

"For a woman who liked to parade around town wearing an old flannel shirt and blue jeans," Eddie said, "she apparently had a taste for the finer things."

"Yeah, beer drinker in public, champagne aficionado in private," Holly laughed.

"Both Nelson and Dexter raised money for Anderson's political piggy bank, which was open for donations 365 days a year. In the big leagues, state and federal offices, governors, members of congress, senators, and obviously, presidents, chasing after campaign money is a 365-days a year pursuit. But fundraising year-round, even when done in a low-key fashion, is highly unusual in a town as small as Sausalito," Rob added.

"Nelson and Dexter have co-chaired Mary Anderson's numerous re-election campaigns going back to when you and I were in high school, Eddie. Additionally, they both have a long list of appreciative clients who throw in a few hundred bucks when she runs every four years," Rob explained.

"What do they spend all that money on?" Eddie pressed.

"I would assume the usual: yard signs, fliers, newspaper ads, and voter receptions," Holly suggested. "And don't forget, if some of that campaign money happens to migrate over to Anderson's personal account, I wouldn't be the least bit surprised. Of course, you won't know that for certain without an audit. At least until now, no one has been that interested in doing a deep dive into Anderson's fund-raising machine," Holly added as she swirled an olive in her martini glass. "Rob and I are convinced that the consistent support Anderson has received from other city council members is rooted in the fact that she directs some of her donors to them in one fashion or another—which, if correct, is potentially a violation of campaign finance laws. In public filings you'll find donations coming from Nelson and Dexter to her fellow councilmembers who see it as their job to smile and nod approvingly through council meetings as Anderson pronounces her position on everything from building projects to Sausalito's various beautification efforts."

"One of her old political cronies who died last year," Rob added. "A guy named, Phil Hudson, who served on the council with Anderson for fifteen years and voted with her, as best as Holly and I can tell, on everything that came before them. The city just erected a statue of Hudson down by the ferry landing. We believe that was Queen Mary's way of showing her fellow councilmembers that she appreciates elected officials who give her their unquestioning support."

"You see, Eddie, if you run for office and do as you're told, you too could get a statue for your grandchildren to visit one day," Holly laughed.

"Playing the yes-man has never been my thing. Jack Canning can tell you that. Besides, getting covered in bird droppings and having people scratch their heads trying to figure out who the heck Eddie Austin was, is not my thing."

"What's a great honor to some," Rob shrugged, "doesn't necessarily mean much to others."

"So, what was the key to her successfully controlling the city council for nearly twenty-five years?" Eddie asked.

"It's pretty simple. Money is to politics what jet fuel is to aviation. Just try getting a career in politics off the ground without it," Rob winked. "I think it's the number one reason, why so many good people won't go into politics and others quit after a term or two in office. The constant demand to raise money just wears them down. Call it dialing for dollars."

"I agree with Rob," Holly said. "Unfortunately, some take to it like ducks to water, not only raising all the money they need, but raising funds for others. The good news, or at least I like to tell myself this, is that a handful of the successful money generators are honest, cause-driven individuals."

"But what exactly did Nelson and his buddy Dexter get out of being such helpful supporters of the late Queen Mary?" Eddie asked.

"Nelson and Dexter got a good deal more money out of supporting Anderson than they put into her campaigns," Rob suggested. "It's been an open secret among the wealthy in town that if you're buying a property in Sausalito that's going to need massive renovations or updating, Nelson and Dexter are the guys who can, as they say, 'get your project through the process.'"

"Renting my home instead of owning it," Eddie shrugged, "I know nothing about the process you're talking about. Not to mention I have no doubt that whatever money you need is well above what any honest cop could afford. Tell me how this works?"

"Sure," Rob smiled. "The first thing to know is it can be a real nightmare getting through the entire planning process, trust me on that. I've written enough stories on the topic to know."

"I would think it's difficult. No one needs to buy their way through an easy process."

"Exactly," Holly smiled.

"First you start at city hall's planning department. The counter, as they call it. This is where you register your proposal with the city," Rob explained. "Once you've completed a small mountain of paperwork, you move on to the city's design review board. That's followed by the planning commission and then up to the city council for your final approval. If you manage to get through all three steps, it's time to pop the champagne. Insiders call it 'running the gauntlet.' Believe me, coming through with your dream house approved and plans mostly intact is no small feat. Of course, for the home buyers who are willing to put themselves through it, the cost is not really an issue."

"Wow," Eddie said, shaking his head in wonder. "Makes me glad I'm just a humble renter."

"Yes. But remember, not everyone gets caught in the system," Rob continued. "Buy a house, move in, and start living there, you'll have relatively few headaches other than the usual annoyances."

"Such as?" Eddie asked.

"Anything and everything, from the ever-rising cost of property taxes, which people think the Jarvis Act tamed, but that's not at all true for people who bought their homes over the decades since the Jarvis property tax reduction took effect. Add to that water fees, trash collection, and assorted bond measures, and even the humblest of homes in Sausalito, and nearly all of Marin, are out of the price range of working-class people," Rob said.

"But there's a plot twist," Holly added. "If you have the money and the desire to renovate or, God forbid, demolish an older existing house that's seen much better days, and build new from the ground up, you're sticking your hand in the fire."

"And then comes the twist!" Rob added with a mischievous smile.

"What?" Eddie asked, quickly looking back and forth

between his two close friends.

"There's a subplot to all this, it's where the serious money comes into play," Holly explained.

"It's a matter of simple common sense. Why drop well over ten thousand dollars, or a good deal more, having architects and engineers, plus an attorney or two and God knows who else, drawing up plans, filling out stacks of forms, replying to countless inquiries, and so on, if the architect you've chosen to create your dream house can't carry the ball over the goal line?" Rob asked.

"You'd just be spending money and spinning your wheels with no real hope of success," Eddie shrugged.

"Exactly!" Holly nodded. "People with real money know how the game is played. And if they don't, one of their group will take them aside and give them a crash course over lunch at the yacht club, or while playing a round of golf at the Presidio."

"And how is the game played?" Eddie asked with a raised eyebrow.

"If you want to take an old house on a great lot with incredible views and turn it into your dream home, you have to pay the piper. Trust me on this, that price can be remarkably steep," Holly explained.

"The piper is, I mean *was*, Mary Anderson?" Eddie smiled.

"She did not create the system," Rob said, "so much as she perverted it to her use. Think of it as a small town going into the business of creating a speed trap, where suddenly a county road goes from fifty-five miles per hour to thirty. You could put up signs like 'reduce speed ahead,' maybe lay down a couple of rumble strips to alert drivers not paying sufficient attention; but if your actual goal is to enhance the town's revenue you can surprise them. Hit them with an eighty-dollar fine for not noticing the sign that announced a drastically reduced speed."

"But none of this revenue for professional consultants to get you through the design review, planning commission, and the city council, goes into the city's treasury," Eddie pointed out.

"That's right. Anderson designed a system in which wealthy people, hoping to secure their dream house, had to pay a steep price before they could win the approval of the city and get the needed permits to begin their project," Rob explained.

"Nelson and Dexter, along with their staffs, of course, were only too happy to play along," Holly added. "And why not? It's a win-win for all of them. A steady flow of wealthy applicants willing to pay their price has made both design firms very successful."

"I'm guessing a piece of the profits Nelson and Dexter made found their way back into Anderson's pockets by way of campaign contributions," Eddie said with a smile.

"We're pretty sure there's a long line of contractors, builders, electricians, plumbers, interior designers, landscape people, and others, all taking their own slices of a very large pie. They're undoubtedly kicking a portion of their profits back to Nelson, Dexter, and through their own campaign contributions, to Anderson as well," Rob concluded.

"I never knew any of this!" Eddie shook his head, awed by what he had learned. "Talk about an underground economy! It just blows my mind. Sausalito may look like a picture-book, small, sleepy town, but as is often the case, you need to take a closer look."

"There's no need to know any of this unless you're planning on buying a rundown home on a good size lot that you've paid two million dollars or more for, and you're prepared to invest another two million dollars to turn it into your dream house," Holly declared.

"All that's needed is the kind of money my old man calls, 'living in high cotton,'" Eddie concluded.

"You need impressive resources to play at this level," Rob added.

"With the skyrocketing values many of the bigger properties can command both here in Sausalito and across Richardson Bay in Tiburon and Belvedere, these folks are often playing in a four million dollar and up price range," Holly said. "On the upside, if you're capable of coming up with this kind of money and you have someone like Nelson steering your project through the process, you'll come out of it with a home worth a million or more above what you paid."

"So, if you play your cards right, and everyone does what they're being paid to do, you can walk away with a ten, twenty, even thirty percent gain on your investment," Eddie said, giving a low whistle. "That's some pretty slick stuff."

"If you've got the money to play this game, you can do very well for yourself," Rob added.

"I would think for all that it's worth, Nelson and Dexter must have done more for Anderson than the occasional use of a vacation home, campaign contributions, and leaning on friends to support her as well," Eddie suggested.

"You mean like gifts, cash, or other considerations?" Rob asked. "That's hard to say. We know both Nelson and Dexter bundled campaign money for her. How they collect that money would take a deeper investigative dive than anything we've done to this point. It's also possible that Nelson might have taken his own cut of Mary Anderson's action. That would seem to fit with his bringing Andrew Dexter into the picture. Holly and I believe that Dexter kicks back to Nelson, likely based on a portion of the revenue coming into his firm from a boom in residential projects."

"The bottom line is that Dexter served two practical purposes, at least from Nelson's standpoint," Holly added.

"Which were what, exactly?" Eddie asked.

"The first, and likely the biggest, is there was way too much work flowing out of the city's planning department into Nelson's office. With approximately a third of that work now being handled by Dexter's firm, it certainly looks better. You can file that problem under 'an embarrassment of riches,'" Holly laughed.

"Then there's a matter of simple practicality. How much business did Nelson want or need?" Rob asked. "The more projects you take on, the greater the need to grow your support staff and increase your total number of associates. Small, picturesque, waterfront towns don't generally attract the world's most ambitious people. If you're a twelve-plus hour workday type, in the office six days a week, you're going to be doing your thing in Los Angeles, San Jose, Denver, Chicago, New York City—*not* Sausalito. This town attracts wealthy retirees, or people who like making a good living while still taking time to enjoy a martini on their deck and watch the sunset while steaks are cooking on the grill. For the twenty-four-seven types, Sausalito is not their scene. This place is way too peaceful," Rob smiled.

"Peaceful on the surface anyway," Holly quickly added.

"Sounds like everyone was pretty satisfied with their piece of the pie," Eddie said. "Mary Anderson had a steady flow of campaign money for whatever use she wanted to put it toward.

Nelson and Dexter had all the work they could want or handle. And the fat cats, who can afford to play by the city's elaborate project development rules, got a great house, plus a potentially handsome return on their investment."

"It's a great system, other than the fact that it's rigged," Rob said. "Frozen out of the system are a lot of honest, hard-working individuals, who might want to participate in what they think are free, fair, and open elections—only to learn, thanks to Mary Anderson and her followers, they need not apply unless they have first proven their loyalty to the handful of people who are actually running the city. Sure, there are occasional openings on the council, a commission, or board, but you can bet your bottom dollar that Anderson and her team already have someone picked out for whatever important openings arise. Good luck to anyone who thought they could enter this arena without the prior approval of Queen Mary and her loyal supporters."

"Bottom line, this is not about better government," Eddie said, "it's more about lining your pockets with a part of all the money flowing into Sausalito because of quickly rising home values. And you can likely bet your bottom dollar that Anderson was the one pulling the strings."

"As we all know," Rob added, "hot markets cool now and then. But if you look at the price curve of property values in Southern Marin over the past thirty-plus years, the market flattens for a brief time; it even dips slightly on occasion. But overall, the prices keep moving upward."

"Meaning Mike Nelson, Andrew Dexter, and what is likely a long line of subcontractors had good reason to be very satisfied with the backdoor deals they had going with Anderson and her pals," Eddie concluded.

"Absolutely!" Holly smiled. "As Mark Twain once wrote, 'There's gold in them thar hills.'"

"Only now the dirt itself is the gold. Of course, it has to be dirt situated in the right place. And that starts with what is popularly referred to as 'million-dollar views,'" Rob added.

"How about the death grip Mary Anderson has kept on the city council over these past twenty-plus years? Any guess how that game works?" Eddie asked. "To be honest, I pay one percent of the attention you two pay to Sausalito politics."

"Let's go back a bit to the hoops you have to jump through to get any new building project approved," Rob suggested. "Remember, before you can reach Anderson and her fellow city councilmembers, you need to secure the approval of the city's design review board and the planning commission. They're both powerful, but the planning commission is at the top of the food chain. What they approve or deny is ratified or overturned by the city council."

"Anderson has a chokehold on who gets appointed to the design board and the planning commission," Holly explained. "You can, of course, vote against Madam Mayor's wishes, but afterwards you'll never get reappointed to the board, commission, or any other position of authority."

"But why do the citizens on a city board or commission want to serve in the first place?" Eddie asked.

"A majority are retired from their day jobs, or nearing retirement," Rob offered. "For most it's a status thing in the town's social circle. The fact that you were a school administrator in your work life, that's fine, and your service was likely a valuable contribution to society as a whole. Serving on a board or commission, however, will get you a level of attention you never previously had. And believe it or not, for some that's a power trip. Little fiefdoms often attract those who think they should be at the top of the pile."

"Rob's right. Call it big fish in a small pond syndrome," Holly nodded.

"I just don't understand what motivates people to put so much time into these boards and commissions in the first place. Do either of you?" Eddie asked.

"One reason is when that high-tech multi-millionaire wants to add a new wing to his mansion, you suddenly find yourself, and your spouse, invited to some really nice parties," Holly explained. "I can't say that's the only reason, but it's certainly a big part of it."

"She's right, Eddie. It must be fun hanging out with the super-rich. She should know," Rob said teasingly as he glanced at Holly.

"Rob, you know perfectly well that my Scott is an accidental millionaire. He won the birth mother lottery. If not for that, he and I would be clipping sale coupons before bed every night—just like you and Karin." Holly explained as she stuck her tongue out at Rob, causing both he and Eddie to laugh.

"Holly, it's just difficult passing up an opportunity to tease you."

"Then try harder, Rob."

"I will. I promise."

"Is that what you tell Karin on a nightly basis?" Holly asked with an arched eyebrow.

"More or less. But it doesn't mean I'm not really trying."

"The longer you two work together, the more you sound like an old married couple," Eddie suggested.

"We are Eddie. Haven't you heard?" Holly admitted. "All the

arguing with none of the intimacy. It's not a perfect relationship…"

"…But it works for us," Rob said with a laugh. "By the way,
Eddie: you may or may not know that most of these boards
and commissions are occupied by retired citizens, or in rare
instances young professionals who, for one foolish reason or
another, have convinced themselves that they are all that
stands between their community thriving or losing its way."

"Rob's inner curmudgeon is coming out," Holly insisted.

"She's right. In doing my job, I've become a bit of a cynic,"
Rob said in his defense.

"Haven't we all?" Eddie asked.

"Residents get involved with these boards and commissions
for various reasons," Holly added. "Many, actually most, want
to see their community improved—however you define
'improved.' Some have felt ignored by the process. Some,
aggrieved. And joining a commission or board can be their
way of righting a real or simply perceived wrong."

"The way we view it, Eddie, is there are two types of boards
and commissions, and this is true for most of the small towns
in Marin County. There are the less impactful groups like the
library board, fine arts, or parks and recreation commissions.
There are also the fire and public safety boards, the historical
preservation committee, and the chamber of commerce," Rob
explained. "Am I leaving any out, Holly?"

"I don't think so, Rob, but there's always a chance that
Sausalito came up with another board, commission, or
committee since we started this meeting!"

"Sounds like a position for everyone who wants one in a
city of seventy-two hundred people," Eddie declared with a
smile.

"That's about the size of it," Rob laughed.

"And we won't even discuss the event committees for the Fourth of July celebration, the opening day parade for the Sausalito Little League, Santa's arrival ceremony, the annual chili cook-off, and the summer jazz festival at Gabrielson Park. Did I get it all, Rob?" Holly asked breathlessly.

"Let's just say there is no need to retire," Rob nodded. "There are enough commissions, boards, and committees to fill the empty dates on anyone's calendar."

"But that's all a sideshow," Holly said. "Mary Anderson could have been killed for a baker's dozen worth of reasons. But until you can put aside the serious money that was going into and coming out of the permitting process as a possible motive, that's an angle you need to keep near or at the top of your list."

"Holly's right. The real action, I should say the real money, is in the planning commission and design review process. If there are backroom deals going on, that's most likely where it's happening," Rob said, then paused to look at his watch. "Gosh, we've been at this for two hours and we haven't yet discussed what Scott and I came up with at the reception following Anderson's service at Star of the Sea church. Any chance you two can reconvene tomorrow morning? I know it's Saturday. But I'm free because Karin took the kids up to Napa this afternoon to spend the night with the grandparents. She's driving back down tomorrow after lunch and we're going to be two adults all on our own until late Sunday afternoon when her parents are dropping off the kids."

"Wow, a night without the little ones! Sounds nice," Eddie smiled.

"I can be here tomorrow morning, provided it's not too

early," Holly said. "I have enough early days Monday through Friday."

"Say, ten?" Eddie asked.

"Done!" Holly exclaimed.

"I hope we're getting somewhere," Rob wondered aloud.

"I'd like to think we are," Eddie said. "One thing I'm pretty certain about: Anderson, like her dad, worked all the angles. People who do that inevitably push other people aside."

"So, you're thinking that's what led to a violent argument?" Holly asked.

"It's a reasonable assumption," Rob added. "Habitually pushing people around can lead to dangerous consequences."

"It's likely there is more than one person in this town who would be happy to see Mary Anderson knocked off her pedestal," Eddie replied. "Once I have a better idea who those individuals are, I'll hopefully be much closer to finding her killer."

CHAPTER THIRTEEN

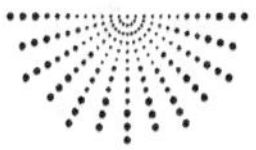

Rob told Holly and Eddie to head home without him. "I want to stay and pull some items together for a jumpstart on next week's editions."

"Never heard the expression, 'when the cat's away the mice will play?'" Eddie's comment to Rob earned him a jab in the ribs from Holly.

"I'm just teasing, Holly."

"That doesn't sound like teasing to me."

Rob heard their conversation continue as they walked down the steps and began their short trips home. The next time he looked at his watch, it was nearly nine. Having done a thirteen-hour day, Rob felt certain it was time to call it a night.

Minutes later, Rob was enjoying a pleasant evening stroll heading north along Bridgeway. He passed opposite the two massive concrete elephants that guard the entrance to Vina Del Mar Park. Then he walked by the busy sidewalk tables at

Poggio's, the Italian restaurant at the base of the Casa Madrona Hotel. The sight of diners enjoying a late dinner caused his stomach to growl out its disappointment that he had not yet eaten. Perhaps he could open a can of beef stew or corn beef hash. That would be the quickest and easiest choice at this time of night.

A few minutes later, Rob was walking down Caledonia Street. As opposed to the downtown district that surrounded the busy two-lane roadway called Bridgeway with an eclectic mix of t-shirt and souvenir shops, jewelers, art galleries, high end clothiers, and a variety of eateries, Caledonia Street caters mostly to the community with small groceries, dry cleaners, hair stylists, a few restaurants, and two bars.

As Rob passed Holly's old apartment building, he could already hear the music pulsing from Smitty's on a typically busy Friday night. The sound caused Rob to smile. How often had he, Eddie, and Holly spoken about the wildly diverse patrons of the longtime neighborhood dive bar? It was quiet through the day with a scattering of old sailors, who were, as the expression goes, "Never drunk on duty; never sober at liberty." It was quiet as well on late Friday afternoons when Eddie, Rob, and Holly held their regular end-of-the-workweek happy hour. But on Friday and Saturday nights, or special occasions such as Giants, A's, Warriors, Sharks, or Niners playoff games, the more than century-old establishment was pulsing with music and voices that could be heard for blocks around.

Being at liberty for just one night, Rob toyed with the thought of walking in. He always remembered that both he and Eddie celebrated their twenty-first birthdays at the old neighborhood hang, a moment they had anticipated since they both turned fourteen. Just as he was nearly beyond the wide-open double doors that beckoned neighbors, strangers, and old friends to step inside and join the party, a hand gripped Rob's shoulder and gave it a squeeze. Rob turned to find Pete Francis, a man who was thirty-plus years his senior and the managing partner of Smitty's for the past two decades.

"Hey, Rob. Where were you earlier tonight? I didn't see you, Eddie, and Holly, for your usual Friday evening end-of-the-week drinks." Pete's Boston accent was nearly as strong today as it was when he relocated to the Bay Area decades ago as an ambitious twenty-something.

"All three of us were swamped with end-of-the-workweek assignments. Putting out four community newspapers every week keeps you pretty busy," Rob replied with a tired smile.

"I can believe it, pal! Come on in and let me buy you a drink," Pete grinned. "Since I read about Madam Mayor's unexpected demise, I've been thinking about giving you a call. Perhaps we were destined to run into each other."

"I'm all ears, but I was on my way home to an empty house. I haven't eaten since lunch."

"That's no problem," Pete said with a pat on Rob's shoulder. "I'll have Mike fix you up a burger with fries and a salad on the house."

"I can't say no to that, Pete. Karin and the kids are with her parents up in St. Helena for the night. To be honest, I wasn't looking forward to going home and opening a can of hash for dinner."

"Follow me, my friend, I've got you covered."

Pete led Rob through the back and past the kitchen, where

he asked that a burger, "with the works," be brought back to his office.

Moments later, Pete sat down at a large desk with a swordfish wall-mount trophy behind him. A small brass plate was embossed with the date and place the creature was caught.

Rob pointed up at Pete's prized catch. "Key West, Florida? I'll bet that was a memorable day."

"It was! A few pals and I go fishing outside the gate two or three times a year. But it's nothing like fishing off the Florida Keys. Beyond beautiful."

After a quick catch-up—including a summary of Pete's two sons, both of whom were now married—Pete shared with Rob photos of his four grandsons, who ranged in age from six to twelve.

"All happy and healthy," Pete declared.

Rob dug into his burger and fries moments after it was put in front of him. He reported that Karin was well, and their children were "getting bigger by the day."

Once Rob's plate was cleared, Pete came around to the issue he wanted to discuss. "I can't say I'm going to miss Mary Anderson."

"You're not alone in that sentiment, Pete. Sometimes I think she had as many detractors as admirers."

"Why do you say that?"

"I cover local politicians in a half-dozen different towns in Marin County. Some politicians are loved and admired, but about a third or more are disliked and distrusted."

"I certainly don't know half as much about Marin County politics as you do, but I can tell you this much, I doubt any were as crooked as Mary Anderson."

As Rob often did in his work, he quickly considered how he could respond to Pete's provocative declaration.

"I have a pretty good idea that she wasn't shy about leaning on folks with money to contribute to her campaign fund, and she encouraged people to give generously to causes she supported, like the jazz festival and the historic preservation center."

"Rob, I'm pretty sure that 'civic pride' routine of hers was all a cover. She could come up with reasons one-to-twenty as to why you should support this or that cause. But I'm convinced a good amount of the money I and others gave her found its way into her pocket."

"Couldn't you tell her to back off? That business was slow, expenses were up, and so on?"

"I tried that, Rob."

"And…"

Pete laughed as he got up, opened a second bottle of Guinness and handed it to Rob. "Anderson says to me, 'You and I need to talk.' She comes in here, sitting where you're sitting right now…"

"And?" Rob asked with increasing interest.

"She goes into this routine about how residents on Caledonia, and up on Locust and Turney streets as well, have been complaining about the noise coming out of here on Friday and Saturday nights. Then she adds, 'I've been taking a lot of heat for you. The least you can do is support a cause that is important to me and benefits the city where you live, work, and prosper.'"

"Wow. Sounds like a pretty polished pitch. Did she define what amount of money she was hoping to get from you?"

"Absolutely. I don't think Mary Anderson was the least bit

shy when it came to leaning on people for money, free labor, products, whatever she thought she could get. Bottom line, she wanted a monthly 'contribution,' as she called it, to her 'Better Sausalito Now Fund,'" Pete explained, using air quotes for the name of Anderson's fund.

"How much did she want?"

"Five hundred bucks a month. In turn she would do all she could 'to keep her fellow city councilmembers from taking up the issue of weekend noise abatement on Caledonia Street.' Those were her exact words. And since we're the neighborhood's noisiest spot on a Friday or Saturday night, it was pretty obvious that the time had come for me to pay up or shut up."

"I'm guessing you did as she suggested?"

"I didn't think I had much choice."

"How many years have you been supporting this fund of hers? Which, by the way, I've never heard a word about."

"Six years now."

"Six years? Yikes! At five hundred a month, times seventy-two months, that's…"

"Thirty-six thousand dollars and counting!"

"That's some serious money, Pete."

"Absolutely! But after I thought about it, I concluded it was my only choice. We could quiet things down a good deal by shutting the front double doors to the place on Friday and Saturday nights, but our business would drop by a third, possibly more."

"Why is that Pete?"

"Couple of reasons. The temperature, as you know, is nearly always cool in Sausalito. When we get busy, particularly on Friday and Saturday nights, just the number of people in here causes the place to get considerably warmer. We open the doors at night to help the air circulate, but the music, the chatter and laughter pulsing out of here attracts people driving or walking by. Just about everyone of a certain age is looking for a party. Once they hear this place rocking, people laughing and having a good time, they know they've found the party."

"You're right about that. Whenever Karin and I are coming home late, not something that happens often now that we have two little ones, it always feels like we're missing the party when we walk or drive by."

"I don't like taking five hundred bucks out of my bottom line every month, but I can't think of a logical alternative. I could save the money and tell her 'No!' Or give her less than what she wanted every month. But in the end, I thought paying her in full was my best move. Now, the big question is…"

"Who is going to come knocking on your door from the, what was the name she used for this fund of hers?"

"The 'Better Sausalito Now Fund.'"

"That's an odd name," Rob said with a short laugh.

"Everything about it is odd to me. It's nothing more than a shakedown scheme."

"I'm guessing you're right about that, Pete. Do me one favor; call me when and if someone comes around to collect your next monthly payment. It would be very interesting to know who is taking up the supposed good work Mary Anderson left behind."

Rob came home to an empty house, thankful for the opportunity to have a peaceful night after such a long day. Come the morning he would share with Eddie and Holly the explosive story he had just heard from Pete Francis.

Just how wide and how deep did Mary Anderson's scheme extend was Rob's final thought as he slipped into a well-earned night's sleep.

CHAPTER FOURTEEN

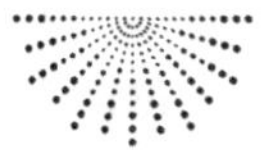

Waking up to silence is a rare experience for a parent of two young children. Once up, Rob dressed quickly and headed for the office. He was anxious to add to the head start he had established on his coming week's workload.

Rob learned long ago that the secret to making time pass quickly was simple: stay focused on tasks which require your immediate attention. First on his agenda for the coming week was the Wednesday release of the Sausalito edition, leading with Mary Anderson's funeral service at Star of the Sea Church.

The mere thought of reporting on a sampling of comments made by various speakers in tribute to the late mayor put a knot in Rob's stomach. It was similar to feelings he had previously when putting into print laudatory comments spoken of someone Rob knew to be less than praiseworthy. It always brought to mind the advice of Rob's journalism instructor,

Professor Pratt, at San Francisco State. "The job of a free press is not to serve as a conveyor belt for garbage. Don't put into print that which you know or have reason to suspect is untrue."

Rob's job brought into focus the difference between academic ideals and publishing realities. In every community he needed to tread more lightly at times than he wished. But at one point, or several each week, he found himself writing a story that given the choice, he would not do.

Publishing four different editions, in four different parts of the county, meant having many influencers and advertisers to please. It was not always possible to keep all his readers engaged and satisfied. Case in point: the ongoing coverage of Mary Anderson's life and death. He had no choice but to detail her long years of service and acknowledge the many ways in which she impacted the community and its residents. He never doubted that a sizable portion of his readership would have enjoyed a more critical examination of Anderson's record as a public servant. Perhaps that was coming in the not-too-distant future. But for now, Rob knew in a small, tight-knit community, praise of the recently deceased mayor needed to precede criticism.

Rob's only choice was to present the facts that were available to him and Holly at press time. Last week, Anderson was a dedicated public official whose body had been found buried in the debris of her wrecked home. Then, to everyone's shock, it was learned that she had been violently attacked just hours before the landslide, causing even her most faithful and vocal supporters to wonder what series of circumstances might have brought her to such a surprising end.

Rob now had reason to believe that Anderson was, to put it

politely, abusing the powers of her office. In a bizarre twist, the act of nature that buried Mary Anderson appeared to be uncovering her misdeeds.

What needed to happen now was clear: Follow the story, report the facts, and keep moving forward.

The first draft of next week's Sausalito edition was, at least for the moment, headlined:

Mayor Anderson Laid to Rest. Investigation into Her Death Begins.

Rob didn't doubt that over the next seventy-two hours, that lead headline could change one or more times.

Rob gathered up a sampling of laudatory comments from the mayor's service. He knew most of what was said were half-truths, at best. His one hope was in the fullness of time, the whole truth would be revealed to all who cared to know it.

He was still at work on his lead article when Eddie and Holly walked in.

"How's the one-night bachelor?" Eddie asked. "Did you behave yourself?"

"I did stop off at Smitty's," Rob confessed.

"You dog!" Eddie reacted with a laugh. "Meet anyone interesting?"

"Cat's away, Rob?" Holly asked with that frequently deployed raised-eyebrow stare of hers.

"Calm down, you two. I'll have you know Pete Francis invited me to come in. He wanted to talk to me privately, so he took me back to his office. When I told him Karin and the kids were up in Napa for the night and I had worked late and not eaten supper, he had his kitchen bring me a burger and fries—and a couple of my favorite beers to boot!"

"Wow," Eddie said smiling. "Pete's a good guy, but generally not big on handing out free food and drink. He must have had something important on his mind."

"He did, and you're both going to flip when you hear what it was."

"What?" Holly asked breathlessly.

"Wait a minute," Eddie said, putting his palm forward like a cop stopping traffic. "Let me guess. Madam Mayor was shaking him down."

Rob slapped his forehead. "You do have some serious skills of deduction! How did you figure that out?"

"Easy. It's something I've wondered about for a long time. In a town as dead as Sausalito can be nearly every night of the year, how is it that Smitty's can be rocking out with music and people partying—not just inside, but on most weekend nights, out on the street as well?"

"True, considering 'late' in Sausalito means anything that happens after ten," Rob replied.

Holly snickered. "Bingo!"

"How much was Madam Mayor squeezing Pete for?" Eddie asked.

"Five hundred a month, for something called 'The Better Sausalito Now Fund.'"

"Wow," Holly said. "That's certainly a creative title."

"I never heard of any such organization. I'm going to check with Sacramento to see if it's a registered charitable organization. I'm guessing it's not," Rob smiled.

"She might have had a half-dozen other names like that she was using," Holly countered.

"I wonder where she was opening these accounts and parking the money she was taking in?" Eddie asked.

"West Bay Savings and Loan," Rob and Holly said in unison.

"You two really do work like one mind," Eddie said, shaking his head in amazement. "How did you both hit upon West Bay Savings?"

"Holly," Rob said. "Tell the man."

"It's simple. Cora Jones, the branch manager of West Bay, and Mary Anderson were longtime pals. Cora organizes Anderson's annual birthday luncheon over at the Spinnaker Restaurant for eighty or so of Queen Mary's nearest and dearest. West Bay also sponsors a lot of Sausalito's annual events: Santa's Arrival, Friday Night Jazz at Gabrielson Park, the July 4th Chili Cookoff, Opening Day on the Bay. Yada, yada, yada."

"Interesting," Eddie said, smiling. "It's just one happy family. At least for those with the right connections."

"I don't know if Cora knew all, or nothing, about Anderson putting the squeeze on business owners like Pete Francis. But if Queen Mary had one, five, or fifteen different accounts like this Better Sausalito Now Fund," Holly explained, "Cora Jones was a pal whom Anderson could rely on to open these accounts with few if any questions."

"Seems like this story gets more interesting by the minute," Eddie announced as he sat back on Rob's blue couch, the one comfortable piece of furniture in *The Standard*'s two-room office. "I suppose taking a share of the money pouring through the offices of her two favorite architects was likely just one of her reliable sources of cash."

"She might have had a dozen others for all we know," Holly shook her head in amazement.

Rob shared the details of his conversation with Pete Francis. When he finished, Holly wasted no time before declaring, "I knew her majesty was a crook!"

"Holly, you think a lot of our fellow citizens are at least somewhat shady," Rob laughed.

"If by shady you mean crooked, I plead guilty as charged. As for Queen Mary lining her pockets with money from a variety of people, I'll bet the house on that."

"I wouldn't bet a dollar against that. You've been proven correct too many times," Rob countered. "Rum runners, buccaneers, houses of prostitution—this town has got quite a history of shady characters. Deadwood, South Dakota, had nothing on old Sausalito."

"Perhaps more shoot-outs," Eddie smiled.

"Probably so, but there are plenty of ways to rob or swindle someone without putting a gun to their head."

"True, Holly," Eddie nodded. "But before we take too long a stroll down Sausalito's shady lane, we have to stay on task. If we can unravel some, or most, of Mary Anderson's dirty deeds, we could hit upon her killer as well. Nothing motivates arguments faster than the question: "How do we split the cash?""

"Agreed!" Holly and Rob exclaimed in unison.

"Additionally, anyone Anderson was shaking down is a potential suspect," Eddie said. "The first thing I'm going to do Monday is pay a call on Pete Francis. I think there's a reasonable chance he knows other merchants in town who might have been under Anderson's thumb. Or, at least has a few businesses he suspects have been targets for Madam Mayor's Sausalito fund. I'm sure none of them were pleased to take a portion of their monthly net income and turn it over to her."

"I don't think that approach would work, Eddie," Rob said. "Business owners want to stay out of anything that has a whiff of scandal. Particularly a scam allegedly run by our newly sainted Madam Mayor. On the other hand, I think they'll talk with us provided we assure them it is strictly on deep background. They need to know whatever they tell us will not appear in the paper until such time, if ever, that they tell us they want to go public."

"This is going to be like the cat with the ball of yarn," Eddie said. "The more we pick at it, the more it unravels."

"Some people are going to take this badly," Holly said. "They'll accuse us of tarnishing the blessed memory of a dedicated public servant who died tragically."

"You and I know we could never sit on a story like this. I agree with Eddie, let's chip away until the whole story can be told. Meanwhile, we have to make sure every headline and every story is rock solid. Mary Anderson's supporters will be waiting to pounce on us the moment we do anything they view as besmirching the great mayor's reputation. Sausalito's Ladies of Liberty will, no doubt, lead the charge. If our facts are airtight, all they can do is pout and ultimately embarrass themselves before the rest of the community."

"The thing that amazes me is the level of greed some people have," Eddie murmured. "Although, considering I'm a cop, I shouldn't be too surprised."

"By 'some of the people,' I assume you mean Mary Anderson?" Rob asked.

Eddie nodded. "Yes, but I suspect this was more than a one-person operation. As you just suggested, Anderson didn't secure all those votes for projects she wanted approved all by herself. If that's the case, you can bet the house that Pete Francis is far from being the only businessperson in Sausalito whose pocket Mary Anderson picked."

Rob nodded. "I have no doubt that Anderson raked in a good amount of cash, and I'll wager she re-invested a lot of that money in running her political machine."

"But why, Rob? WHY?" Holly asked impatiently.

"Here's my guess as to why: Money fueled Mary Anderson's political machine. Go back to what we discussed yesterday afternoon: Anderson's scam with Nelson and Dexter. In order for that to work, she had to know that she had at least three votes on the planning commission, three votes on design review, and two votes along with her own on the city council. Without delivering on pledges to get projects approved, what good was Anderson to any of these high rollers or their architects? Those same satisfied applicants who told their wealthy friends that Nelson and Dexter had the know-how to get their projects through would go looking for another town—say, Tiburon, Belvedere, Mill Valley, and other places—happy to have them build their mansions there."

"Makes sense, Rob," Eddie nodded.

"None of us doubt that you need a lot of money to fuel the kind of operation we think Anderson was running. And we agree that it's a real stretch to think Anderson would put a nickel of her own money into her election campaign, no less helping to elect other candidates," Rob added.

"Mary Anderson was smart enough to know that money is to political campaigns what fuel is to a plane. Without it, you're not getting off the ground," Holly said. "I'd wager that this Better Sausalito Now Fund, is one of several such funds she had going."

"I would not bet five cents that you're wrong about that, Holly. When former elected officials are asked what they liked least about running for office, nearly all point to the endless job of raising money for their campaigns," Rob explained.

"That makes sense," Eddie said, as Holly nodded in agreement.

"I think we agree that none of the money used to buy support from council, board, or commission members, came out of Mary Anderson's pocket. Agreed?" Rob asked.

"Perhaps she contributed a small amount from her own personal savings, but no more than that," Holly said.

"I'm guessing she was more her father's daughter than any of us imagined," Rob added. "If you wanted to control the political life of a community, being able to fund the campaigns of your chosen candidates, in part or in whole, is a pretty good way of keeping the body politic of any community under your thumb."

"So, you're suggesting that Queen Mary recruited candidates for the city council, boards, and commissions, and funded their election efforts and-or recompensated them personally?" Eddie asked.

"Yes, Eddie, I am," Rob smiled. "I know it's a stretch. But if she was raising a lot of dark money, aka unreported, it's a logical place for most if not all of that money to go."

"You're on a roll, Rob, so keep going," Holly smiled.

"If you were Mary Anderson, there's really only two seats you needed to control."

"Two votes plus your own and you have a lock on the city council, correct?" Eddie asked.

"Absolutely," Rob nodded. "And that explains why Queen Mary was supported so often for the seat of mayor during the annual council reorganization meeting. Each one of the councilmembers would revolve the honor of serving as vice mayor, but Anderson kept the top job. A few times over the past quarter century when the council elected a different individual as mayor, it was when Anderson suggested she stand down for a year and give the job to someone else. I assume she also directed them regarding who that person would be."

"Her stepping aside only happened once every four or five years," Holly added.

"I don't doubt that every time she counted and re-counted a growing pile of cash," Rob said, "some of that money found its way into her pocket as well. But that was not the motivating factor in her scheme. That was simply an added benefit of sitting on a pile of cash. I think her real ambition was to control every aspect of the city's operation."

"That's a solid theory, Rob," Eddie said as Holly nodded in agreement. "I also think that the argument that led to her death was rooted in her not sharing control of the city, the money she was raking in, or most likely, both."

"One thing Holly and I have never done is interview Lester Harriman."

"Who's that?" Eddie asked.

"A widower who lives on a fixed income over at the Pine Street Apartments. He became the chair of the planning commission two years ago," Rob replied. "How someone like Lester Harriman landed in that position struck Holly and me as strange. But, if we investigated everything that struck us as peculiar in Sausalito, we'd have to give up publishing a weekly newspaper in three other communities in Marin. Better still, go into the business of being private investigators."

"Hey, wait a minute—I know Lester Harriman!" Eddie exclaimed. "He's one of the old guys who play chess on the sundeck outside the senior center. I've played a couple of games with him while Sharon was keeping an eye on Aaron and his little pals at the Hammer playground. Harriman seems like a nice guy. Pretty good chess player too."

"I agree. He is a nice guy," Rob nodded. "The only thing I'd like to know is how a guy like Harriman finds himself on the planning commission—and as its chairperson no less. He's not involved in housing, design, or any related field I've ever heard mentioned."

"I don't think having any expertise in the actual field of home design and/or planning and construction would have anything to do with why you would be appointed to a Sausalito board or commission," Holly suggested. "It's more of a who-you-know, as opposed to what-you-know game. There are five seats on the Sausalito Parks and Recreation Board, and rarely are any parents of young children appointed, although they are the ones who most frequently use the parks or participate in the city's organized youth and recreation programs."

"Holly's right. You don't need any connection, professional or personal experience, and so forth, to be appointed to one of Sausalito's boards or commissions."

"Personal and political connections, however, is the dividing line between the chosen and the countless thanks-but-no-thanks candidates," Holly added.

"The old who-you-know, not what-you-know game," Eddie smiled. "You said Lester Harriman was retired. Do you know what he did during his working life?"

"As it happens, I do," Rob said. "He owned a crab trap supply business in one of the warehouses near Fisherman's Wharf."

"I don't think I ever knew anyone in that business," Eddie shrugged.

"In San Francisco it's huge," Rob responded. "In a good crab season those equipment leasing operations take in serious money. In a great season, it can be like printing money."

"How did you get so knowledgeable about the crab business?" Holly asked.

"My dad had a pal who was in the business. They served together in the military and stayed close after their service. The problem with the crab business is you've got to be able to hold on through those bad years when there's something like a toxic bloom caused by an El Niño. Crabs eat the bloom, people eat the crabs, and you can get a whole bunch of sick people. So, for one reason or another, during certain years, crabs are deemed unsafe for human consumption. When that happens, the value of a sixty-million-dollar harvest drops to zip. You have to be able to hang on through a bad season. Like a lot of other areas of the food business, it's like playing the stock market: great return one year, hanging on by a thread the next."

"Setting the ups and downs of various crab seasons aside," Holly said with a roll of her eyes, "I know another individual who easily qualifies as a head scratcher: Stan Pollock, the chair of the city's design review board. He moved into the subsidized senior housing project on Bee Street a couple of years ago after his wife died."

"Who's that?" Eddie asked.

"Pollock worked in commercial insurance, if I remember correctly. I did short bio pieces on him and Harriman, which is nothing unusual. I write something about every new board or commission member, including parks and recreation appointees. If nothing else, it allows us to fill empty space on a slow news week."

"Any idea how these two appointees got chosen?" Eddie asked.

"With four communities to cover, we always wind up with more questions than answers by the time Friday rolls around. That's particularly the case in Sausalito. But Holly is right, like Harriman, you could call Pollock spectacularly unqualified. The fact that they both serve as chair makes the appointments that much stranger."

"Eddie, I don't think either of these guys ever looked at a set of building plans before they were appointed." Holly shrugged. "Give me a minute. I think I can pull up a comment I got from Mayor Anderson at the time Harriman was made chair of the planning commission."

Holly searched her computer for a moment. Tapping her index finger to the screen, she exclaimed, "Here it is: 'Lester Harriman Appointed Chair of Sausalito Planning Commission.'"

Holly took a few moments to scan the two-hundred-and-fifty-word news item and quickly came across the comment by Anderson she had vaguely remembered. "'I'm very pleased with the appointment of Mr. Harriman as chairperson of our planning commission. Lester is a longtime resident with great affection for this small but famous city. I look forward to working with him and his fellow commissioners as they endeavor to preserve the unique heritage of Sausalito...' Yada, yada, yada," Holly said as she moved her hand in a circular motion. "Now, if Anderson had been honest, I think she would have said, 'Mr. Harriman was chosen because he will vote as instructed and keep a careful eye on applicants or fellow commission members who have been uncooperative in following my wishes. Those who follow the recommendations of the board and hire the right design firm will be quickly passed along to the city council for final approval. Uncooperative applicants will find their projects in limbo, leading to a series of long and costly delays or permanent setbacks.'"

"You're dreaming now," Rob chuckled.

"The work both of you have done convinces me that Anderson and her supporting cast were running a well-oiled machine. I don't know whether to be appalled or awed by what she accomplished. I suppose I'm a bit of both."

"Eddie, in covering Sausalito, we often have the same reaction. On one hand, you feel a heavy hand pressing down on the scales of justice and perverting it. On the other, you find yourself wondering how far the stain of corruption spreads, and if there are any limits to the number of transgressions and misdeeds these people are capable of committing," Holly explained.

"If we do a deep dive into Mary Anderson's past, we could be in for a long slog," Rob cautioned. "Don't get me wrong, I'm very much in support of doing that. But we have to do it with our eyes wide open. It's certainly not something we're going to do out of idle curiosity. If we cast a shadow across Anderson's legacy, it will be like shooting at a wild boar. You get one shot. If you miss the target, you'll be in for a world of hurt."

"Is that a dramatic way of saying you're concerned about taking a foolish risk that perhaps offers little in return?" Eddie said with a smile.

"Exactly, it's not like Anderson was running for a state or federal office," Rob replied. "But this would surprise you: even in a relatively small town, the reports of each candidate's campaign expenditures show that costs can add up quickly.

And I strongly suspect that Mary Anderson never intended to pull a dollar out of her own pocket to cover the cost of her campaigns or contribute in one way or another to those who, if elected, pledged to support her agenda."

"She was as tight with a buck as that nasty old father of hers," Holly added. "And all those holiday parties she hosted every year at the community center for three hundred of her nearest and dearest friends? I doubt she ever put a dollar of her own money into covering the cost of any of those events."

"You ever go to one of those parties, Holly?" Eddie asked.

"No, but Scott has. I didn't want him to, but he feels he has to do something now and then to represent his late mother. Henrietta was a stalwart supporter of Anderson, as are all the Sausalito Ladies of Liberty."

"That name, 'Ladies of Liberty,' cracks me up every time I hear it," Eddie smiled. "With Henrietta's money, she didn't need a favor from Mary Anderson, or anyone else.

"That's true, but remember Henrietta's late husband, Elijah, had a penchant for buying commercial and residential real estate, both here in Sausalito and all over the Bay Area," Holly explained. "If property ownership and management is your business, then having friends at city hall can come in handy."

"Trust me, pal," Rob added, "when it comes to misbehaving politicians, I have no doubt that Anderson was high on the list. Not by the standards of a New York, Chicago, Dallas, or Los Angeles, perhaps, but for this part of the world, in a town of fewer than eight thousand residents, she was one smooth operator."

"The love of money is the root of all evil," Eddie grinned.

"Timothy 6:10," Rob announced.

"How did you pull that one out of your hat?" Holly asked.

"Karin and I were playing a Bible trivia game last night, and that was one of the questions. I missed. Hopefully I'll remember it the next time it comes around."

"If you guys want to expand your circle of players one night —you, Karin, along with Eddie and Sharon—don't invite Scott and me," Holly chided.

"I'm afraid Sharon and I would have to pass as well. Both of us remember Sunday School as the time between when we got out of bed on a Sunday and when we were free to go off and do something fun with our friends. Now, if you want a foursome for movie trivia, give us a call." After some thought, Eddie added: "Both of you have given me a lot to think about. Could you forward me a list of planning commissioners and members of the city's design review board? Plus, any bio information on Anderson's two favorite architects, Mike Nelson and Andrew Dexter."

"No problem, Eddie. We keep a file on board and commission members. And over the years we've gathered a lot of information on Nelson and Dexter as well. You never know when you're going to have to pull together a last-minute obituary," Rob explained. "Most of our boards and commissions are stocked with seniors, so obit readiness comes in handy."

"Good. Put an asterisk next to anyone sixty or younger. Where there's ambition, there's an increased chance for misbehavior. That doesn't mean seniors, like perhaps Pollock and Harriman, won't take what doesn't belong to them; they just have less inclination to do so."

"Mary Anderson was a senior as well," Holly said.

"I'm aware of that. And I'll tell you one other general rule: cons and fraudsters rarely get out of the game. They can start at eight and stay in until they check out at eighty. It's pretty incredible. I've always believed it's just a part of what makes them tick."

"Sounds like a lifetime attraction to misbehaving," Rob suggested.

"Some get out of the game, and a few do manage to reform, but the attraction of easy money can be as addictive as any drug. I see it all the time. Call it creative accounting, or a dozen other descriptions. This certainly holds true for cops as well. In Anderson's case, I think she learned long ago how access to political power can be turned into a saleable item. Once she developed a taste for putting a squeeze on the Pete Francises of the world, she was hooked. Of course, at this point we don't know who was her first, or for that matter, her last. I'm guessing we're going to be pretty amazed when all her schemes are unraveled."

"So, you agree with Rob and I that our esteemed mayor fell victim to the lure of easy money?" Holly asked with a mischievous smile.

"More so with each passing day. A criminal investigator's first rule: Follow the money! It looks like a good amount of cash was coming her way. Whoever walloped her thought he was not getting his fair share of the loot."

"Not all of the money coming her way was locally based," Holly added. "There are a lot of contracts Sausalito hands out: construction, electrical work, road and sewer projects, to name just a few. Most of those firms are based outside of Sausalito."

"If we're right about Anderson's shakedown of Pete Francis being one of many, you're going to need a court order to open her records at West Bay Savings," Rob suggested.

"Agreed," Eddie nodded. "There's a good chance that

Anderson's shakedown of Pete Francis, and her rigging of the permitting process for various projects, were just two aspects of her operation. Deposits dropped into her account will hopefully fill in many of the blanks all three of us have at the moment."

"I don't know about the two of you, but I'm starting to feel like we're going down a rabbit hole," Rob suggested.

"You might be right. Still, I have to keep pushing forward. Only with time will we know if we were moving in the right direction. For all we know, Mary Anderson was killed by a jealous lover. As for poking a sleeping bear, I'll deal with any and all growling regarding the investigation when and if it comes my way or yours."

"Anderson's network ran wide and deep," Rob offered, knowing full well how big a story he and Holly were now chasing. "I'll bet the bank that this is going to be bigger than anything the two of us imagined. The closer we get to unraveling the truth, the more people we're going to make nervous—which is an excellent reason for holding our cards close to the vest."

"If we're right, there's a good chance that someone out there got tired of paying Anderson's extortion demands," Eddie said. "What you both told me yesterday about her likely scheme to shake down wealthy home buyers puts in play an additional list of possibly aggrieved individuals. Someone who paid the price for everything to go according to plan, but still got their project rejected. The more people she pushed around—or worse, double-crossed—the longer my list of suspects."

"However, this plays out, it's going to shake this town like a seven-plus quake," Rob said, delighted to be sitting atop such a huge story.

"By the way, we never discussed if you or Scott came away with anything from Anderson's service Thursday afternoon," Eddie stated.

"As we suspected going in, it was slim pickings. Worse still, I had to listen to speakers all declaring what a fantastic, brilliant, dedicated public servant Mary Anderson was. Trust me, it wasn't easy."

"Wow! Better you than me, pal," Holly grinned. "I did get one piece of news from my sweet snoop."

"What's that?" Eddie asked, hoping to hear anything that might make this case a little less challenging.

"Scott got cornered by Kayla Fox."

"Kayla Fox? Her name is on my list of neighbors living near Anderson," Eddie said. "But I'm not sure I remember her."

"Eddie, you know her," Rob said with a laugh. "She's the old woman who came out of her house to complain about the noise every time we used a leaf blower to clean old man Anderson's deck."

"Oh my God—*Kayla Fox*! She's still alive?" Eddie said shaking his head.

"Apparently. At least Scott thinks so. He and Kayla had an entire conversation."

"I guess the old dear still has her hearing," Rob laughed.

"When we were teens," Eddie explained, "we thought Kayla Fox had pulled baby Moses out of the reeds."

"I'm happy to report that she's not quite that old!" Holly smiled.

"So, what did she have to say?"

"Fox said she was awakened three times the night Anderson was killed. The third time was the slide. But the first was at ten-fifteen, when she heard loud voices coming from Anderson's place. One of the voices sounded like that of a man. She drifted back to sleep, but not long after at   "

"Ten forty-five," Eddie jumped in, "she heard a car screech as it pulled off Anderson's parking deck."

"How did you know that?" Holly asked with obvious surprise.

"We haven't discussed who, if any, of Queen Mary's neighbors I've been able to speak with so far. Only one gave me something that might be of significant value." Eddie turned to Rob. "It came from our old sailing coach, Sean O'Hara. He lives across the road from Anderson's place, one house over from Kayla's. Sean said he heard a car come screeching off her parking deck at ten forty-five. All of us know the sound tires can make on rain-soaked wood. Particularly when you're going in reverse on an upward slope. Sounds like a noise Aaron makes when he's playing with his train set: *EEEERRRR!*" Eddie let loose with an irritating sound. "But I was hoping to corroborate what I was told. So, hearing ten forty-five confirmed is very helpful."

"If the loud voices Kayla Fox heard were part of an argument that Queen Mary had with her mystery guest, wouldn't her killer have high-tailed it out of there in a lot less than thirty minutes?" Holly asked.

"Not necessarily," Eddie replied. "After she fell back and cracked the back of her head, there's no way of knowing exactly what happened."

Rob and Holly nodded in agreement.

"Her killer might have been a partner in her shakedown racket and convinced she was not turning over his fair share of the take. At this time, we don't know how much money she was taking in. Could be tens of thousands, or hundreds of thousands of dollars collected over two or more decades," Eddie shrugged. "After she was out cold, her assailant might have used that time between when Fox heard shouting and when she was reawakened by what most likely was her assailant's noisy departure. And even if he left, screeching tires and all, that doesn't mean our mystery suspect did not return later after he cooled down from what undoubtedly was a violent argument."

"Sounds to me like Anderson's slaying was the result of a conversation gone wrong," Rob suggested.

"You are a master of understatement, Rob," Holly smiled. "My guess is that Mary Anderson's killer was likely angry about something when he arrived at her door on that dark and stormy night."

"Sounds like a mid-century film noir staring Lizabeth Scott and Dan Duryea," Rob suggested.

"Crooked politician attacked, massive landslide, and a long list of suspects," Eddie nodded.

"It certainly has all the ingredients."

"After the killer walloped the poor dear, you think he might have gone looking through her house for money he thought was owed to him?" Holly asked.

"That seems like a logical guess. I can suggest a second reason," Eddie replied.

"What's that?" Rob asked.

"Her attacker might have been searching for an accounting ledger."

"You think Anderson kept a record of her collections or other items related to her activities?" Rob asked.

"Seems logical," Eddie replied. "If her racket was as big as we suspect, she had to keep some form of a ledger, either digitally or good old pen and paper to keep her side business straight."

"That makes sense," Holly nodded.

"It is equally possible Anderson's killer might have rushed around her house trying to rid the place of evidence that he had been there," Rob offered.

"Hah!" Holly exclaimed.

"What's so funny?" Rob asked.

"Her killer running around straightening up a home that hours later would be smashed by a massive mudslide, that seems funny to me."

"You're right, Holly," Eddie noted. "With what that slide did to her home, at least the front two-thirds of the place, it's hard to imagine a murder scene more totally ruined, short of an all-consuming fire."

"I suppose you did a sweep of the part of her house left standing?" Rob asked.

"I had the county's forensics team up there most of Monday afternoon, shortly after Max informed me that we were dealing with a crime scene." Eddie replied. "Unfortunately, whatever happened to Anderson must have occurred in the front half of the house where her body was found. Keep in mind, the section of the house that went down the hillside included the home's entryway, the living room, den, kitchen, and a guest bathroom. Of course, the team searched the back portion of the home that was sitting basically untouched by the slide. That included three bedrooms, two additional bathrooms, and two walk-in closets. I felt pretty certain any evidence that would have aided our investigation was in the section of the house where her body was recovered. Still, the forensics team looked for hairs and fingerprints in the undamaged portion. Anything that might help us identify her assailant. Zip, nada, nothing! Whatever the killer might or might not have been searching for, he left no evidence of his presence in the back half of the house. Knowing that he might have mortally injured Anderson, my theory is he took time in the entryway, perhaps the kitchen, the living room, and other areas of the house, wiping away any fingerprints he might have left. Bottom line, there's a good reason he didn't get out of there in a hurry. And if this case ever comes to trial, the fact that he assaulted her then spent approximately thirty minutes in the house afterwards without dialing 911 for assistance, will likely put the noose around his neck, if not literally, then figuratively."

"So, what's your next move?" Rob asked.

"I've got two neighbors confirming ten forty-five as the approximate time the assailant fled the scene. I'm comfortable for now with that timeframe. I'd like to learn a good deal more about Anderson's shakedown schemes. In the near future I'm going to have to talk with Cora Jones to see what, if anything, she's willing to share."

"What if she's uncooperative?" Rob asked.

"I don't doubt that she would like to be. However, this is a homicide, first, second or third degree. A slaying in which the victim was a prominent citizen of the community. Getting a court order will involve a brief delay, but that shouldn't be a problem," Eddie shrugged. "In a situation like this no judge is going to be interested in dragging his or her feet, placing more time between law enforcement and the perpetrator. And detailing the money flowing out of what we assume are multiple accounts is potentially just as beneficial as knowing what checks are being deposited into one or more accounts."

"So, you're feeling pretty confident that her putting the squeeze on merchants, and God only knows who else, could be the key to finding her killer?" Holly asked.

"Following the money has been a reliable key to unlocking a mystery in countless investigations," Eddie noted. "Of course, there could be other sparks that ignited Anderson's slaying. Jealousy, for one. The killer could have been a jilted lover."

Holly shuddered. "Oh Eddie—who could possibly be romantically involved with Queen Mary?"

"Spend a year doing my job and you'll be able to imagine people doing a number of things you never thought possible. From broken promises to cheating over how the loot is divided, the old expression is true: there is no honor among thieves. The goal is to eliminate the obvious scenarios before you move to solutions statistically less likely."

"While you pursue your investigation, I want to send Holly off to pluck what I suspect is a piece of low-hanging fruit," Rob said.

"What's that?" Holly and Eddie asked in unison.

"I'd like you to talk to Mike Banks down at The Lazyjack Bar. He's managed that place for years. Holly, as I'm sure you remember, worked for Banks several years back. If Mary Anderson could shake down Pete Francis for disturbing the nightly peace along Caledonia Street, it's reasonable to assume she leaned on Banks for doing the same thing in downtown. We've been getting letters from readers for years about noise coming out of The Lazyjack."

"Before Scott caused me to quit the singles life, even after I worked there, I spent a fair amount of time at The Lazyjack, hoping to find Mr. Right. Mike and I have been friends for a long time. That's a great idea, Rob. I'd be happy to speak with him."

"It's likely Anderson shook down several merchants, barkeeps, restaurant operators, and God only knows who else. As of today, we have no idea how long Anderson's collections list ran. A solid next step is to do what we can to fill in at least some of those blanks."

"When we get a look at her bank deposits that should tell us a lot," Eddie smiled.

"I'll say one thing for Anderson: she was one busy politician," Rob shook his head in wonder.

"There's a good chance that her final argument was over how to divide a pretty big pie," Holly added.

"A pie that might have been bigger than any of us originally imagined," Eddie suggested.

Rob and Holly nodded in agreement while imagining a variety of headlines suggesting sensational developments to come.

CHAPTER FIFTEEN

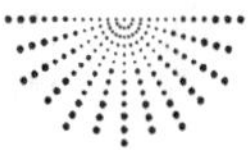

On Monday morning, Holly entered the office at eight. She was unusually upbeat for the start of another long workweek.

"What has you so up and at 'em this early?" Rob asked.

"This whole Mary Anderson thing has me tickled."

"Hopefully you're not amused by her having been killed?"

"No, Rob, not that. I'll admit I wasn't one of her fans, but I wouldn't wish the way she died on anyone. Well, almost anyone. What has me so tickled is that the pious old crows in Sausalito, who for years have been praising the wonderful work Anderson has done on behalf of her community, are in for the surprise of their lives. They're going to be dining on humble pie when Queen Mary's dirty secrets come bubbling up to the surface."

"You're absolutely right. We've all heard the line, 'jaw dropping disclosures;' we're going to see some stunned expressions on people's faces when this mess gets untangled and put in print for the whole town to see. Speaking of getting to the truth, are you going to stop by The Lazyjack tonight to speak with Mike Banks?"

"No need, Rob. I spoke with Mike last night."

"From the size of the smile you're wearing, I'm guessing Queen Mary had her hooks into Banks as well."

"Bingo! And for the same amount she was pulling out of Pete Francis. Even the same fund, 'Better Sausalito Now.' Five hundred bucks per month, thank you very much!"

"Gosh!" Rob shook his head. "Anderson really had quite the side business going. It's surprising to me that she didn't take a vacation in Lake Como, Italy, every year instead of Stinson Beach."

"If not that, at least go slumming in Maui. But wait, Rob, the story gets better. Mike laughed off the whole thing. He thought of paying Anderson every month as just another expense of doing business in Sausalito. He claims to have been making payments for over three years, but here's the best part."

"What?" Rob asked excitedly.

"Mike's brother, Rowland, who owns the souvenir shop—Sausalito Memories, over on El Portal, close to the ferry landing—he's been contributing to a different fund; this one is called, 'Keep Sausalito Beautiful.'"

"What's Rowland paying?"

"Two-fifty a month, according to Mike."

Rob gave a long low whistle. "Looks to me like our suspicions were correct. Anderson was some operator. I suppose she had a sliding scale for what she estimated was her target's monthly net income."

"How would she have any idea about the size of their income?" Holly wondered aloud.

"I'm guessing Anderson looked at their business license, permit papers, and most importantly, city sales tax records. She wouldn't be able to hit their monthly net income right on the nose, but with that information she could come pretty darn close."

"Wow, Anderson was the real deal when it came to being a top-of-the-pile crooked politician."

"I'm starting to think Queen Mary may have been putting the squeeze on every tourist trinket and t-shirt shop, burger and pizza joint, bar, coffee shop, bakery, and restaurant in Sausalito."

"Could be," Holly laughed. "At this point, I don't know what to think. She might have been leaning on Bill Vogel for a monthly donation if he wanted to hold on to his position as the town's fire chief!"

"Holly, you can't accuse the old buzzard of having had a lack of ambition!"

"That's certainly true, pal."

Both wondered how far Anderson's shakedown racket actually extended. After a few moments of silence, Rob was the first to speak. "This is a huge scandal that's been going on right under our noses, I'm somewhat embarrassed to admit."

"I'm surprised we didn't stumble across her scheme sooner. You would think one, or more, of these business owners would have come squealing to us. Most likely insisting that they serve only as an unidentified source, of course," Holly added.

"Apparently everyone Anderson was leaning on thought they'd be in for a world of hurt if they reported what was going on, and she ever figured out who squealed."

"You're right, Rob. Plus, they might have seen it as a form of protection money. Kind of a tax you hate to pay, but you don't want to find out what will happen if you choose not to hand over your money."

"That's probably why Pete Francis felt free to let me in on Anderson's racket only after she was found dead. It was obvious he was angry about taking six thousand dollars every year out of his bottom line. Pete's not a guy whose feathers get ruffled easily. But he met her demands and kept his mouth shut. Even though he hated paying her."

"I don't doubt that every business owner she leaned into resented what she was doing, but ratting her out to us, or any news outlet, just wasn't worth the risk."

"And for right now, it's anyone's guess as to how many years Anderson was playing this game," Rob added. "She might have been pressing city contractors to throw some money her way as well. Road paving, sewer replacement and repair projects, and more. All those contracts every city gives out on a regular basis can be worth hundreds of thousands of dollars. Millions in a big city. A one or two percent in kickback isn't such a terrible price to pay. Particularly if you're burying the payoffs into your job estimate."

"When that happens, Rob, it's the average citizen who is paying the tab."

"At this point it's reasonable to assume that Anderson was sitting on a small fortune," Holly said, staring out the window and looking at a row of shops on the other side of Princess Street that catered to the tourist trade. "Those shops directly across the street from us, places we see every day of the week, might all have each been paying Anderson a monthly stipend. At least this explains why hanging on to her position as mayor was so important. Her legion of fans thought it was her cease-less dedication. Nice sentiment, but not true!"

"Anderson clearly recognized that it's not easy to squeeze people when you don't wield the level of power that can make their lives pleasant or miserable."

"I can remember when I worked at the Lazyjack, a month did not go by without someone threatening to go to the city with a complaint about the noise coming out of that place. Particularly on a Friday or Saturday nights when they had a live jazz trio—something they still do every weekend. The back of Mike's place sits at the bottom of a steep hill. Above are a number of private residences. The sound rises up just like it does in an amphitheater. You might be two or three hundred feet away, or more, but it can still sound like that jazz group is playing in your backyard. Not to mention the voices of patrons trying to talk over the music."

"So, resident complaints fell on deaf ears, pun intended," Rob suggested with a smile.

"Exactly. Anderson would hold a public hearing, once every couple of years, regarding noise coming out of the place. She'd sit, along with the other councilmembers, listening to a line of citizens complain and simply wait them out. Mike and I both attended, more to observe than to speak and now I know why."

"It was a shrewd move on Anderson's part, to hear out the neighbors," Rob smiled. "She knew the number of locals who enjoy going to The Lazyjack to hear some great jazz on weekends far exceeded the relative handful of neighbors who complained about the noise the live music caused. Not to mention the voices of patrons who had one too many and were trying to make themselves heard over the music. If you vote against the handful of neighbors, they'll be disappointed, most likely angry, and unlikely to vote for you when you're up for re-election. But on the whole, far more voters would be angry if you went against the bar having live music than the support you'll get for shutting it down."

"Spot on, Rob, that's almost exactly what Mike told me. Those council hearings were an opportunity for uphill neighbors to blow off steam. They didn't get what they came for, but their grievances at least were aired."

"But then why hand over five hundred bucks every month to Anderson?" Rob asked.

Holly shrugged. "I believe Mike's thinking was similar to what Pete Francis told you Friday night."

"Telling Anderson thanks, but no thanks, and waiting to see what, if anything, happened, just wasn't worth the risk."

"Exactly, Rob. And you have to admit, it makes sense. As Mike explained," Holly looked down at the notes she had written after their meeting, "'If Anderson wasn't able to make trouble for me related to having a jazz trio play on weekends, she could find other ways to make my life miserable and take a bite out of my bottom line.' I have no doubt Mike was right about that. Better to hand her a small part of your monthly take and think of it as another monthly expense item."

"You're right, Holly. And I can't argue with Mike's logic."

"I don't want us to get ahead of ourselves, Rob, but I'm confident Madam Mayor had her hands in more pockets than we imagined."

"Agreed. That's becoming clearer by the day. If you can't create a problem for people, you're not going to be worth five dollars a month, no less five hundred! But if you want to get down into the weeds of the city's codebook, the do's, and don'ts that any business needs to follow, there are countless violations that can be either enforced or ignored. Without that codebook, you're threatening these business owners with a gun that shoots blanks. Until Pete Francis sat me down Friday night, we thought Anderson's rigging of the planning and design approvals was the total extent of her scam. Now, I feel foolish to have ever imagined that."

"Given the amount of money on the line in the approval process for new residential construction, it's still probably a sizable chunk of her annual take," Holly added.

"You would think. But the further we go following the trail of Anderson's misdeeds, the more you wonder: just how far this scandal will spread?"

"The court order that Eddie's getting for her banking records will hopefully answer some of our biggest questions."

"That's so true, Holly. It will be especially interesting to see who, if anyone, takes over her monthly collections."

"I wonder what kind of service Anderson was performing for someone like Mike's brother, what's his name?" Holly asked.

"Rowland Banks. Eddie and I knew Rowland when we were at Tam High. He was two years behind us. Played junior varsity basketball, just like his big brother Mike. I think I'll stop by Rowland's place on my way home this evening. He probably closes around six, like most of the downtown merchants. Anderson must have had some angle with him. If she leaned on Rowland for a monthly check, I strongly suspect that the half-dozen other souvenir shops in Sausalito were paying into her scheme as well."

"You have to say one thing for Mary Anderson."

"What's that Holly?"

"She saw an opportunity and ran with it."

"You're right about that. What I really want to know is what role, if any, did her ambitions play in her death?"

"In her case, Rob, I think ambition was spelled M-O-N-E-Y!"

"She was more like her dad than you or I ever guessed. I don't suppose any amount of money would have ever been enough."

"I would love to know the answers to two questions."

"What are those, Holly?"

"One, what was her total monthly take? Two, what in the world was she doing with all that money?"

CHAPTER SIXTEEN

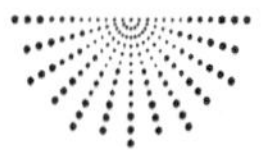

Shortly before six that evening, Rob walked the three short blocks from the front door of his office on Princess Street to Rowland Banks' shop on El Portal.

Rowland was straightening out racks of souvenir sweatshirts and jackets, which had been picked over by tourists since he opened at ten that morning. His last two customers of the day walked to the counter to purchase matching sweatshirts that featured an artist's rendering of the huge stone elephants that stand on either side of the entrance to the small public garden known as Vina del Mar Park, located directly across from Rowland's shop. The elephants have stood there for over a century. They are two of just a few remaining artifacts of San Francisco's 1915 Pan Pacific Exposition, which celebrated the city's return from the devastation of the 1906 earthquake.

The elephants, nicknamed by Sausalito's children as "Jumbo" and "Pee Wee," were originally constructed of papier mâché. Amazingly, most likely a result of the area's relatively mild winters, it took twenty years for the two giants to fall into disrepair. In 1935, at the height of the great depression, it was impossible to find the needed funds to replace the beloved creatures. At that point, it seemed certain that these twin giants would soon be headed to the city dump. Then, an idea was put forward: allow the originals to serve as molds, pour in concrete, and finish the work with a light gold patina. Along with a fountain, also from the exposition, they have served as symbols of Sausalito ever since.

Once Rowland thanked his last two customers of the day as they hurried out to catch the evening's final departing ferry returning to San Francisco, he turned to Rob and said, "Mike called earlier today and told me I'd be hearing from you or Holly. I'm happy to talk about Mary Anderson as long as you keep my name and the name of the shop out of the paper."

"No names needed. I'm talking to you strictly off the record."

"Good. The only reason I pay these people is to make sure they stay off my back. I don't want them to think I'm trying to make trouble. If I wanted to do that, I never needed to pay them in the first place."

Rowland's response caught Rob off guard. Mary Anderson was dead and buried. Clearly, the long shadow she cast still intimidated this merchant and most likely many others.

"As I'm sure you're aware, your brother Mike has been paying into a fund called, 'Better Sausalito Now,' but Mike told Holly that you pay into a different fund called, 'Keep Sausalito Beautiful.'"

Rowland snickered at the name. "That's right. They can call it whatever they want, it's just another excuse to take money out of the pockets of merchants who already pay taxes, fees, and everything else the city can think to throw at us."

He paused for a moment to look closely at what he hoped was just a bit of dust on one of his more expensive plush souvenir jackets. Rowland swatted at the spot with the palm of his hand and was glad when a small clump of dust fell to the floor.

"You're never going to sell these items without letting the customers touch, feel, and try them on. Unfortunately, some walk in with hands that have just finished working through a package of caramel popcorn, a slice of pizza, or worse, a greasy hamburger. No matter how thoughtless any one customer might be, you need to keep smiling and keep selling. Just like paying Anderson, it's all about the money. Believe me, Rob, it's not for the thrill of being here six or seven days a week that I do this."

Rob took a deep breath, hoping to reset the conversation. Rowland was clearly not a happy camper, and Rob had begun to wonder how cooperative he was going to be.

"Rowland, I'm here to talk to you about your support of Mayor Anderson's Keep Sausalito Beautiful Fund. How long have you been a contributor to the fund?"

"You're sure my name and the name of the store won't appear in the newspaper?" Rowland asked again.

"Absolutely not! Mike, Eddie, you, and I have all known each other since high school. I'm just trying to understand what Anderson was doing raising money for funds that Holly and I can find no mention of in the city's records. As I said, this is for research only. Your name and the name of your shop will never appear in print in connection to this story until such time, if ever, that you ask for your comments to be made public."

"Okay, Rob. I get what you're saying. Just remember, I'm putting two-fifty a month into the hands of these people in the hope of not landing on their list of uncooperative merchants."

"No names of individuals, no names of businesses." Rob said once more, wondering what it was about the deceased mayor that made Rowland so uncomfortable.

"You want to know how long I've been making monthly payments?" Rowland said, scratching his head. "I make a notation of it in my accounting ledger. I'll double-check later, but I think it's been approximately three years. That's at least nine thousand dollars by now. And honestly, I could have used that money for the store, for inventory, or a dozen other things I'd rather done."

"Did Anderson come and pick up a check from you every month?"

"No, I guess the amount she was squeezing me for was on the piddling side. I know Mike's been kicking in double my amount. Five hundred a month and that's been collected by our beloved late mayor. Every month I handed my check over to Lester Harriman."

Rob wrote quickly and nearly dropped his pen when Rowland named Harriman as his monthly collector. Harriman, the surprise choice for the chairmanship of the Sausalito planning commission. Perhaps he had earned his prestigious appointment in exchange for his service as one of Anderson's loyal lieutenants?

"Rowland, I want to be clear about how this came about. It was Mary Anderson who first asked you to contribute to this fund, correct?"

"Absolutely!"

"How did she explain the need for you to make a monthly payment?"

"Rob," he said with a laugh, "that I recall as if it happened yesterday. I was pretty taken aback when she showed up one evening about five minutes before my usual six o'clock closing. Anderson explained they were putting together a special fund for the enhancement of the ferry arrival area and creating an improved level of care for Vina del Mar Park and El Portal. There were insufficient funds in the city's treasury to do either and she was hoping to gather the support of merchants in the immediate vicinity between the park and the ferry landing to make it financially feasible."

"Did you tell her you would think about it?"

"I did my best to keep smiling, even though I wasn't happy about handing over that amount of money every month of the year. I'm already paying a long list of taxes and fees to the city, county, and state, some of which are monthly, and others annual. It's no secret that this has not been the best of times for the tourist trade, but I also thought that saying 'no' was probably an unwise choice. Anyway, she asked me to think about it and told me she would be back in a week or two for my answer."

"And was she?"

"Actually, she got to the door, walked out, then turned around and came right back in."

"Had she forgotten something?"

"I suppose you could say that. She walks up to me and says in a friendly, casual sort of way, 'By the way, those few items you have on that small display rack outside the store will have to be moved back inside, along with that 'buy one hat, get a second hat for half price,' sign. Having them outside the store is a violation of Sausalito's city code eight-two-seven.'"

"How did you take that?"

"I took it the way I think she intended. Pay up or think what life will be like when you're expected to be in compliance with every single line of the city's codebook. Perhaps she has all the possible code violations committed to memory, but I doubt that. My guess is she looks for something to give her request a bit of added punch. I think she did a quick check of the city's codebook before paying me a visit and knew exactly what she could do to rattle my cage if I did not immediately agree to her request for a monthly payment."

"So, it was when she walked back in that you told her you were onboard with the monthly amount she requested?"

"I sure did. It felt like my best choice. I thought if I kept her waiting a week or more for an answer it was likely she would raise my expected monthly contribution by another fifty bucks or more. Removing those few items on the outside rack and taking away that half-price sign would potentially put a bigger dent in my sales than two-hundred and fifty bucks a month she was looking to lift out of my pocket. From that point on, I agreed to be a monthly contributor to her Keep Sausalito Beautiful fund. Whatever that means."

"Have you seen any improvement in the park or the area around it since you started kicking in your monthly contribution."

"Not a thing. For all I know Anderson was putting the money toward spa treatments. Or treating herself and a friend to dinner in the city once a month."

"Has Lester Harriman been around in the past week or two?"

"Came by just a few days ago to collect my monthly check. I guess the mayor's good work, whatever that is, goes on without her."

Rob thanked Rowland and assured him, for a third time, that his name, and the name of his shop, would not appear in *The Standard*. At least, not in connection with this story.

After leaving, Rob walked up to Bridgeway, turned right and headed north, his usual route when walking home from his office. As he passed Jumbo and Pee Wee at the open gate to the small pocket park, Rob wondered what he would have done had he been in Rowland's shoes. Probably, he concluded, the exact same thing. Very few people are willing to stick their hand in the tiger's mouth to see if it's inclined to bite.

Pay the money and consider it part of the cost of doing business. That was undoubtedly his safest choice.

Rob pulled his phone out and pushed the speed dial preset for Eddie.

"I just had a meeting with Mike Banks' brother, Rowland."

"I haven't seen him in a long time. What's he up to?"

"Among other things, paying into one of Mary Anderson's slush funds."

"Gosh, she was dedicated to being served by the public."

"You mean serving the public."

"Not from her perspective," Eddie laughed.

"Where are you now?"

"Just came through my front door five minutes ago."

"Do you have a few minutes to talk about what I just learned?"

"I do, actually. Sharon took the little man to a late afternoon T-Ball practice. By now the game is probably over and the kids are running around the playground, hopefully wearing themselves out. Come on by!"

"I'm walking past the back of the fire station right now coming up on Caledonia Street. I'll be there in five."

When Rob arrived, the front door of Eddie and Sharon's home was already shaded from the late afternoon sun by Sausalito's city hall, which sits directly across from their home. The building was converted decades earlier from Sausalito's Central School into the city's civic center, which now housed the council chambers, meeting rooms, municipal administrative staff offices, the senior center, recreation center, library, and the town's history archive.

A moment after Rob pressed the front door buzzer, he heard Eddie call out, "It's open, come on back."

Rob walked down a long hall that provided cool relief from an unexpectedly warm afternoon.

"What's up, pal?" Eddie asked cheerfully.

"You're in a surprisingly chipper mood."

"I can't be grumpy all the time. I got a pile of paperwork cleared off my desk in record time and got out of work early. That'll put me in a good mood any day of the week. So, you've been following the money trail of our late, not so great, mayor?"

"Eddie, I feel like the guy who thought he was getting close to his destination, only to find he had another hundred miles to go." Rob proceeded to relay the details of his morning meeting with Holly and his just-concluded conversation with Mike Banks' kid brother.

"Wow! That story makes me feel rotten for all the times we picked on Rowland when we were hanging out with Mike. I would think trying to make your living as a retail merchant in a small tourist town is tough enough without having Madam Mayor lift money out of your back pocket twelve times a year."

"On the upside, you'll be happy to know Rowland appears to have recovered from all those times we picked on him. Although he does seem a bit dyspeptic over the state of retail sales in the tourist district. You can't blame him; online buying has made life tough for most retailers."

"Yeah, you're right. There was a time if you wanted a souvenir jacket, sweatshirt, hat, or whatever that said Sausalito, Carmel, Santa Barbara, Hollywood, Yosemite, Disneyland, or a dozen other places in California, you needed to have actually gone there or have a friend or relative bring it back for you. Now you can go online and buy anything from anywhere."

Rob relayed his conversation with Rowland, concluding with Anderson's not-so-subtle hint that if Banks decided not to contribute to the fund, he'd be held to the letter of the city's codebook.

Eddie whistled with surprise. "Anderson wasn't shy about playing hardball. Nothing like having a countless number of rules and regulations to motivate the hesitant to get onboard. Further evidence, if needed, that our late mayor knew how to play hardball."

"Agreed. Now here's the best part: Lester Harriman has been the contact person picking up Rowland's monthly check."

"Wow," Eddie said with a smile. "These folks had quite the

racket going. Time to put Harriman up on the big board of suspects. This other guy you were talking about on Saturday…"

"Stan Pollock, chair of the city's design review board…"

"That's the guy. He was likely one of Anderson's collectors as well, I imagine. Wow oh wow, Robbie my boy, you are sitting on one hell of a story."

"I know it, brother. What's your next move?"

"I've got to get the county started on filing a court order for the release of Anderson's bank records. When we crack open her list of 'donors,'" Eddie said, using air quotes, "I'm hoping we'll be able to assemble a monthly collections list of thirty, forty, or more. But who knows? Anderson might have been taking a bite out of every business in town. Right now, we're still feeling our way around the edges of what could easily be the biggest scandal that's ever hit this town. No small accomplishment considering some of the shady characters that have passed through Sausalito over the last hundred and fifty years."

"I keep going back to one simple thought: What in the world was Anderson doing with all the money she was collecting?"

"Rob, your guess is as good as mine."

"You think all this will lead to why she was struck and died after what we suspect was a violent argument?"

"You would hope. But I've been doing my job long enough to know that there are never any guarantees. When you find this level of illegal activity, not to mention a cash spigot that we reasonably assume Anderson controlled, the chance of violent crime often follows. There's a lot of truth in that old expression, 'There is no honor among thieves.' I see that in my line of work just about every day of the week."

"Any guess as to who might next turn up dead?"

"Rob, if Anderson's death resulted from an argument over how the loot gets divided, my guess is whoever was part of this scheme is most likely my prime suspect—or my next victim. Buried treasure, in this case, I assume piles of cash, can motivate people to take all sorts of risks. Buckle up pal, this could be one wild ride."

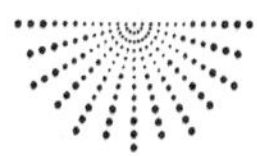

CHAPTER SEVENTEEN

Tuesday morning began with Rob filling Holly in on the details of his conversations with Rowland Banks and Eddie.

Holly listened in disbelief. "Wow, Rob, this story is like a spreading stain. I thought the secrets of the Gossiping Gourmet stunned Sausalito. That was a good deal smaller than the size of this scandal. A long-serving, highly honored mayor, known throughout Marin County, was operating a massive shakedown scheme. A racket that quite likely has a connection to her death. In Sausalito's long history of odd characters and bizarre stories, this one might take the prize."

"You're right, Holly. And, we haven't yet approached answering one of the most puzzling questions."

"Which one is that Rob?"

"What in the world did Queen Mary do with all the money she collected? I mean, can you imagine? I suspect it was thousands of dollars per month. Her father left her a home, way up on Sausalito Boulevard no less. That place must be worth three million by now if not more. God only knows what else he left his only child. Unless she had some kind of massive gambling addiction, what did she do with the loot? She never married, never had children, I just don't get it."

"I find it bewildering as well. All I can think is this puzzle still has a slew of missing pieces."

"I'll bet you're right."

"I'm glad that Eddie is getting a court order to see what Anderson actually stashed in one or more accounts at West Bay Savings. Hopefully, that will answer many of our questions. Right now, Rob, we're just guessing how much money her scheme took in. But if she was going after small retail tourist shops like Rowland's, she was likely leaning on half or more of Sausalito's businesses."

"Her bank records should answer a lot of those questions. Let's hope we're both right about her connection to West Bay. I hate the idea of sending Eddie off in the wrong direction."

"Certainly, she and Cora Jones were very chummy whenever we spotted them together," Holly said confidently. "If she kept her money in town, I'd be very surprised if it were anywhere else."

Rob took a sip of his coffee. "But what I suspect will still be missing is any accounting ledger. If we're right, Anderson had her hooks into a long list of businesses. When I learned from Rowland that Lester Harriman was collecting a monthly payment from Sausalito Memories, that was a big step forward."

"Harriman's involvement begs the question of whether Anderson's other spectacularly unqualified appointee, Stan Pollock, is also in the collections business. Distinguished chair of Sausalito's design review board by day, bag man for Anderson by night. If it applies to Harriman, it could easily apply to Pollock. As we told Eddie, both are totally unqualified for the positions they currently hold."

"Geez, Holly. As the expression goes, I suppose this is a puzzle wrapped in an enigma."

"Frankly, I think there's cause for hope."

"Why is that?"

"For starters, Rob, it's been less than ten days since half of Anderson's home was swept away, and that began a landslide of revelations about her conduct as a long-tenured public servant."

"You're right! So much has happened over a short period of time that it feels a good deal longer than it has actually been."

"The first shocker came from Max Brownstein when he informed us that Queen Mary had been killed hours before a flood of dirt, rocks, and broken trees slammed into her home," Holly added.

"You and I have long suspected that Anderson was crooked, but as we explained to Eddie, we have three editions, other than Sausalito's, to put out every week. Both of us would love the luxury of being able to take a story like how our small city has been under the thumb of Anderson and her crowd for over two decades and do a deep dive into the political rot that has caused."

"But we just don't have the time to do it all, and have a life outside the office as well."

"Absolutely, Holly. But it's ironic to think that the landslide that buried Mary Anderson uncovered what might be our most explosive investigative work since I took over the paper from George Benton."

"True," Holly nodded.

"Our job right now, on top of all our other weekly tasks, is to stay on the Anderson story and see where it leads. Later today we transmit this week's Sausalito edition for print. Tomorrow at this time it will start landing in mailboxes. We need to make some decisions now about how much of what we now know we want to print."

"What we have now leads to many more questions than answers."

"I agree, Holly. So, let's start by putting together a follow-up story on Anderson, beginning with last Thursday's funeral."

"Good, Rob, send me your notes and article draft on the service at Star of the Sea and we'll go from there."

As Holly grabbed her coffee and rushed off into her office, Rob wondered for another few moments about where this story would take them, then reset his thoughts and began the long slog through another busy day.

As Rob and Holly's meeting was ending, eleven miles north, Eddie and Sheriff Canning's discussion on how to proceed in the Anderson case was beginning.

"Any developments, Eddie?"

"A few shockers for sure, Jack. And they were uncovered by my buddy and his assistant editor at *The Standard*."

"Wow!" Canning smiled. "*The Standard* is the little newspaper that could. For a shoestring operation, your pal and his number two, Holly...something..."

"Cross."

"That's it! She's a firecracker. Easy on the eye, as well. Don't repeat that," Jack added quickly. "Together, they have pulled off some amazing stories. Marin County's answer to Woodward and Bernstein," Jack laughed. "So, what did they dig up on Sausalito's not-so-beloved Madam Mayor?"

"Well, I'm glad you're sitting down."

"That good?" Canning's expression was a blend of surprise, anticipation, and satisfaction.

"She's had some kind of shakedown operation going for at least the past six years, perhaps longer. The first Rob knew about it was this past Friday night when the managing partner of a popular bar in Sausalito—a guy named Pete Francis—told him that Mary Anderson had been squeezing him for five hundred bucks a month for the last six years. That's thirty-six thousand dollars to date!"

"OUCH! I always suspected that woman was an operator. But I never imagined anything like this. A lot of her devoted fans in Sausalito are going to be walking around in a daze when this bit of news falls out of the sky."

"It gets better." Eddie leaned closer.

"I'm all ears."

"Just in the last two days, Rob and Holly have uncovered two more targets she was leaning on. They feel, and I concur, they're probably just looking at the tip of the iceberg."

"My God! What was Anderson thinking?"

"No idea, Jack."

"Who are the other two she was putting the touch on?"

"The Lazyjack, on Bridgeway. Also, at five hundred a month. And..."

"The Lazyjack!" Canning interrupted with obvious surprise. "My wife and I love that place! We go there on a

Friday or Saturday evening, at least once a month, when they have a jazz trio playing that we like. They consistently have some great music. What's the other place Anderson was putting the squeeze on?"

"A place called Sausalito Memories. It sells sweatshirts, hats, jackets, mugs. Typical Sausalito souvenir shop. It's located just a block from the ferry landing."

"Same five hundred a month?"

"Nope, two-fifty for this place. Apparently, she had a sliding scale, and when the owner was slow to agree to her price, Anderson cited a couple of civic code violations like a small display outside his front door."

"Let me guess, the owner quickly agreed to pay the monthly amount she wanted. And she must have suggested something regarding what she planned to do with the money."

She claimed it was to fund improvements to the ferry landing area, which is steps away from the front door of Sausalito Memories."

"The two bars make out checks to the 'Better Sausalito Now Fund.' The souvenir shop writes a monthly check to the, 'Keep Sausalito Beautiful Fund,'" Eddie further explained.

Jack whistled at the thought of Mary Anderson's audacity.

"Here's the thing, Jack: if Holly and Rob are right, we're just scratching the surface."

"Go on…"

"Anderson collects the monthly checks from Smitty's and Lazyjack, but the chair of the city's planning commission, a guy named Lester Harriman, picks up a monthly check from Sausalito Memories. Harriman is one of two high-ranking appointees that Rob and Holly describe as quote, 'spectacularly unqualified,' for their positions."

"This is unbelievable. Who was the other collector?"

"Most likely, a guy named Stan Pollock. He's currently the chair of the city's design review board."

"Wow, Eddie. It's just amazing what Rob and Holly pull off on what I assume is a shoestring budget."

"You're right, Jack. I attribute it to hard work and a determination to get as close to the truth as they possibly can. But shaking down local merchants and barkeeps is only half the story."

"There's more? Wow! They've hit the small-town newspaper jackpot this time!" Jack laughed.

Eddie went on to detail Rob and Holly's theory about Anderson pushing renovation and construction contracts for new and renovated homes toward two firms, Mike Nelson's and Andrew Dexter's.

"That's potentially tens of thousands of dollars in kickbacks being pushed her way as well," Jack said shaking his head and growing more amazed by the scope of this scandal.

"Rob and Holly might need to borrow the investigative staff of *The Washington Post* to reel this fish in," Eddie smiled.

"I wish there was something I could do to help."

"Actually, there is, Jack, and it's a very important aspect of their investigation."

"Sure, Eddie. What do you need?"

"Rob and Holly are confident that all of the accounts for these various funds were opened by Mary Anderson at a small Sausalito-based bank called West Bay Savings. I'd like to get a court order to see what accounts Mary Anderson kept there. Anderson, Harriman, and likely Pollock are, or were, bringing in a lot of money every month; it would be nice to see where it came from and where it has been going."

"Absolutely!"

"Two other accounts are likely these fake civic improvement funds like Better Sausalito Now and Keep Sausalito Beautiful. If Rob and Holly are right about Anderson's close relationship with West Bay Savings, getting a court order would allow us to examine exactly what funds she was depositing into one or more those accounts. Equally important, what checks she's been writing out of those accounts. That information has the potential of helping us break this manslaughter case wide open if she was making payments to one, two, or more co-conspirators. As you and I both know, when you find significant amounts of money the chances for one or more of the players to get greedy increases."

"Eddie, none of that should be a problem. All this grows out of an investigation into her death and the search for her attacker. As soon as we're done, I'll refer it to our legal staff; if they run into any static, I'll call Judge Botherton. He'll bring the hammer down in a hurry. No one has more years and more experience in Marin County's legal system than Botherton."

"Terrific. Until then, I'm pushing ahead with the investigation into her killing."

"Anything to report on that front?"

"I'd say the most significant thing in the last few days has been what Rob and Holly have dug up about these two bars and a retailer being leaned on by Anderson. If those two are right about the money that has been flowing through Anderson's racket, there's an excellent chance that whoever killed her is someone connected to that money flow."

"Follow the money, right Eddie?"

"It's a theory that works for us ninety-five percent of the

time. You'll never get far as a criminal investigator if you ignore the greed factor."

"You're right about that, Eddie. Really good work on the part of your newspaper pals. There are times I get frustrated with journalists, but I'd hate to see what would happen to our society without them."

"Agreed, Jack."

"You know, I had a pal in the county DA's office many years ago when I started as an investigator. He used to say that Sausalito was the meanest little town in the old west."

"Sounds like he knew what he was talking about. I've heard that as well."

"I think you're in for a wild ride. Keep me posted. Let me know if you need any help. And don't worry about delays; Botherton will cut through any red tape. If I remember correctly, and I'm pretty certain I do, the good judge wasn't a fan of your hometown's late mayor. For that matter, I don't know anyone in Marin county politics outside of Sausalito who was."

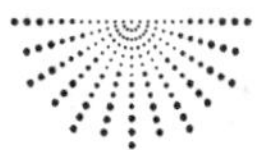

CHAPTER EIGHTEEN

When that week's edition of *The Standard* began arriving in mailboxes early on Wednesday morning, outrage was not a strong enough term to describe the reaction of Sausalito's premier social group.

Rob knew it would be impossible to satisfy all his readers. Given her years of service there were those who thought Mary Anderson was a saint. Then there were a significant number of voters who believed she had vastly overstayed her welcome. Rob chose not to reveal even half of what they had learned about Mary Anderson over the past week. But he knew he would be derelict in his responsibility to the community if he did not share at least part of the information they had gathered.

This approach allowed Rob and Holly a chance to shake the trees, as California's walnut ranchers do at harvest time, without damaging their prospects for a far more significant yield in the days ahead. Additionally, by giving the community a peek at the growing body of evidence *The Standard* was collecting, it may encourage some citizens, businesspersons, and other stake holders, to come forward and share their stories.

There were two aspects of the Mary Anderson investigation that Rob was ready to stake his reputation on: first, there were many more shakedown targets than the initial three businesses they had uncovered; and second, the money, coming in and going out, was not being reported or spoken of publicly by the late mayor or anyone else in her circle.

Those facts alone created a breathtaking violation of the transparency rules that govern campaign or nonprofit civic improvement contributions. Since Anderson never acknowledged the financial support of these merchants and none of these funds were detailed in any campaign filings, Rob chose a provocative, but relatively cautious headline:

Late Mayor Raised Thousands of Dollars in Unreported Funds.

Holly wondered if he was being overly cautious. "Don't you want to do something a little stronger than that?"

"If we had our hands on Anderson's banking records right now, trust me, I'd be coming at more directly. But for now, I'm fine with underselling the story. Think of it as a fishing lure. If I know the Ladies of Liberty, they'll jump at anything that impugns the blessed memory of Queen Mary. The only headline I could run that would not raise their ire is something like: 'Proposals for Statue Honoring Late Mayor Gather Momentum.'"

"Hah! You're right about that, Rob. I suppose our letters to the editor column next week is going to fill up quickly."

"I have no doubt. If they knock themselves out and send us enough letters to fill an entire page, that's one less article we'll need to cook up for next week's Sausalito edition. Let them throw a few punches our way. You and I know there are ninety-nine chances out of a hundred that this story is going to get bigger and uglier over the next two weeks."

"You're right Rob. Let them throw their tantrum now. Before long they'll wish they hadn't rushed in knowing half of the story."

Less than an hour after the Sausalito edition of *The Standard* began dropping into mailboxes, a flurry of morning phone calls resulted in an emergency meeting at the home of Alma Samuels, the longtime leader of the town's premier social club, The Ladies of Liberty. In Alma's sunroom, the club's key members gathered for a light lunch consisting of chilled cucumber soup and a small plate of chicken salad.

Nearing one hundred, and always a fussy eater, Alma had grown even pickier in recent years. Her list of ailments and complaints grew ever longer. Still, she was resolute in her determination to hold on to the club's presidency as long as she could draw breath.

Most times when this circle of friends gathered, they shared a healthy dose of gossip. There's always other people's lives, marriages, divorces, and affairs to chat about, often disapprovingly. But on this occasion, Alma was determined that everyone stay on task. Moments after she reviewed the front page of this week's paper, Alma knew quick action was needed. The very idea that Mary Anderson acted improperly, in any fashion, was simply unacceptable.

"We all know why we're here," Alma began in as strong a tone as she could muster. "I'm very concerned, as I'm sure all of you are, with this week's front-page story in *The Standard*. Mayor Anderson is one week in her grave, and already Rob Timmons has shown his intention to do whatever he can to ruin her good name. Timmons must be persuaded that this type of scandalous reporting must stop immediately!"

"I don't believe a word of any of this," Marilyn Williams added enthusiastically. "Where does that man get such ridiculous, I should say scurrilous, stories?"

"That's what I'd like to know!" Beatrice Snyder thundered. "Rob Timmons, and that so-called community newspaper of his, is going to upset a lot of people by smearing the cherished memory of Mary Anderson. After twenty-five years of dedicated service to this community, her legacy deserves a great deal better than empty accusations of improper campaign contributions!"

"I'm not surprised by anything that man writes," Robin Mitchell announced, anxious to join the chorus of outraged members. "The question we should be focusing on now is what we intend to do about this."

"Write letters!" Beatrice declared. "If that doesn't make Timmons realize his behavior is unacceptable, we'll push for advertisers to boycott the paper." Bea's face and neck reddened with anger, causing concern among her fellow club members given her long-standing issues with elevated blood pressure.

"I think we're getting ahead of ourselves," Ethel Landau

cautioned. "We would be wise to adopt a wait-and-see attitude."

The room went suddenly silent.

As opposed to Alma's natural inclination to strike back quickly, Ethel frequently cautioned moderation. Behind Alma, however, stood the full force and fury of approximately three hundred women representing many of Sausalito's most prominent families.

After several moments of awkward silence in which each of the women sensed that Alma was about to speak, they waited patiently, anticipating their fragile leader's opinion on the matter. "An interesting thought, Ethel," Alma said softly. "I'm not a fan of Rob Timmons, but I can still remember how all of us felt when he and that county detective friend of his unmasked Warren Bradley's true identity and, in so doing, humiliated all of us."

"That's very true, Alma," Ethel added. "All of you should keep that in mind. We all suffered great embarrassment when we vigorously defended Warren Bradley, better known now as the Gossiping Gourmet. Timmons said Warren was a fraud. Whether we liked it or not, he uncovered the information that proved Bradley was a fraud.

"Now he claims several businesses in town were pressured by Mary Anderson to give to various funds, the purpose of which remains unclear. There is the suggestion that this money was undeclared campaign contributions. In his piece, Timmons acknowledged that the investigation is at an early stage. If all this comes out to be one huge misunderstanding, I'll be the first one to write a letter demanding a full apology and retraction. Mary Anderson gave over twenty-five years of her life for the betterment of this community. Her memory deserves to be honored, and her good work in keeping runaway development under control should be recognized."

After several moments of awkward silence, the group once more waited for their leader to speak. Alma gathered her thoughts and her strength. Finally, she growled softly, "As much as I'd like to see that nasty Rob Timmons and his childhood friend, Eddie Austin, pack up and leave our otherwise peaceful community, Ethel is correct to point out that our defense of Warren Bradley was a time of terrible humiliation for all of us. We placed our faith in Warren and suffered great embarrassment because of that."

Each of the assembled unhappily nodded in agreement.

After a few more moments of silence, feeling a rare surge of urgency, Alma added, "Having said that, if any of you wish to write to Mr. Timmons, I encourage you to do so. Remind him that there has been no one in the history of our small but wonderful city who has been more highly honored than Mary Anderson. Perhaps Mr. Timmons should invest less time chasing scurrilous accusations and more time demanding that Detective Austin, and the Marin County Sheriff's Department, bring the investigation of her slaying to a swift and satisfactory conclusion. Those who have known and admired our late mayor's unprecedented dedication hope, wish—no, *demand*—that her killer be brought to justice!"

Alma's adoring acolytes busied themselves making notes of her shared wisdom. They left their luncheon ready to complain bitterly to Rob Timmons that while any and all allegations of misconduct must be investigated, it does not change the fact, as Alma exclaimed, that "a killer walks among us and must swiftly be brought to justice!"

Within three hours of leaving Alma's hastily arranged meeting Robin Mitchell, who often listened quietly and then proceeded to do whatever she thought best, had found more than a dozen members of her circle to write letters denouncing Rob Timmons and *The Standard* for questioning "the unimpeachable integrity of Sausalito's late, great mayor."

By noon on Friday, the letters—resulting from phone calls by Mitchell and her longtime friend, Marilyn Williams—were pushed through the ground floor mail slot of the old Victorian that served as home to *The Standard*.

For the past forty-eight hours, Holly had been wondering when, or if, the long-established Ladies of Liberty would speak out on behalf of the mayor they had vociferously supported for more than two decades. She got her answer when she saw a pile of envelopes, in various pastel colors with floral or nature designs on two of their four corners, sitting atop their usual daily mail delivery. Each was addressed: "Letters to the Editor, Sausalito Standard."

"Oh Rob," Holly said teasingly as she re-entered their offices and placed the letters on his desk, "I counted fourteen. The Ladies of Liberty apparently read this week's issue, and they were moved to share their thoughts."

"I don't suspect any wrote in praise of our tireless effort to provide outstanding journalism."

"We'll have to open them to see, but I wouldn't hold my breath, pal."

"Trust me, I'm not."

"Let's start opening at least some of these envelopes and see what Alma's devotees have to say," Holly added.

"I'm surprised they pulled this kind of effort together in less than forty-eight hours."

"I'm not, Rob. They were all adoring fans of Queen Mary. She supported nearly all of their pet projects, so I could see them jumping in with both feet."

"Still, I'll be surprised if Alma wrote. She and her besties were in a twist after the embarrassment they suffered over their dear departed gossip columnist."

"We won't know if we've heard from her until we take a closer look, Rob."

"Agreed! But I'm guessing Alma held back. Even at one hundred, she's sharper than most of her fellow Ladies of Liberty members."

"Either that, Rob, or she no longer has the strength to hold a pen. Of course, if we don't find a letter from her this week, it doesn't mean one is not coming next week."

"Holly, whenever Alma wanted to gripe about the fire department to her pals down at city hall, my dad would be called in to see that her complaints were addressed. Afterward, frustrated by the way she was able to ruffle the feathers of local politicians, Pop would say, 'That woman runs on battery acid.' You know, he might have been right about that."

"I didn't know she caused your dad headaches when he was fire chief."

"At one point or another Alma Samuels has caused everyone who works, or worked, for the City of Sausalito a headache. It's always been one of her many talents."

"You're probably right, Rob. But they can carp as much as they like. With the amount of page-space we're going to need to run all these letters, it means, as you suggested earlier, one less feature we'll need for our next edition. So, at least for this week, the Ladies of Liberty are okay in my book."

"What they don't realize is that we held back from our article a number of facts that we pulled together in the past few days. We've got a pretty good idea of what's coming, and we know there's an excellent chance that the Mary Anderson story is going to get a whole lot worse than what we've already put into print. And this is before we begin unraveling the whole Anderson, Nelson, and Dexter shenanigans regarding new residential construction projects. If we're right, and I'm pretty sure we are, a story about money pouring into those two design firms, along with a healthy kickback going to Mary Anderson, will be as bad, if not worse, than questionable campaign and civic contributions."

"You know, Rob, we work hard, but we do have fun."

"Especially when we can catch a group of well-connected socialites lavishing praise on someone they thought they knew well."

CHAPTER NINETEEN

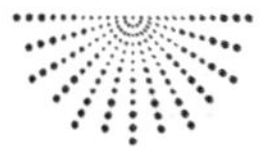

A closer review of these letters revealed that, run in their entirety, they would have covered over two pages in a weekly community newspaper that only exceeded twelve pages in the weeks before Christmas.

"Are you sure you know what you're doing, giving this collection of letters from the Ladies of Liberty a full-page spread?"

"I'm pretty sure I do, Holly. They're demanding apologies and retractions. As this story unfolds, they're going to learn the hard way why, as the expression goes, you should never get into an argument with someone who buys ink by the barrel."

"That's true, Rob. Here's another expression these people could learn from: 'Look before you leap!' They only knew that Mary Anderson stood with them in holding back any and all threats, real or perceived, to change in the community. Maintaining the status quo has always been their battle cry. And Anderson was a faithful adherent to that view. But look closer at all the players who danced to Anderson's tune and you find numerous projects that have been approved."

"It's mostly political gamesmanship, Holly. Change being good or bad, like beauty, is largely in the eye of the beholder. That's why if you look at past minutes of the planning commission, or the design review board, even before those boards were chaired and populated with Anderson's appointees, you'll find laughable inconsistencies in what elected officials claim is their goal and the final changes you'll find a decade or two later."

"Based on what we've learned so far regarding Anderson, the light at the end of the tunnel, which Anderson's admirers think is coming, is a freight train filled with revelations they're not going to enjoy reading."

"That's the news business, Holly. Lots of people jump to conclusions, but when the story plays out, they're often shocked to discover the whole truth."

Minutes before Eddie arrived for a second Friday cocktail hour held privately at Rob and Holly's office, Rob once again went to Venice Gourmet to pick up snacks and a four-pack of Guinness beers. He left Holly and her martini shaker to do what little else was needed to help make the transition from workspace to Friday evening gathering spot.

By the time Rob got back, Eddie was already stretched out on the overstuffed blue couch in Rob's office.

"You certainly look comfortable," Rob smiled.

"This has been one helluva week. It's time for me to lay down or fall down. Preferably, with a Guinness in my hand."

"Here, this should help." Rob said, handing Eddie a beer, which he promptly opened as he flashed a smile. "Tastes like the weekend," he announced happily.

"Long week?" Holly asked.

"Long? Yes, but an excellent one for moving the Mary Anderson case forward."

"What did you find out?" Holly asked.

"First, let me fill you in on some new developments. The scam she had working with Dexter and Nelson of squeezing home buyers for under-the-table cash payouts in order to secure their dream house was child's play compared to her sweeping up monthly payments from every restaurant, bar, coffee shop, ice cream parlor, art gallery, clothing and souvenir trinket retailer in Sausalito. Remember last week how the three of us wondered if we were seeing the tip of the iceberg? BINGO! Two bars and a souvenir shop barely scratched the surface."

Simultaneously, Rob and Holly, whose jaws hung open in disbelief, both experienced a sense of shock and elation. Their suspicions regarding the scope of Anderson's impropriety were actually below the mark.

"Wait a minute," Holly said, choking on her first sip of a chilled martini. "For you to know all this, you must have already gotten Bloody Mary's banking records out of West Bay Savings."

Suddenly, Rob felt an all-too-familiar panic whether he had the capacity to cover a story of this size and scope. "How did you pull that off? I mean getting into her account this quickly."

"It was surprisingly easy, I'm happy to say. I met with Jack

Canning on Tuesday morning, after my Monday evening conversation with Rob regarding Rowland Banks. Turns out that Jack was no fan of Queen Mary. More importantly, Marin County Judge Pete Botherton found Anderson, how did he put it? Oh yeah, 'Consistently obnoxious!'"

"Interesting, isn't it? When you step outside of a small town's echo chamber," Rob shrugged, "you begin to realize how many people were less than impressed with Mary Anderson."

"Thanks to Canning and Botherton being onboard, a court order went through in forty-eight hours. By yesterday afternoon, I was invited to a meeting with Cora Jones at West Bay Savings to discuss Anderson's financial relationship with the bank."

"I would love to have been a fly on the wall for that meeting!" Holly chuckled. By this point, she was too excited to give her Friday afternoon martini a second thought.

"Was Jones cooperative?" Rob asked.

"Very! She played the unknowing innocent, which I think we all agree is likely not true. If looking the other way while Mary Anderson opened several accounts into which she dropped surprising amounts of money was a problem, Jones used the excuse of being a busy bank manager with, as they say, great aplomb."

"Aplomb? Very nice, Eddie. You've been working your crossword puzzles again."

"Thank you for noticing, Holly. Not everyone would."

"Enough, you two." Rob said in a rush, anxious to hear the details of money passing in and out of Anderson's accounts.

"Holly, I think your boss wants some specifics about just how badly Sausalito's long-serving mayor misbehaved."

"I'd like to know that myself," Holly replied.

"To be honest, there was so much there, it's hard to know where to begin."

"Well, try, Sherlock, before my head explodes," Rob growled.

"Alright, Watson, calm down. For starters, Anderson kept three accounts: the one you and Holly stumbled upon, which Pete Francis and Mike Banks checks dropped into. There was a second account, which Rowland Banks was making a monthly contribution. Her third account she called, 'Onward Sausalito.' Interestingly enough, based on checks being paid out of that account, it's the only one at least partially dedicated to Queen Mary's political causes."

"She was creative," Holly said. "You have to give her that."

"Not to mention persistent!" Rob added. "Speaking of which, how many businesses did Anderson have on the hook?"

"Get out your notepads because you're going to want to write down some of these numbers. From what I've seen, twenty-eight restaurants and bars, all paying by check in amounts between three hundred and seven hundred dollars per month. As for shops like Rowland's, there were five more of those. That brings the total to six, at two-fifty each. Coffee shops, ice cream parlors, pizza kitchens also paid one price: one hundred and fifty per month. We don't have any corporate chain operations, so I don't know if she would have gone higher on places like Starbucks, Peet's, or Jamba Juice. And she also clipped the four art galleries in town for monthly contributions of three hundred bucks each."

"Incredible!" Rob said softly taken aback by the size of Anderson's operation.

"Wow," Holly added. "This is much bigger than anything we

imagined."

"What was her monthly take?" Rob asked.

"All totaled, she was taking in seventeen thousand two hundred per month."

"At that rate," Holly said, tapping on her phone's calculator app, "she would have collected $206,400 per year! That might be chump change in Washington, but in Sausalito, a town with a little more than seven thousand year-round residents, that's a remarkable haul!"

"Wow!" Rob said slowly shaking his head. "I think I'm feeling a little lightheaded."

"Of course, those kinds of numbers would never be possible if Sausalito did not swell from two to ten times its population, depending on the time of year. During holidays and the Labor Day Weekend Arts and Music festival, we grow to over twenty times our year-round population," Holly pointed out.

"I wonder why she didn't lean on the two big bicycle rental operations near the ferry landing?" Eddie asked. "On summer and holiday weekends, they seem to be busy, from early morning until closing time."

"Maybe she never got around to talking to them," Holly suggested with a shrug. "As it was, she had to be one busy lady, even if she had the help of one or more collectors."

"Speaking of collectors, anything in the bank statements about Harriman and Pollock?"

"Yep! She wrote a check to each one of them for seven hundred and fifty dollars per month. Harriman was paid out of one of the accounts and Pollock's take came out of another."

"Anyone else get a check?" Holly asked.

"None that went out of her accounts at West Bay. But here's

another important fact to keep in mind: she pulled a significant amount of cash out of each of those accounts every month. Right now, there's no telling where all that cash went. She might have put some, most, or all of that cash into her pocket. Or…"

"She might have put additional cash in Harriman and Pollock's pockets," Rob said. "You could argue that each of them was rewarded with their appointed positions. But having one of the design board members in your pocket, and another vote on the planning commission, is a benefit that cuts both ways."

"How so, Rob?" Eddie asked.

"For one thing, there is a transcript of what the design board and the planning commission members do when they are seated in public session. But when they go into closed session, it's like a jury deliberating. No official notes are taken, and no recordings are made that document those discussions for later review by the public."

"What do you suppose Anderson was concerned about?" Eddie asked.

"It could have been several things. But it was important to Anderson that she have a trusted set of eyes and ears to report on whether each member of those two bodies was doing what was expected of them. Her value to Nelson and Dexter turned on getting needed approvals through a maze of city regulations. Drop the ball on that aspect of the operation, and Anderson's worth to Nelson and Dexter vanishes.

"Here's one other fun fact you don't know regarding that third account I mentioned earlier, Onward Sausalito. From what I could see going through her accounts, it was used to collect payments from Nelson and Dexter. And you'll love this:

some of the engineering and construction firms that were at the top of Nelson and Dexter's vendor list were also contributors to Onward Sausalito."

"Speaking of Nelson and Dexter, any idea how much Anderson was taking in from her planning and design approvals?" Rob asked.

"Each statement's income varied significantly. I suppose that should be expected, depending on the number of construction projects going through the city's tangled planning process during various months. For example, the money deposited into Onward Sausalito would take a noticeable drop when we had a heavy rain season that extended over several months, times when construction slowed or halted altogether. This was particularly noticeable starting in mid-November and ending in late February. But overall, it was a pretty consistent and impressive level of deposits. Low months would be in the three to four-thousand-dollar range; peak dry months, when construction jobs are moving ahead at full speed, had deposits as high as twelve thousand dollars. When combined with the haul from restaurants and retailers, you're not taking in the kind of money that will allow you to buy an island in the Caribbean, but it came to about a quarter of a million dollars per year. Tax free!"

"Not a bad side business for a supposed dedicated public servant," Holly laughed.

"And once again, there were regular cash withdrawals made from this Onward Sausalito fund as well," Eddie added.

"Incredible!" Rob scratched the back of his head the way he always does when presented with an unimaginably huge story. "I feel like a kid on Christmas morning, I'm not sure what to tear into first."

"I have one suggestion," Eddie offered. "Start with interviewing the chairpersons of the design review board and the planning commission. I'm guessing that's the weak underbelly of her various scams."

"You're right! That is a great place to begin," Rob said, already planning his next move. "Go straight to the source. But what exactly am I looking to get out of them that I don't already have? I don't want to get in over my head and do anything to trip up what you and your department might need regarding Harriman and Pollock. I imagine both are potential suspects in Anderson's death."

"Don't worry about stepping on my toes, pal. This has been your story and Holly's since the day after Mary Anderson's body was buried by that landslide. You got a lucky break when Jack Canning was unavailable after Max examined Queen Mary's body and quickly realized she had been killed hours before the slide occurred. If not for Canning playing golf that day with Judge Botherton and hanging a do not disturb sign on his office, that report on Anderson would have come out that Monday instead of Tuesday. Rather than being a day ahead of *The Independent*, you would have been a full day behind. So, as long as the newspaper gods are smiling down upon you, call Pollock and get him to agree to an interview. Once you have him lined up, get a hold of Harriman and do the same. You know neither one of them is going to be willing to talk with you the day after your next edition comes out."

"But Eddie," Holly said, "what's Rob going to get out of those two, other than a bucket of lies about the work they do safeguarding Sausalito from runaway development? It'll just be more of their usual blather."

"I don't doubt that they'll feed him a load of malarky. But it would be nice to get them on record talking about the late mayor and see how they answer questions about her unreported campaign contributions—which, by the way, I thought was a wonderful opening gambit by both of you on the subject of Anderson's unexplained cash haul," Eddie said.

"The average city council campaign is going to run anywhere from ten to fifteen thousand dollars—tops. Two to three hundred thousand is easily ten to twenty times more what anyone should or would spend on a race to win one of five seats on the Sausalito City Council. And that's to cover the cost of a campaign you only need to run once every four years. Granted, you may do a voter meet-and-greet once a year, but that's coffee and donuts. That's pocket change given the cash haul Anderson was raking in."

"Rob's right, raising all that money on an annual basis is inexplicable. Which leaves one very obvious question: If not for her re-election campaign, where or to whom did all that extra money go?"

"I'm guessing it went to countless other things that likely had little, if anything, to do with her campaign or civic causes and projects she wanted to support," Eddie replied. "I will say one thing for Anderson: she was at least smart enough to not write big checks to herself. As I said, the only two individuals she wrote payments to were Harriman and Pollock. And even those checks were for relatively modest amounts."

"I assume most or all of the money going out of those accounts came in the form of regular and significant cash withdrawals," Rob said.

"Yes, that's correct. The deposited funds were drained out by frequent cash withdrawals, most often for the three-hundred-dollar daily cash limit. Anderson did write certain checks made out to 'Cash' for higher amounts. But that was never more than once every few weeks."

"What's your next move, Sherlock?" Holly asked.

"Actually, I'd love to hear what Harriman and Pollock have to say for themselves. As the old expression goes, 'There's no honor among thieves.' Those two might have been working in tandem, or one might have been playing his own little game. Either way, we have good reason to suspect one or both of them got greedy."

"If the week we just finished had not been so busy, I would have reached out to them already," Rob responded. "I know at least some of what I want to ask those two. More to the point, what is it you'd like to know?"

"After you go through your checklist—the 'when did you come to Sausalito,' family, professional background, and so on—I'd love to know how they respond to questions like: How did you become interested in holding a position on the planning commission and design review board? Noting gently, of course, that neither has any background that prepares them for serving, no less chairing, the board or commission on which they serve. How long have they known Mayor Anderson? What do they think about Mary Anderson having a significant number of unreported campaign contributions?"

"In other words," Rob said with a smile, "make them sweat a bit?"

"More than just a bit, I suspect."

"Eddie, do you really think either of them had anything to do with Mary Anderson's death?" Holly asked.

"Let's just say Anderson's accounts make it clear that both of them were knee deep in whatever she was doing. Not to mention Rowland Banks fingering Lester Harriman as his monthly collections guy."

"And perhaps, Harriman or Pollock was the other voice that Kayla Fox heard arguing with Anderson half an hour before she heard a car driving away!" Holly added. "One of them might have spent the time between that argument and when she heard a car screeching its way off her parking deck looking for what I imagine was a very substantial stash of cash. In fact, while Kayla Fox overheard an argument between a man and a woman, that does not eliminate the possibility that both men were in her home the night she died."

"If that were the case," Eddie said, "they could have found some of her haul because the fire and rescue guys and our county forensics team found no significant cash either in the wrecked portion of the home or the back section left standing."

"So, for all we know, Pollock, Harriman, or both, are sitting on a significant pile of cash at this very moment!" Rob exclaimed.

Eddie nodded. "That's a real possibility. In any event, now that I've gotten a good look at Anderson's accounts over at West Bay, I'm much further along than I was last week at this time."

"Wow! Longtime mayor and political boss knocked off by a high-ranking city officials! What a terrific story that would make!" Rob announced with obvious excitement.

"Don't count your chickens before they hatch, pal," Eddie suggested. "There could be other unexpected twists in this story before I'm able to make an arrest."

"I won't, Eddie," Rob said excitedly. "But every small-town journalist has a right to dream of landing a really big story every now and then. And this one is looking like a gem."

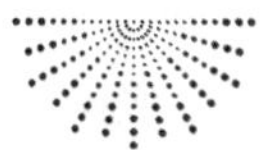

CHAPTER TWENTY

By Sunday night, Rob could think of little else other than his upcoming interviews with Stan Pollock and Lester Harriman. Having called them Saturday morning, he was delighted that both agreed to meet Monday. He scheduled Pollock for eleven, and Harriman soon after, at twelve-thirty. The first day of the workweek is always busy, but Rob was hoping to get some usable quotes from both of them for his next Sausalito edition.

Regardless of how the interviews went, friendly or hostile, it was certainly worth Rob's time and effort given the information Eddie shared with Holly and him Friday afternoon.

There was little doubt that by now both of them had seen last week's edition with the headline that stirred so much attention and conversation throughout the small town. Rob was reasonably certain that Pollock and Harriman would confer with each other prior to meeting with him. In fact, their responses to Rob's request for an interview time were nearly identical: "I know I have a busy day on Monday," each explained, "but give me an hour or less and I'll ring you back to tell you if I'll be able to work meeting with you into my schedule." In a little less than an hour, Pollock called saying he would meet. "I had to shift a couple of appointments to accommodate your request, Mr. Timmons, but I can make eleven o'clock on Monday work. Please try your best to be on time!"

Just five minutes after getting off the phone, Harriman returned Rob's earlier call and confirmed a twelve-thirty meeting. These two reminded Rob of an old expression he learned from his father: "They act like Frick and Frack."

Rob was so amused by Pollock and Harriman's obvious coordination with one another that he went online to learn how the term originated. Rob learned that Frick and Frack were a pair of famous ice skaters, both from the Swiss city of Basel. They performed with the Ice Follies in the mid-Twentieth Century. Their movements were so well synchronized that they gained world-wide fame. In so doing, their names became forever linked with the idea of two individuals working in perfect coordination.

Rob had a restless sleep anticipating Monday's interviews with two potential suspects in the death of Mary Anderson. Thoughts regarding what might have occurred between the three apparent conspirators that brought about a deadly confrontation on a rain-soaked night kept coming to mind. Was he putting himself at risk? That was unlikely, Rob reasoned. Still, it added to his inability to have a restful night.

Shortly before six, Rob threw back his side of the blanket and attempted to quietly leave the bedroom.

"What time is it?" Karin muttered, clearly displeased to be awakened at such an early hour.

"Almost six," Rob said softly, not wanting to be heard by the children sleeping in the two bedrooms across the hall.

"Come back to bed," Karin pleaded.

"I have to write down a few questions for my interviews with Pollock and Harriman today."

Karin sighed. "Do what you have to, but please don't wake the kids! I was hoping to sleep until seven if possible."

"I'll be quiet," Rob promised. Gently, he kissed her cheek then slowly and softly he shut their bedroom door.

Rob walked downstairs to a room that doubled as a laundry area and a home office.

The sun was peeking out from behind Angel Island, which sits to the east of Sausalito, positioned between the Tiburon Peninsula, the East Bay, and San Francisco.

It would have been easy for Rob to simply enjoy the spectacle created by the rapidly emerging light upon a large body of water that, just minutes earlier, had been shrouded in darkness. But two potentially contentious interviews were just hours away, and Rob knew he needed to be well prepared.

Rob was experienced in the art of uncomfortable interviews. He had done many of them during his years publishing *The Standard*. But like all interviews, amicable or contentious, the best results occur when you come well prepared.

Even though Rob had put out a story in the previous week's edition regarding Anderson's unreported cash donations, he had no reason to think that Pollock and Harriman believed they were currently on Rob's radar. The story made no mention of who contributed to these funds, nor of how the money was collected.

It was uncertain that either of them already knew about the court order presented to West Bay Savings, but it was possible that Cora Jones had let one or both of them know that Eddie Austin had been given access to Anderson's bank records. While that would not reveal which, if any, of the collections were made by Harriman or Pollock, it would show checks written to both men from one or more of Anderson's accounts. Rob concluded that it was a safe bet Jones and West Bay would maintain a low profile on the questionable nature of Anderson's monthly haul. That included having limited, if any, contact with Anderson's co-conspirators.

It was probable that by now Pollock and Harriman were cut off from those funds derived from Anderson's shakedown of local merchants, but that would have been triggered by Anderson's death as opposed to anything *The Standard* had put into print.

Both men likely agreed to the interviews because, at least for now, they were hopeful of continuing their endeavors— perhaps with the help of the new acting mayor, Julie Phillips, who had long been a booster for all of Anderson's positions and legislative proposals.

Shortly before eight, Rob showered and dressed, walked down Caledonia Street on his way to the office. He felt satisfied that the questions he had prepared for both men would draw them out or, perhaps, cause them to refuse any further cooperation. He was anxious not only to see how they responded, but their comfort or discomfort in discussing the late mayor.

The first three hours of Rob and Holly's Monday began by reviewing editorial content for the week ahead: stories written, and those yet to be composed.

Mill Valley was opening an expanded recreation center. Corte Madera was holding a public meeting to discuss renovation and expansion of their popular public library. And San Anselmo was reviewing a new flood preparedness plan.

Time, as it always does, moved quickly for two very busy people. Pollock had left Rob a voice message Saturday morning on *The Standard*'s office line explaining that he had arranged for the two of them to meet at City Hall, where he had secured the use of a private room off of the ground floor's senior center.

Determined not to be late, Rob walked into Sausalito's civic center building a few minutes before eleven. By fifteen minutes past the hour, Rob was simultaneously annoyed and a bit amused by Pollock's failure to appear at, "Eleven sharp!" The exact words Pollock used in his voicemail message.

Rob tried both Pollock's cell and home phone numbers. He failed to pick up either line.

Did Pollock change his mind, or perhaps get cold feet and decided to blow off our meeting? Rob wondered. Concluding that was unlikely, Rob left and went across Bee street, which borders the north side of the civic center. He went directly to the main office for the senior complex. There, he ran into one of his dad's old fire department crew, Cal Pierce. After smiles and a handshake, Cal, who looked considerably older than the last time Rob saw him, shrugged when asked if he had seen Pollock. After he explained the meeting, they had arranged, and Pollock's insistence that he arrive promptly at eleven, Rob asked, "It's odd that Pollock would vanish without a follow-up call, don't you think?"

Cal shrugged. "Let's go over to his unit and take a look. In case you don't know, Rob, and just between us, Stan's not the world's nicest guy," Cal said quietly as they walked along a winding path toward Pollock's one-bedroom unit. "He does make a big deal about punctuality. I had a new shower head I was installing in his unit last week and he was apoplectic when I showed up thirty minutes late! I'm used to some of these older folks being on the fussy side. But Pollock can be a real pain in the rump, if you know what I mean!"

As Rob remembered, there never was anything subtle about Cal. He stood behind the big, but now somewhat stooped, former firefighter as he pushed the front door buzzer.

No response.

Cal then pounded with the side of his fist. "Stan? You in there?" he barked. "Sometimes you got to speak up with these older folks. I should know, being one myself."

Cal waited a few moments more before banging on Pollock's door a second time.

After several more buzzes and knocks, Cal turned to Rob and said, "Wait here, Rob, while I go get the passkey."

"Is that okay, Cal?"

"Of course, it is. This is a senior center. Now and then we have a resident die, without giving us any notice." Cal laughed at his own words, showing a bit of the macabre humor firemen develop over years of service.

"Sure," Rob agreed. As he waited for Cal to return, he wondered again if Pollock had gotten word of Eddie examining Anderson's banking records. Perhaps Pollock panicked and decided his time would be better spent meeting with Harriman, deciding how they would explain their role in what by now had the unmistakable feel of a growing scandal.

When Cal returned, he banged his fist one more time on the center of Pollock's front door, almost as if he was jabbing at the midsection of an opponent during one of the amateur league bouts that Rob's dad took him and Eddie to when they were teens.

Growing impatient, Cal slipped the passkey into the lock and opened the door. The unit's neat appearance seemed to fit with Pollock's personality, a fastidiousness that came through when he was speaking from the center chair of the five-member design review committee.

No lights were on in the apartment. Rob followed closely as Cal first checked the kitchen, the living room, the bathroom, and then the bedroom. Its door was closed. Cal gently rapped a partially opened fist against the bedroom door.

"Stan," he called out. "You in there, Stan?"

He twisted the knob slowly and opened the door. The room's floor-to-ceiling horizontal blinds were closed and let in very little light. Cal flicked the overhead light switch, and to Rob's relief the bed was empty and looked as if it had been left undisturbed from the previous night.

"Perhaps Stan spent the night out, or he left early. Maybe he just forgot you two were supposed to meet."

"I seriously doubt that Cal. He was really insistent I meet him at eleven over at city hall. Said he had a busy day and could give me no more than thirty minutes. If he had something come up, it's strange he didn't call to reschedule."

"Sounds to me like he blew you off. But what do I know?" Cal shrugged. "We need to get out of here. If he comes walking up to his unit in the next couple of minutes and finds the two of us snooping around, I'll have hell to pay." Cal gave Rob's shoulder a gentle nudge toward the front door.

Less than five minutes later, after two calls Rob made to Eddie's cell went straight to voicemail, Eddie rang back.

"You done interviewing Pollock?" Eddie asked immediately. "Get anything interesting out of him?"

"He was a no-show," Rob said.

"You're kidding!"

Rob went on to detail the past hour, ending with Cal entering Pollock's empty unit. "I've got a 12:30 with Harriman, so I better get myself over to his place."

"Let's hope he's there waiting for you," Eddie said.

"No kidding! Otherwise, I'll have a big hole in this week's Sausalito edition. It's just really odd. Pollock was so insistent I be on time, telling me twice how busy a week he had coming up."

"I guess he and Harriman have to pick up the slack, now that Mary Anderson is not there to help with collections," Eddie said. "Actually, I would think that scam they've been running is all but dead without their Queen Bee scaring people into handing over their monthly contribution."

"We'll see. The chairmen of the planning commission and design review board can make an applicant's life pretty miserable if they choose to do so," Rob declared. "I'm not saying any of these businesses have a project coming up before either of their committees at the moment, but people in high places tend to have friends in high places."

"Valid point," Eddie conceded. "I've got to scoot. Call me when you finish with Harriman. Hopefully he'll be an interesting interview. Better still, maybe he knows where you can find Pollock."

It took Rob just five minutes to walk down Caledonia Street. He passed three different eating establishments that were already filled with locals enjoying their lunch break. He hung a right at the corner of Caledonia and Pine and passed the newly built retail shops that took the place of the town's one and only movie theater that closed several years earlier. He walked the short distance uphill to the Pine Street Apartments, which looked as if it had been torn from the pages of a nineteen-sixties California picture book. Rob double-checked Harriman's unit number before knocking on the door. By then, it was precisely 12:30. After two more knocks, and several times pushing a buzzer that was screwed into the door frame, Rob put down his satchel. At this point he couldn't help but think that this was not going to be his lucky day.

Rob remembered that the affable Tommy Hana managed the Pine Street Apartments. Tommy was one of a handful of Sausalito natives not scared away by the Bay Area's rising prices, thanks mostly to the fact that the owner was a friend of Tommy's dad who gave him a great rate on a one-bedroom unit in exchange for his work as the property's on-site manager.

Frustrated and hot from a midday sun that was starting to

burn through the light jacket he was wearing, Rob tried to call Harriman. The call went directly to voicemail. As Rob slipped the phone back into his jacket pocket, he heard a familiar voice calling his name. "Rob? Is that you, man?" He turned to his right and was happy to see Tommy smiling and walking toward him.

Rob explained the situation. Hana shrugged, stepped around Rob, made a fist and banged the side of his hand on the center of Harriman's door.

"Les, you in there? You've got a visitor, pal," Tommy said loudly.

After a minute Tommy turned to Rob and shrugged. "Looks like old Lester stood you up."

Rob explained that he had just come from Stan Pollock's place. "He had a meeting with me at eleven. Never showed up. Now Harriman's a no-show." From getting out of bed before six until this moment, Rob felt like his entire morning had been a colossal waste of time.

"Wow, Rob. First Pollock, now Harriman. I always tell the wife that those two are like Abbot and Costello. You rarely see one without the other."

"My thought exactly, Tom. Only I call them Frick and Frack. And for some reason they both decided to stand me up today."

"Hey, I'm not supposed to do this, but I am the guy with the master key to all the units. Why don't you head out to the street for a minute and let me step inside and just check that he's okay. Generally speaking, local politics aside, Lester's a good guy. If he said he'd meet you here, and he never called to cancel, I'm a little concerned that he and Pollock were both no-shows."

Rob waited back out on Pine Street, stewing over the fact that his entire morning had been a colossal waste of time.

Tommy walked back out moments later, shrugging his shoulders and saying, "Got me beat, Rob. Sorry man. Whenever he turns up, I'll tell Lester you were here looking for him."

Fifteen minutes later, Rob was back in the office. "What a colossal waste of time!" He said to Holly, before flopping into his desk chair. "We'll have to punt. What can we put on the front page of this week's Sausalito edition?"

"Not sure about a lead story at the moment," Holly replied. "But we got even more missives today from the Ladies of Liberty's letter writing campaign."

"I'd sooner shoot myself in the foot than give those old crows any more space for their nonsensical carping."

"Things aren't quite that bad. How about leading with Enrico's Pizza opening a new location on Bridgeway?"

Rob groaned. "I'd sooner shoot myself in the other foot than do that."

"Sounds like we're going from bad to worse. Something will turn up by tomorrow. I'd hate to see you shoot yourself in the foot. There would go those Sunday nature hikes you like to take with Karin and the kids."

"Don't worry about me doing something stupid. I'm just a frustrated at the moment. Maybe between now and tomorrow's deadline, good fortune will once again smile upon our humble weekly newspaper."

CHAPTER TWENTY-ONE

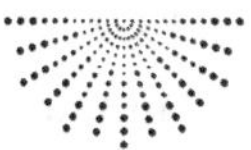

Rob's dyspeptic mood followed him home that night. To make up for a restless night, he decided on an early bedtime.

He was thankful when he woke at seven and realized he had slept for nine full hours. Karin was already rattling around in the kitchen; Micah and Alice were engaged in their first argument of the day. Just as he was about to step into the shower, his phone began to vibrate on the bathroom sink's aging powder blue tile countertop. The display said "Eddie."

"You already at work?" Rob croaked, still suffering from morning dry mouth.

"Yeah, I'm at work. Got called in about twenty minutes ago. At least the call was close to home," Eddie said with a chuckle.

"Where are you?"

"I'm over on the waterfront at Dunphy Park. You know those two guys who stood you up yesterday?"

"Sure, Pollock and Harriman. What about them?"

"They washed up on shore overnight, each wearing nothing but a pair of boxer shorts."

"WHAT?"

"They're dead, Rob. Very dead indeed. They either went for a midnight swim, or more likely, some not-so-friendly pirate made them walk the plank."

"I'm on my way! Be there in ten or less."

Rob flew out the door in such a hurry that Karin saw only a blur that called out excitedly, "Eddie found Harriman and Pollock! They're both dead! I'll call you as soon as I get done."

Karin shook her head and wondered if there was any other small city in all of California where the bizarre seemed routine. Well, at least it keeps Rob busy, she thought as she called the children to come have their breakfast before it got cold.

Rob, wearing an old pair of khakis, worn out tennis shoes, and a faded blue sweatshirt that said across the front, "Sausalito July 4," ran down the steps that led from his parking deck onto Napa Street. Two minutes later, he had crossed Bridgeway near Galilee Harbor and stepped onto the green, open expanse of the newly revitalized public park.

From there, Rob could see the scrum of police cars pulled alongside two Sausalito fire and rescue vehicles close to the water's edge. As he neared, Rob could see Eddie. He was crouching down for a closer look at one of the two bodies that had earlier been carried from the rocks at the water's edge to gray tarps that had been spread across newly planted grass.

To Rob's surprise, Harriman and Pollock were barely recognizable. Both, as Eddie had mentioned, were disrobed with the exception of their boxer shorts.

Harriman, the heavier of the two, was in even worse shape than Pollock.

Rob nodded a silent greeting to the assembled police and firefighters, all of whom he recognized, and who in turn recognized him. The upside, or downside, depending on your personal preference, of life in a small town.

Crouching down next to Eddie, Rob said, "This explains why I was shut out on my interview appointments yesterday."

"Seems like they were otherwise engaged. Well, they gave you a better story than any interviews would have."

"You're right about that, pal. I was convinced these two coordinated with each other on a regular basis. But I never imagined anything like this."

"Have you eaten yet?" Eddie asked.

"No! I ran out of the house just as Karin was preparing breakfast. How about you?"

"Running on empty."

Rob marveled at Eddie's ability to separate his appetite from the unexpectedly gruesome aspects of his job.

Eddie spoke with several officers at the scene, scribbled down a few remaining notes, flipped his small pad closed, then turned to Rob and said, "Let's walk down to your place and grab some grub to go at the Lighthouse Café along the way."

"Sounds like a great idea," Rob declared, wondering how long it would be before he regained his appetite.

The two said their goodbyes and headed south on Bridgeway.

Twenty minutes later, carrying eggs, sausages, and toast, along with two tall coffees, they walked through the chilled morning air, saying little to each other.

"I suppose our food will be cold by the time we get to your

office," Eddie suggested.

"That's why I'm glad Holly and I figured out where we could place a microwave in our cluttered space," Rob replied.

"I didn't know you had done that. That's good news."

"Just got it a couple of months ago. Too often both of us picked up something hot, walked into the office, answered a call, or whatever other distraction might be going on, and the next thing you know your hot food is no longer hot."

"Rob, where else but Sausalito would two seniors, with questionable backgrounds, end up at the water's edge of a popular weekend picnic spot? I got called at six-fifteen this morning about your two missing city officials. That was a lousy way to start my day!"

Rob shrugged. "On the upside, I've got my lead for tomorrow's Sausalito edition," Rob smiled. "Twelve-plus hours ago I had nothing to put on the front page other than a rehash of what we've already put out on Mary Anderson. I'd say my lead story is now significantly more interesting."

"Good for you, pal! As for me, this case just got far more complicated. I knew my luck with the Bill Bent case wasn't going to last. I just didn't want to think it would end so soon. Harriman and Pollock turning up as a pair of floaters just put an exclamation point on that suspicion."

"I suppose you can't be certain that the Harriman and Pollock deaths are connected to Mary Anderson's death."

"You're right, I can't. But there is a ninety-plus percent chance that they are!" Eddie said confidently.

After a healthy breakfast, both Rob and Eddie were feeling better prepared to discuss the morning's developments. Just as they were about to start, Holly walked in and said, "What are you two up to this early in the day?"

"Sit down, kid," Eddie said. "We've got a story for you."

"Oh my God, now what?"

Holly's eyes got wider as Eddie recapped his early morning call to Dunphy Park.

"Unbelievable!" She announced dropping back into her chair. "Rob, you've got an infinitely better lead for this week's Sausalito edition than you had yesterday afternoon!"

"That's what I just told Eddie!" Rob announced reaching out to exchange a fist bump with his office mate.

"I'm glad you two are pleased with the story that just landed in your laps. Now I'd like us to spend a little time considering what in the world happened to these two distinguished gentlemen?"

"I don't know if I'd call them 'distinguished,' Eddie." Holly suggested with a half-smile.

"Eddie, I assume you're thinking, as I know I am, that Pollock and Harriman were up to their eyeballs in Anderson's scam," Rob suggested.

"Scams, plural," Holly added.

"Indeed, scams," Rob nodded.

"There's a good possibility that Anderson's attacker was also involved in the deaths of Harriman and Pollock," Eddie said while drawing a doodle of a hang man on a scrap of paper.

"You know, I had taken to thinking of Harriman and Pollock as Frick and Frack," Rob announced.

"Why Rob?" Eddie asked.

"When I called them at the end of last week to set up those interviews for Monday, it seemed clear that they were coordinating their movements with one another. Both of them were reluctant to agree to being interviewed or agreeing to a time and place. When I checked back with them, both explained they were now open to meeting with me but made similar suggestions about the scope of my interview."

"That makes sense," Holly nodded. "I think it's all but certain that they were both lieutenants under Anderson's command."

"You make it sound like this was a military operation," Eddie said with a smile.

"In a sense, I think it was," Holly responded. "Even though we've only interviewed Pete Francis at Smitty's, Mike Banks at the Lazyjack, and Rowland Banks at Sausalito Memories, the pattern seems pretty clear. And thanks to your access to Anderson's banking records, most importantly her check deposits, we have an extensive list of businesses that she'd been hitting, from Jack's Bikes at Gate Five on the north end of town, to Sal's Pizza on the south end of town. If we took a Saturday and picked a half dozen of the places on Anderson's list, I'll wager several of them had Harriman as their pick-up person. And others probably had Pollock."

"There could have been other collectors," Rob added, "but I think Anderson was smart enough to keep it a tight little circle. I'm betting that Anderson was the setup person for all of these businesses, and Harriman and Pollock were merely loyal foot soldiers."

"Yes. Anderson probably handled collections herself for older accounts like Pete Francis over at Smitty's," Holly added.

"I'm going to get out of your way so the two of you can go to work. I've got to go bug Max. I'll call you before your Sausalito edition deadline this afternoon and let you know if Max has any early word on how our two floaters, Messrs. Frick and Frack, wound up on the shores of our small, but rarely boring, city."

CHAPTER TWENTY-TWO

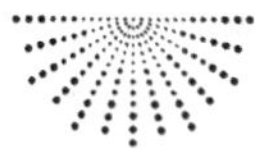

Eddie entered Max's examination room just before eleven. The good doctor, standing between the two bodies he had first seen two hours earlier, was obviously deep in thought.

"What have you got for me, Max?"

"A pair of stiffs, but I think you already knew that." Max responded with a grin.

"Agreed! My question is how did they arrive at this sad state?"

"My best guess is it was a race between drowning and hyperthermia. Jumping or being pushed into the cold, choppy waters of San Francisco Bay can kill you in a variety of ways, but those are the two most common. I suspect that one or more individuals assisted them on their way out of this world."

Eddie frowned. "You think they were made to walk the plank?"

"In a manner of speaking, yes! It's reasonable to assume that both of them, reportedly of sound mind, were inebriated when they went into the water. In fact, their blood samples already tested positive for the presence of alcohol. But I think I have a scenario that might fit how these two met their demise, as they say in murder mysteries. Corny ones, anyway."

"And that was?"

"Remember, Eddie, I'm just expressing a theory. But it seems perfectly plausible to me, so let me share it with you."

Eddie grinned, nodded, and said, "I'm all ears, doctor."

"I think someone took these two out for an early evening sail on the bay," Max explained. "It's my understanding that both of these gentlemen were Sausalito residents, so it's likely that the boat they boarded was docked somewhere along the Sausalito waterfront. Sunset this week has been right around six-fifteen. Last light occurs just after seven. These two bodies floated up at Dunphy Park. I'm quite sure, given the conditions of the two victims and their stomach contents, they had been in the water for approximately thirty-six hours."

"An educated guess is that they went into the water around sundown on Sunday night," Eddie replied. "They were scheduled to be interviewed by my pal, Rob Timmons, on Monday. He was disappointed when both were no shows. Now we know why. But how did it take that long for them to float back to shore?"

"Could have been one of many factors," Max pointed out. "First, tides and cross currents in the bay can, as you know growing up here, be a pretty wild show. Second, they may have floated in or near Galilee Harbor, close to Dunphy Park, the previous day, and got stuck in the mud at low tide. Then, just as easily, their bodies floated back out Monday night, finally washing up where they were found early this morning."

"As they say, what the tide taketh away, the tide returns," Eddie shrugged. "So how do you figure they went from on the boat to in the bay?"

"The fact that they were both found wearing only their underwear was what got me thinking. You see, if I wanted to kill these two…what are their names again?"

"My buddy Rob calls them Frick and Frack."

Max nodded. "For demonstration purposes, those names will do just fine. Suppose I invite Frick and Frack out for a sunset cruise. I lower my boat's anchor somewhere between Sausalito and the Tiburon Peninsula. Just as the sun is setting, I offer them alcoholic drinks: a good brandy, say, or a fine Scotch. Perhaps a Bourbon. I lace both of their drinks with what has become known as the date rape drugs: Ketamine, Ecstasy, or Rohypnol, any of which would serve the killer's purpose. All three of these drugs have no taste, no smell, and require only a small dose to do the trick. Not only would Frick and Frack be feeling no pain, but they would also be open to any number of ridiculous suggestions."

"Such as their host saying this would be the perfect time for a swim," Eddie says.

"Exactly! Now, laughing and acting as carelessly as a couple of high school kids, they strip down to their underwear. Perhaps their host did as well. The three of them are ready to jump into the increasingly dark and frigid water when their host, promising to join them in a moment, explains there is something that needs looking after. He says, for example, 'I just need to check that my port and starboard lights are on, so that any other boat approaching will be able to see us anchored here.' Heckle and Jeckle, I mean Frick and Frack, jump in just as carefree as a couple of schoolboys. Meanwhile, their killer isn't checking the boat's lights. He's starting the engine and slowly moving away, probably with his two passengers ignoring him, laughing, and enjoying what they unfortunately think is the happiest night of their lives."

"More like the last night of their lives."

"Exactly! If you wanted to dispose of two people, that's not a bad way to accomplish the goal. Vicious and cold-blooded, but certainly a clean kill."

"What do you say the following day to your guests in the unlikely event that they are picked up by another boat before drowning or dying of hyperthermia?" Eddie asked.

"In the event they're rescued, the boat captain can say they both got a little too drunk, started horsing around, and fell into the water. It was getting dark, and the tide carried them out of sight. Given my suggested scenario, their age, and the bay's water temperature, there's an excellent chance that the last time their killer would have seen these two alive is when they went into the water."

"Wow! That certainly makes sense. But I've got to tell you, Max, that sounds like a stone-cold killer."

"Eddie, you can't be in my line of work and not pick up a few smart ways, and occasionally some very dumb ways, of eliminating people who, for whatever reason, some individual wants gone."

"I suppose you're going to need a few weeks for the toxicology report to come back, confirming your theory that both these victims were drugged."

"Unfortunately, it'll be four weeks or possibly a little longer before we get definitive test results. But I just can't imagine our two floaters jumping into the bay and going for a swim on the strength of one stiff drink or, more ridiculously, they actually thought it was a good idea. These aren't two older gentlemen visiting from South Florida. Locals know how cold the bay's water can be. But lace their drinks with Ecstasy and any ridiculous suggestion seems like a good idea."

"Max, I got to hand it to you, that scenario makes perfectly good sense."

"I assume these two were up to something that was, let's just say, coloring outside the lines?"

"That they were, Max. I suspect whoever was their boat captain was looking to get his cut, and their cut, of what was a substantial amount of cash."

"People are capable of doing a lot of bad things. Throw a substantial amount of money into the mix, and their temptation to misbehave increases by a factor of ten."

Rob was wearing one of those goofy grins that tells Holly he's having a wonderful day. The lead story of this week's Sausalito edition, which he had so worried about just twenty-four hours earlier, seemed to be writing itself. He worked through lunch, not only detailing the recovery of the bodies of two city officials but explaining how their deaths might be connected to the death of Mayor Anderson.

"I've had some good and bad days since I bought The Standard, but I'll remember this as one of the great days," Rob declared.

"I know how cranked-up you get when you feel you're sitting on a great story, but really, Rob, try to show a little sympathy for the deceased." While Holly's tone was admonishing, she understood Rob's relief going from having no lead story to a front-page they would likely remember for years to come.

"Trust me on this Holly, neither Harriman nor Pollock are deserving of our sympathy. I'll bet the bank that they were up to their necks in whatever games Mary Anderson was playing. For that matter, they might have run part of this racket themselves. They both worked regularly on planning and design approvals. I strongly suspect they were in for a cut of whatever was coming in—not just from merchants and restaurants, but also likely kickbacks from Dexter and Nelson. It's safe to assume that there were also kickbacks from construction contractors as well."

"My guess is that most, or all, of those funds came in the form of cash, which likely was never placed into her account. I strongly suspect that in addition to all the other money flowing into West Bay Savings, she had a pile of cash, some of which might have been handed directly to Frick and Frack for the good work they did at Anderson's behest."

"Another possible reason why there was such a significant gap between the time Kayla Fox heard voices shouting and when she was awakened a second time by a car screeching off of Anderson's deck."

"Agreed! For all we know that side business was taking in as much cash as any other aspect of Anderson's operation."

The balance of Rob and Holly's day passed so quickly that the afternoon deadline for the Sausalito edition seemed to close in on them like an unexpected squall rising in the turbulent waters of the Pacific outside the mile-wide opening into San Francisco Bay, named by the earliest Spanish explorers as Puerto d'Oro, and later translated into English as the Golden Gate.

"Well, everything looks good for this edition," Holly declared. "I've read over all the editorial copy twice. The only thing left is a frontpage headline."

Rob had been thinking about this edition's headline since he laid eyes on Pollock and Harriman early that morning. Somewhat like the proverbial kid in a candy shop, he had so many choices, Rob didn't know which to pick. Finally, he settled on a headline similar to the paper's previous week, in which he raised the issue of the late mayor collecting thousands of dollars in unreported contributions. He wanted to ratchet up the pressure on Anderson's supporters, and any conspirators yet to be revealed, without going all-in on a case that he knew, at this point, remained untried, unproven, and unresolved.

"How about this, Holly: 'Deaths of Two Sausalito City Officials Heightens Mystery Over Mayor Anderson's Past.'"

"Great! Sounds ominous while still leaving us a good amount of wiggle room for our next edition," Holly declared happily. "Alma and the ladies will be apoplectic when they see this front page!"

Rob chuckled. "It's the least I can do for my most devoted readers."

CHAPTER TWENTY-THREE

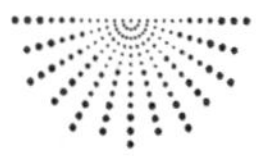

For Alma Samuels and her group, what they read in *The Sausalito Standard*'s latest edition fell well short of what they were hoping to see. Granted, Rob gave the Ladies of Liberty a generous amount of space, in which they were able to state their grievances over the previous week's coverage of Mayor Anderson. However, this latest issue left Alma's acolytes perplexed and troubled over what might come next.

"Step by step, this is becoming ever more maddening!" Alma complained to Ethel Landau while both shared tea and sympathy in her mansion's sunroom late Wednesday afternoon. "That man and his so-called newspaper, are destroying the legacy of good government that Mary Anderson worked hard to establish over a period of twenty-five years!"

"I find it upsetting too," Ethel muttered. "But at this stage I think we should, as you suggested last week, wait and see how this story concludes. Rob Timmons managed to embarrass us beyond anything we could have imagined after we backed Warren Bradley to the hilt. Regardless of what we think of Timmons, Bradley was indeed a fraud with a very disturbing past. I know you felt as I did that Warren was above reproach. Sadly, we could not have been more wrong."

"I agree! But it's inconceivable to me that Mary Anderson was, what's that terrible term…"

"Shaking down?"

"Yes, shaking down nearly every business in Sausalito for contributions to various funds. And to what end? The whole thing makes no sense!" Alma insisted.

"I'd like to agree without reservation, but there is something I know about Mary that I'm afraid you don't."

"What could that possibly be? I knew Mary for a very long time. I'll grant you her father was an unpleasant character with a questionable past, but that shouldn't tarnish all the good Mary did for Sausalito."

"Agreed! But what I heard has nothing to do with the sins of Mary's father. Julie Phillips and I had tea together this past Friday. I don't know if you were aware of what she shared with me, but I was certainly shocked by what I learned."

"Ethel, what in the world are you talking about?" Alma asked anxiously, fearing, as she often did, that her aging heart might not withstand another unexpected shock.

"You know, of course, how Julie and other members of the city council had unswerving loyalty to Mary, praising her leadership and so on. Most importantly, every year supporting Mary for another term as mayor, as opposed to revolving the honor among each member of the council as they did prior to Mary's quarter-century of service."

"Yes, of course, I'm aware of her long success in holding

onto the position of mayor! I've always thought their continued support of her was in recognition of her excellent work and the strong leadership she brought to her position."

"Alma, I'm afraid there was more to it than just that."

"Go on!" Alma's obvious agitation, along with the reddening of her neck, caused Ethel concern that she might be pushing her decades-long friend too far and too quickly. Still, having said this much, Ethel had no choice but to complete this unpleasant news. She took a deep breath, looked Alma in the eye and said, "Julie said that Mary approached her many years ago and suggested she run for an open seat on the council."

"There's nothing wrong with that!"

"That's not the troubling part of what Mary did. Over the years, lots of councilmembers have recruited and supported numerous citizens for the council, often suggesting that they start by applying for a position on one of the city's boards or commissions and then, as the expression goes, move up through the chairs. A commission, board, or committee member becomes a vice chair, eventually a chairperson and then stands for elected office as a member of the city council if they have the desire, ambition, and commitment to serve at that level."

"Yes, that's the way it's always been. What did Mary do that was different?"

"When they were ready to run for a seat on the city council, Mary funded their campaigns."

"SHE WHAT?" Alma said in a voice louder than any she had used in a very long time.

"Worse still, she gave Julie cash and told her to report the money she handed her as miscellaneous cash donations. In other words, cash donations of one-hundred dollars or less."

At this point, Alma could feel her heart rate increasing.

"You mean to say that Mary essentially funded Julie with her own cash and instructed her on how to misrepresent the source of her campaign donations?"

"I don't know if it was her own cash or money she bundled from other supporters. Julie did have some checks from neighbors and friends, all of which were reported. But Mary directed her on how to bypass the state's reporting requirements by largely underreporting cash flowing into her campaign, or ignoring disclosure requirements altogether."

"Ethel, how could they do that?"

"I'm not sure, but it's not difficult to imagine how it could happen. The county and the state are woefully understaffed. Regulators have to keep an eye on thousands of individual council races in a state with over forty million residents and nearly five hundred towns and cities. It is a near impossible task, given the level of funding support needed for truly effective oversight of a system of that size."

"I just don't know what to say, Ethel. I've always believed in the ancient advice that where there's smoke there's fire. It's highly doubtful that funneling money to Julie Phillips, disguised as small cash contributions, was a onetime incident. I didn't press Julie for specifics, but she made it clear that she wasn't the only member currently serving on the city council who was offered financial support by Mary."

"Ethel, you need to speak to Marilyn Williams and Robin Mitchell. Tell them to stop this flood of letters to *The Standard*. I might disagree with Rob Timmons far more frequently than I agree, but I strongly suspect he knows more about Mary

Anderson than he's putting into print as this time. Once again he's likely leading the Ladies of Liberty down a primrose path knowing we'll soon be confronted by a series of ugly truths."

"You're suggesting we just go silent on the whole matter?" Ethel asked, surprised that Alma would back down at any point.

"The discovery of Mr. Pollock and Mr. Harriman, dead and nearly disrobed, is warning enough that we're walking down a blind alley. There is something evil going on here that none of us, at this point, can claim to understand. I can't take pen and paper out of their hands, but this is going to end badly! The more we defend Mary Anderson and her co-conspirators, the worse the final outcome will be. We must put an end to our support right now!"

"Quite a story you put out today!" Eddie barked into his cell phone while driving back to Sausalito late Wednesday afternoon. "You're lucky to have friends in high places."

Rob laughed. "Don't I know it, pal. Who would have ever guessed we hated each other back in elementary school?"

"Good thing our teachers and parents finally convinced us to let bygones be bygones."

"On a more current note, this week's edition turned out to be much better than the one I thought I'd be putting out." Rob was still feeling the rush of excitement that rolled over him Tuesday morning when Eddie had called to report that Pollock and Harriman had floated ashore at Dunphy Park. "So, what's up? Got any more dead bodies washing up along Sausalito's otherwise picturesque waterfront? Perhaps Dexter, Nelson, or both?"

"No, sorry Rob, it's been a slow day for corpses floating in off the bay. But I do want to tell you and Holly about the theory Max Brownstein laid out for me regarding Frick and Frack."

"Sure, we're ready to take a break. Just sent tomorrow's Mill Valley edition off to the printer. Our lead story was about a budget dispute they've been having over the cost of reseeding their Little League fields. Exciting stuff!"

"Sounds like a must-read."

"Very funny! We're up for talking a little murder and mayhem whenever you get here."

"See you in ten."

Holly returned to Rob's office a few minutes later. When she heard that Eddie was on his way to discuss Pollock and Harriman's time with the county's medical examiner, she replied, "I don't know about you, pal, but I'm not discussing a double homicide without a double martini. And as long as we're talking drinks…"

"I wasn't talking drinks…"

"Okay, then when I go around the corner to Venice Gourmet, you want me to pass on picking up a couple of beers for you and Eddie?"

"I didn't say that either. Anyway, it is past five…." Rob said, more than ready to set aside the rest of his work for the following day. "You're right, Holly, that is a good idea."

"I'll be back in ten. Tell Sherlock not to start without me!"

It was five-fifteen by the time Holly returned. Handing Rob and Eddie their beers, she rushed to her office and pulled out a glass, a drink shaker, a bottle of Stoli, and some olives she kept in the fridge for emergencies.

Walking back into Rob's office, Holly fell backwards into the comfortable embrace of Rob's blue couch: the one, and only, piece of furniture in their two-room office that Holly truly appreciated. She took a long slow sip of her martini. "So, what does Max think happened to Laurel and Hardy?"

"Max called them Heckle and Jeckle," Eddie said with a laugh.

"I'm sticking with Frick and Frack," Rob smiled, lifting his beer in a salute to his two close friends.

Eddie detailed the how and why of Max's theory regarding Pollock and Harriman. Then he sat back and gave Rob and Holly a minute to consider the scenario and see if they thought it plausible.

"Holly, if it's okay with you, I'd like to dive in first. No pun intended."

"Go right ahead, Rob. I'm perfectly happy to sit here and sip my martini."

"I think Max's theory is plausible. However, having not gotten the opportunity to interview either of these gentlemen..."

"We've heard!" Eddie and Holly said in unison, then laughed.

"If both of them had enough sense to dress themselves in the morning, they had enough sense to know that only a crazy person jumps into the middle of San Francisco Bay to go for a swim with night approaching," Rob said. "A couple of teens or twenty-somethings are likely to do just about anything, but two older adults, particularly ones local to the area, know that the bay's water is frigid year-round, and hypothermia can occur in surprisingly little time. If they went for a swim in their skivvies, given the time of day and their age, they were on something, as Max suggested, a good deal more powerful than a twelve-year-old Scotch."

"I agree with Rob," Holly said. "These two are not members of the San Francisco Polar Bear Club that does those annual bay swims, during the day of course, between the city's shoreline and Alcatraz Island. These are two older gentlemen in not particularly good shape. I can't imagine someone their age doing anything that foolish without being loopy."

"I sat in on a couple of meetings of both the planning commission and design review board," Rob added. "Neither Pollock nor Harriman struck me as the foolish, whimsical type. Arguably, not as knowledgeable or well-prepared as they should have been. But they were both thoughtful and deliberate despite their limited grasp of the issues."

"I have to agree with Max as well," Eddie said. "I've seen several people hopped up on Ecstasy, and to say that they have taken leave of their senses can be an understatement. Additionally, they're highly suggestive. And if someone poured them a scotch or bourbon laced with Ecstasy, they'd be open to all sorts of crazy suggestions."

"I assume neither corpse showed any signs of violence?" Holly asked.

"Zip. No bruising, no signs they were restrained either. They weren't made to walk the plank. We can be quite sure of that," Eddie added. "If their bodies took any hits when they were in the water, such as colliding with a loose piece of floating wood, banging against some rocks or whatever, that occurred after they died so there was no bruising. Another reason I support Max's theory is that neither body showed any signs of restraint. They were not abducted, thrown into the back of a boat, stripped down to their underwear, and thrown into the bay without their bodies showing signs of a struggle—not to mention the bruising that would occur if they had been constrained. It's simply not plausible. As odd as the scenario might seem, I think Max hit the nail on the head with his theory."

"I imagine whoever arranged for Frick and Frack's evening swim might be the same person who dispatched our late, not so great, mayor," Rob suggested.

"I second that notion," Holly added.

"I've been thinking that too," Eddie said. "It's like this book I've been reading by the guy who killed Pluto."

"Huh?" Holly asked as she raised an eyebrow. "Are you talking about the planet that got demoted to a non-planet, or Mickey Mouse's four-legged friend?"

"Holly," Rob said, "Eddie's always been a big astronomy nut. When we were teens, he wanted to go up on Mount Tam any night we had a meteor shower or a lunar eclipse."

"Guilty as charged," Eddie admitted with a smile. "I'm not sure what it is, but nothing wows me like a star-filled night when you're in a remote place like the Mendocino coast, or how clearly you can see countless stars at the outer edge of the Milky Way when you're in a desolate spot like rural Montana. Anyway, I was reading this book by the American astronomer, Mike Brown, who first suggested that Pluto was not really a planet."

"Yeah, why is that?" Holly asked. "It didn't seem fair to give Pluto the boot."

"It's several things, but the author's main argument is that all the other planets in our solar system, whether a giant like Jupiter or a far more modest planet, like Earth, clear the space of their own orbits. Pluto is too small to do that. In fact, there are several small planets within Pluto's range that are what astronomers call 'Pluto-like objects.'"

"And so…" Holly asked, anxious to get back to the topic of murder.

"Here's the catch. Astronomers have come to recognize that there is a pronounced gravitational pull occurring far beyond Pluto's orbit. Many who have studied this phenomenon think it's our solar system's actual ninth planet because something is causing this gravitational pull of smaller objects that are near Pluto or a good deal farther out. The point is that this object is often thought of as the dark planet because its presence, for now anyway, is only known because of its gravitational effect on all these other objects at the far reaches of our solar system. Much farther from our sun than Pluto."

"You're suggesting there's another player in this whole Mary Anderson scheme?" Rob asked.

"I am. And I feel pretty strongly about this," Eddie said.

"So, you think whoever walloped Anderson on that dark and stormy night also disposed of Harriman and Pollock," Holly said.

"That's my theory," Eddie replied confidently. After a long pull of his beer, Eddie added: "Someone who was in on Anderson's scheme and perhaps got kicked to the curb. For all we know it could be the person who first suggested the scam she's been running these many years. I'm going to take the next couple of days and do a deeper dive into Mary Anderson's banking records. I might be running in circles, but there's a reasonable chance that I'll find my hidden co-conspirator in those records. In a nutshell, we know that Mary Anderson had two people directly tied to her scheme, Harriman and Pollock. But I feel pretty confident that there was at least one more player in their game."

"Someone who got cut off from the cash spigot the three of them shared," Holly smiled. "Makes sense to me."

"What about our two favorite architects, Nelson and Dexter?" Rob asked. "Any chance your mystery partner in crime is one or, perhaps, both of them? We already know they're not playing with clean hands."

"I don't see either of those two as stone-cold killers. Happy to rake in lots of extra money? Absolutely! Glad to benefit from payoffs and bribes? Undoubtedly! But candidates for doing wet work? That would be a stretch. I think Nelson and Dexter are strictly white-collar criminals. Neither of them would be willing to play at the level of Harriman and Pollock's killer. I grant you both it's nothing more than a theory. But I think it works."

"You do what you need to do, Sherlock." Rob said. "All I ask is when you find the killer, let us know first."

"I always do, pal. I always do!"

CHAPTER TWENTY-FOUR

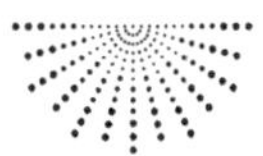

Ethel Landau thought long and hard about calling Rob. Twice she dialed his number from her ancient, but still performing, flip phone while sitting alone in Sausalito's Langendorf Park. This small, secluded spot was a short walk from her home on Pearl Street. She would have called from home, but after the many times her husband had heard her complain about *The Standard*, she didn't want him to think she was losing her mind.

Ethel took one more look around to make certain she was alone. Other than a couple of crows that chattered noisily, she was surrounded only by silence and a gentle breeze.

The Standard's phone rang just once before Holly picked up and energetically announced, "Standard Community Newspapers! How may I direct your call?"

Holly's greeting was a bit officious, Ethel thought, for what she knew was a small community newspaper with a fulltime staff of two. Further evidence, she thought, that its publisher had an exaggerated sense of self-importance. She took a deep breath and said, "This is Ethel Landau. I'd like to speak to Rob Timmons."

It took Holly a moment to catch her breath and reply. "I'll have to put you on hold to see if he's available. Wait one moment, please."

"That's fine."

"What's up?" Rob asked, looking up from his laptop as his hands kept moving quickly across its keyboard.

"Ethel Landau is on the phone for you," Holly said softly. "I wonder what she's up to?"

Rob looked up at the ceiling and sighed. "Why don't I take the call, then I might be able to answer your question. Meanwhile, get back to work."

But Holly stayed put, having no intention of doing anything other than listening to at least Rob's side of the conversation.

"Ethel, how are you? I haven't seen you since the Sausalito Arts Commission's holiday party. What can I do for you?"

There was a brief pause, after which Rob said, "That works for me... I'd be delighted... Then tomorrow morning it is. I'll be at your place at eight."

After a brief pause, Rob said, "Nice speaking to you too. Enjoy the rest of your day."

In less time than it takes to switch on a light, Holly exclaimed, "What was that about?"

"Ethel is 'concerned,' as she put it, that this whole Mary Anderson thing could spiral out of control, whatever that means. She thought it would be, in her words, 'wise if we two met to discuss where this story was going.'"

"What do you make of that?"

"I'm not going to bet the bank on this, but I think Ethel and her ancient leader…"

"Alma Samuels?"

"Correct. I think they know we've caught the tiger by its tail. And if they didn't sense that last week, Frick and Frack washing up at Dunphy Park before dawn on Tuesday doubled their concern that this story is not going to end happily for Mary Anderson and the political machine she left behind."

"In other words," Holly said, "this whole affair could be a huge black eye for the Ladies of Liberty. I suspect they're still a bit gun-shy after their favorite gossip, Warren Bradley, crashed and burned in such spectacular fashion."

"Agreed! They walked into the middle of that one," Rob smiled. "Hopefully, Ethel and Alma are waking up to the fact that just because Mary Anderson supported their sentiments concerning 'undesirable changes to our community,' that did not make her a person of high moral character," Rob explained.

"In Mary Anderson's playbook, all of the long-held beliefs of the Ladies of Liberty that we must 'hold back the tide of future development' evolved into the old scheme of pay-to-play. You could do what you wanted, provided you were willing to pay the right design firms to draw up your plans and get them approved by Anderson's design review board and planning commission. Anderson was never interested in putting a moratorium on new development so much as turning it into her personal cash cow," Holly laughed.

"I suppose you should say, 'One of her cash cows.' It was not about setting standards for equitable governance or controlled development, but it had everything to do with increasing her own political power."

"Looks like the myth Mary Anderson so carefully built is

going to come crashing down. Ironic to think it all started with a landslide!"

Rob shook his head in amazement. "Actually, Holly, it started with whoever argued with Anderson in the hours before the slide. If that slide had never occurred, in one day, or possibly several days, her body would have been discovered by someone she employed to clean her place, or a member of her inner circle wondering why she wasn't answering her phone. Anderson was in no way the isolated senior who goes days or weeks before someone wonders where they might be."

"You're right, Rob. It was Max revealing the fact that she had been struck in the hours before the slide that begged the obvious question: What was her attacker's motive?"

"If I had to guess, I think Anderson cheated her attacker out of his cut of the monthly take. Eddie spoke with two neighbors, both of whom heard a car peeling out of her driveway, and one of whom heard the actual sounds of an argument that Eddie believes, rightfully in our opinion, occurred between Anderson and her mystery guest."

"Find that guest, and you'll almost certainly find her killer," Holly added.

"And you'll probably find the boat captain who suggested Harriman and Pollock go for an evening swim in the bay."

That night, after Micah and Alice had been delighted by a bedtime story their father told of a mouse that roared, Rob retreated to his office to memorialize his thoughts on how the schemes of Mary Anderson quickly unraveled in the days following her death. He sensed, as any good journalist would, that the story he had been chasing over the last two weeks was moving toward a conclusion.

More than any other aspect of Anderson's undoing, Rob kept coming back to Eddie's suggestion about the presence of an unseen player in this small circle of conspirators. He agreed with Eddie that it was most likely one single person who was behind the deaths of Anderson, Harriman, and Pollock. He or she possibly played an important role in creating Mary Anderson's political and financial machine. An individual, who had managed to stay in the shadows, arguably made one terrible misstep in taking Harriman and Pollock out for an evening boat ride, almost certainly drugging them, and then suggesting they go for an evening swim. Before their slaying, the assault on Anderson that led to her death could have been sparked by a number of factors, from a lovers' quarrel to a scheme Anderson was involved in, which had remained, at least until after her death, unrevealed.

But Harriman and Pollock were directly tied to Anderson's control of the city's permitting process for new and renovated construction. In all likelihood, Anderson had suggested to both of them that they submit their names for boards, which they still served upon at the time of their deaths.

Whatever grievance Anderson's killer had with her, he likely had the same grievance with Harriman and Pollock. Eddie went to speak with several of the business owners caught up in Anderson's web to see if they ever dealt with any collector other than her, Pollock or Harriman, and came up empty. Nevertheless, he remained convinced, that her assailant was somehow connected to Anderson's pay or risk her vengeance schemes.

Friday morning at eight, Rob presented himself at Ethel's front door. She had told her husband ten minutes earlier to walk down to The Lighthouse Restaurant for breakfast, knowing he would not return home for an hour or more.

Ethel had coffee and an assortment of teas at the ready. She also put out a selection of breakfast pastries, purchased the night before at the nearby grocery, Mollie Stone's.

They sat on either side of her kitchen's butcher block table. After a brief exchange of pleasantries encompassing the weather and the current ages of Rob's children and Ethel's grandchildren, Ethel came around to the reason she needed to talk with him.

"Yesterday, I shared with Alma Samuels some disturbing information regarding Mary Anderson. It appears that for many years she selected candidates for vacancies on the city council, and then covered the expense of their campaigns by giving them direct cash contributions."

At first Rob couldn't believe what he was hearing. He fought the temptation to jump out of his seat and shout, "WHAT?" The story he had worked for the past weeks was even bigger than he had ever imagined.

"Ethel, that's incredible!" Keeping an even tone, Rob made every effort to control his surprise.

"Incredible was my reaction precisely," Ethel said dispassionately. "I know very little about California's political contribution disclosure requirements, but I have little doubt that what Mary did was a violation of campaign finance laws. If I understand correctly, an individual can give a check or cash donation of any amount, between a single dollar and one hundred dollars, without the candidate needing to report the donor's name and address. I'm sure you know more about these matters than I do."

"If forty people each gave you a check for one hundred dollars, you're only required to report the total amount of money you received. In that example, four thousand dollars would be listed as miscellaneous cash contributions. If all those same people gave you a check for one hundred and one dollars," Rob continued, "you're required to provide the name and address of each donor. I believe the consensus of the state's legislature when they settled on this amount was that people should be able to attend a backyard cookout in support of a candidate and donate a relatively small amount in cash, or personal check, without overly burdensome reporting requirements."

At that point, they both paused for a moment. Ethel knew Rob would have several questions.

"I don't suppose you would like to tell me who shared this information with you?" Rob began.

"I can't violate the confidence in which this information was shared. I can tell you it is from a very well-placed, and highly reliable source. Apparently, Mary Anderson had made a practice of recruiting candidates for the city council and through the use of cash donations, she covered nearly the entire cost of their campaigns. The majority of her chosen candidates came from a pool of board and commission members that she had supported prior to their running for our city council."

Rob could feel the hair on the back of his neck rising. He made a concerted effort to remain calm. "So, these individuals she encouraged to, for example, submit an application for joining the planning or parks commissions or the design review board, provided a class of individuals that would later be considered, if they were interested, in serving on the city council. Perhaps one day becoming the city's vice mayor."

"That's correct," Ethel said.

"I want to be sure I'm understanding you correctly. Mary Anderson would approach John or Jane Doe and say, for example, 'I think you would make an excellent candidate in the upcoming city council race. If you agree to stand for office, I'd be happy to gather cash donations that will cover most, perhaps all, of the cost of your campaign.' Is that a fair summation?"

He waited a moment for Ethel to respond. By her frown, Rob could tell she was not happy about having this meeting or discussing Mary Anderson's illegal behavior. But Ethel Landau, as Rob well knew, was no one's fool. She could not jump halfway into the pool. Having leapt off the diving board, she was committed to following through.

"That's correct, Rob. I want to assure you that I was just as shocked when I heard this as you appear to be now."

"You realize the sum total of this provides a rather dramatic explanation for Mary Anderson's re-nominations to remain as mayor during the city council's annual reorganization. Something that happened only rarely before Mary's tenure. And it apparently assured Mayor Anderson of being able to push through her priorities and full agenda every year."

"I have no idea to what extent her financial support determined the votes other councilmembers cast. I can only agree that considering what she did, it's reasonable to assume she had an undue influence on the votes her fellow councilmembers cast."

"Given the number of years she served on the city council, there's a good chance that every other member serving on our current council was selected and financed by Mary Anderson."

"I think that's a realistic assessment."

"Ethel, I'm grateful to you for sharing all this with me."

"You're a good investigative reporter, Rob. Even if I and others often disagree with your editorial direction regarding growth and change, your competency has never been in question. At least, not by me."

"I appreciate that. Holly and I work hard in the hope that the level of accuracy in our reporting remains high. When you run as many stories as we do in a year, it's all but impossible to get every line correct. The only individuals who get every fact right, every time, are those I call armchair journalists. With the constant pressure of deadlines and attempting to juggle several stories at once, one hundred percent accuracy is a lot harder to achieve in real life than most readers would imagine. That doesn't mean you stop trying to get every aspect of a story correct. And the five Ws, the who, what, when, where, and why, are most important in a story, particularly, a story like this."

Ethel nodded. "Having known you for many years Rob, I believe that you would have kept at this until you revealed every aspect of Mary Anderson's career. At this point, I have only one remaining question: Who killed Mary and why?"

"When and if I have an answer to that question, I'll pick up the phone and tell you myself."

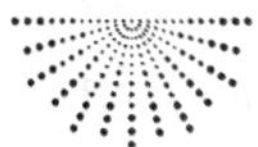

CHAPTER TWENTY-FIVE

After leaving Ethel's cottage, Rob walked down Easterby and made a right onto Bridgeway, heading south toward his office. Within a few blocks he was walking the same route along the waterfront that he takes every morning going from home to his office. He usually enjoyed this walk, but after meeting with Ethel he was too stunned to think about anything other than what he had just heard.

The question running through his mind in an endless loop was simply this: How should he present this story to his readers?

In the years since he had purchased *The Standard* from its founder, George Benton, Rob had developed and reported on several intriguing, and occasionally shocking, stories. The Mary Anderson story was quickly becoming the most interesting of all. The idea that a single politician could so thoroughly dominate the life of one community was something

Rob found amazing. He felt quite certain that in many other places—towns and cities large, small, and in-between—political bosses had seized control of the system, often remaining in power until being voted out, retiring, or, as in the case of Mary Anderson, dying while in office.

Very rarely did the law catch up to them, and rarer still were they successfully prosecuted for their wrongdoing.

Just like Eddie had explained to Rob and Holly two days earlier, there had to be a missing piece to this puzzle: most likely a co-conspirator who argued with Anderson in the hours before the landslide. As Eddie thought, this was likely the same individual who had taken Pollock and Harriman on a one-way trip out on the bay.

Was it the killer's hope that Harriman's and Pollock's bodies would wind up on the Sausalito waterfront? If so, the killer had a knowledge of tide patterns along the Sausalito side of San Francisco Bay that few pleasure craft owners generally possess. Were their deaths a message to other players enjoying a piece of the take from Anderson's scheme? Nelson, Dexter, or possibly others? And, as he, Holly, and Eddie suspected, a player in Anderson's scheme to turn Sausalito merchants and restaurant owners into her own cash machine.

Or was it simply the killer's hope that having died by drowning or hyperthermia, their deaths would cause the maximum amount of shock in a community still reeling from the death of its longtime mayor and the loss of a sterling reputation she had among the majority of residents who followed local news and politics?

As Rob neared his office, he passed, as he did most days, the massive elephants standing guard outside of Vina del Mar Park. He had no idea that just moments before, Eddie had passed that very spot on his way to the Sausalito Yacht Club.

Constructed in 1958 over the abandoned dock of the Sausalito to San Francisco passenger and vehicle ferry, which ended service shortly after the 1937 opening of the Golden Gate Bridge, the creation of the club was described as a labor of love by its earliest members. Over the decades, it became a popular spot: not only for the area's boat owners, but for a long list of community events as well.

Eddie had called ahead and asked if the club's commodore, Eli Warren, would meet him at the club at ten that morning. Eli, a big man with an always pleasant demeanor, greeted Eddie by offering him a coffee and pastry. Eddie, who had finished breakfast two hours earlier, was already hungry and happily accepted Warren's offer.

"So, what can I do for you, Eddie?" the commodore asked.

"I'm just buttoning down some facts on what your log might show for guests here this past Sunday or Monday."

"Do you think Pollock and Harriman might have gone out aboard a boat sailing from here?"

"Eli, this is an active investigation, so I can't discuss any details at this time."

"Sure Eddie, I understand. Well, I wasn't down here at all on Sunday or Monday, so personally I have no idea. But let me get the logbook and you can go through it yourself." Eli walked off, leaving Eddie a few quiet moments to enjoy the view afforded by the club's floor-to-ceiling windows.

Rows of boats, small and big, bobbed gently on the light waves coming in off the bay. The view's effect was, as always, hypnotic. Eddie was reminded of his sailing lessons as a teen under the tutelage of Sean O'Hara. Challenging, but always fun, made more so by their instructor's love of sailing.

A few minutes later, Eli handed Eddie the club's current activity log. "While we make an effort to keep this log accurate and updated, there's always a chance—sometimes a very good chance—that one or more boats went out or returned without being placed in the log. Not too many are missed going out, but coming back in is often overlooked, especially if the member didn't sign in and out of the club or put something on their tab the day they were here. If you don't see what you're looking for under departures, be sure to check the returning boats; you might find the information there."

Eli went off to attend to his chores on a typically busy morning at the club. Eddie removed a pencil from his pocket and lightly used the eraser end to track down each entry. Nothing, outbound or inbound, matched the time parameters Eddie had in mind. Still, he was reasonably certain that Pollock and Harriman began their final journey from here or some point along the Sausalito waterfront. If Eddie could establish where that was and, more importantly, what boat they were on, he believed he had a good chance of unlocking the puzzle of the three deaths he was investigating.

Minutes after Eddie arrived at the Sausalito Yacht Club, Rob walked into his office. Holly had come in shortly after eight. She was nearly an hour into her workday when Rob greeted her.

"So, what did Ethel have to say for herself?" Holly asked immediately. "I hope she didn't waste your time."

"You better sit down, because when I tell you what she told me, you might fall down."

Holly chortled, "From that smile on your face, I guess she spilled some pretty big secrets."

"Bigger and better than anything I could have imagined."

"Something we can use, I hope."

"Absolutely! She has agreed to my quoting her simply as 'a well-placed source.' Additionally, I told her that I was recording our conversation, and on tape she gave her approval as well."

"That's great!" Holly said.

"No, her consent for my recording our conversation was good; what she told me was great!"

Despite facing their final deadline of the week for Saturday's release of the Ross Valley edition, Rob pressed the recorder's play button. As if waking up from a dream, he had to hear it all once again to be sure it was as remarkable as he remembered.

For thirty minutes, Holly sat awestruck by what she heard. Having been present during the recording, Rob was surprised to find that he was even more excited by hearing Ethel on tape. She succinctly described how Mary Anderson recruited and financed candidates who in turn rubberstamped her legislative proposals and her suggested appointees for all city boards and commissions. Essentially, one person had commandeered the levers of power for the entire city.

After hearing the recording, Holly sat stunned. "I'm speechless, Rob—and you've known me long enough to know that doesn't happen very often! She certainly didn't hold back."

"Honestly, I think she was smart to do that. She realized we were closing in on every nasty detail of Mary Anderson's past."

Holly rolled her eyes. "Wow! What do you suppose will happen to Julie Phillips and the other three remaining councilmembers?"

"These are uncharted waters for the two of us, and I suspect for most, if not all, of Sausalito's citizens. I suppose the California Secretary of State's office, with the backing of the governor, will order a new election, perhaps for all five seats on the council at one time. Holly, you have to admit, for what appears to visitors to be a sleepy little picture book town, life in Sausalito is never dull."

Eddie left disappointed. Pollock and Harriman apparently had not departed from the yacht club that Sunday. Not only was there no log entry of departure or return that fit his suspected time frame; members he spoke with were confident in their belief that neither man was at the club on Sunday.

The break in this case he was hoping for would have to come from somewhere else. Eddie headed toward the Madden Boat Yard, which begins opposite the Casa Madrona Hotel and runs parallel to Bridgeway for a distance of over a half mile. A half-dozen piers stretch out far into the bay, providing safe harbor for what seems like a mind-boggling collection of yachts, both motor- and sail-powered craft, each seemingly more impressive than the last. The weather was so perfect that the endless collection of vessels rocking slightly in the gentle swells of a calm day prompted Eddie to take out his phone to capture a photo to share later with Sharon. Both of them had enjoyed strolling along these docks during a countless number of beautiful days. None of those days, he thought, could have been any nicer than this.

As Eddie was passing the storage lockers at the end of Dock B, still looking out at the bay, he nearly collided with his old sailing coach, Sean O'Hara.

"What are you doing here, Eddie? Shouldn't you be out chasing bad guys?" Sean asked with a laugh.

"You're right; I should be getting back to work. I just needed to clear my head and this fresh air feels like the perfect cure."

"Tough day?"

"In my line of work, you have days that are good, bad, and most often, a blend of both."

"Sounds like this is a stay-tuned kind of day for you."

"Did you ever run into Stan Pollack or Lester Harriman around here? I'd sure love to find out how they came to be washed up along the beach at Dunphy Park."

"I vaguely remember meeting one or both of them down here. Perhaps, more than once. If not here, I must have met them at some city function. God only knows we have enough parties and receptions in this town."

"To say the least! Well, I better get back to work. Bad guys to catch and paperwork to complete."

"Good luck, kiddo. I don't doubt you've got a full plate. I'm busy working on my boat. The old joke is really true."

"Which old joke is that?"

"The two happiest days in a boat owner's life: The day you buy your boat and the day you sell your boat."

Eddie watched as Sean walked down the ramp on B Dock. He was surprised by how much Sean seemed to have aged since the time he was his sailing instructor.

Five minutes later he was sitting behind the wheel waiting for the light to change at the corner of Bay Street and Bridgeway. Eddie knew that there were still several pieces missing from the puzzle he was attempting to solve. Suddenly a thought flashed across his mind. He turned left, rather than right, and headed south on Bridgeway. Moments later Eddie was back in Hurricane Gulch driving up the steep hills that brought him back to where this mystery began one rain-soaked night on Sausalito Boulevard.

CHAPTER TWENTY-SIX

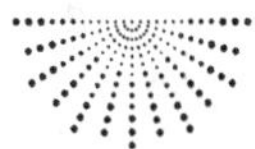

Eddie parked just beyond the driveway for Kayla Fox's home. Stepping out of his car, he noticed directly across from him was the remaining portion of the late mayor's house. Massive blue tarps now covered the gaping holes where the house had been torn in two, a reminder of nature's brute force.

For just a moment Eddie thought about his family being caught in a similar disaster. It was an unthinkable nightmare for him and countless others, who live on these beautiful, but occasionally treacherous hills.

Kayla Fox opened her door after Eddie rung twice, knocked once, and waited patiently. She was dressed in a floral print housecoat and looked just as old as Eddie imagined. Having missed her on his two previous sweeps of homes along the same block as the late mayor's, he was glad that Scott had crossed her path at the Star of the Sea reception following

Anderson's funeral service. But perhaps she could be of additional help.

After a moment of Kayla looking at this thirty-something, tall, handsome man, dressed in a white shirt, dark blue suit, and light blue necktie, Kayla smiled and said, "Eddie Austin, is that you?"

"It is Mrs. Fox," Eddie announced happily.

"What are you doing here?"

"I was hoping you could help me with a few final questions about the night of the slide."

"I'll certainly try. Come in, come in. I'm so happy to see you. But first, you have to give me a few moments to take the tea kettle off the stove. Come sit while I fix us both a cup of tea. Do you take cream, sugar, or both?" Kayla asked as she padded along the wood floor in her slippers, heading toward the kitchen.

"Cream and one teaspoon of sugar, please," Eddie said, realizing his visit would not be quick. Hopefully, however, it would help him find a few badly needed answers.

Stepping into the kitchen, which Eddie assumed looked the same as it had for decades, Kayla pulled a cup and saucer from a cabinet and began pouring cups of tea for both of them. She lifted a plate of chocolate chip cookies and set them down in the middle of the table. If you traded the hot tea for cold lemonade, Eddie thought as he traveled back in time, it was just like he and Rob were teens once again working odd jobs on weekends.

"This is very nice of you, Mrs. Fox."

"It's the least I can do. I'm sure your days are difficult and filled with one or more unpleasant characters. I like to read mysteries, so I know a little about what you must go through as a detective."

Eddie smiled, but said nothing.

"Try one of these homemade cookies."

Eddie took a bite. "They're delicious!"

"Glad to hear you like them. I made a batch twice a week for my husband. They were always his favorites. I now make them just once a week and I'm glad I still do. It makes me think of the poor dear smiling down on me. I certainly wish he was still here."

"Well, I'm glad I'm here to enjoy them with you."

"I'll send you home with some. Now tell me what you're doing. Still working on what happened to poor Mary, I imagine."

"That I am. And I have a couple of questions for you."

"Terrible business. I don't know if I can be of any help, but I'll certainly try."

"When you spoke with Scott Silva at the reception following Mary Anderson's service at Star of the Sea, you shared with him some of what happened on the night of the slide."

"I remember speaking to him. He's a lovely young man. Grew up in Pasadena, he told me."

Impressed and pleased by the elderly woman's memory, Eddie continued. "Yes, I heard that Scott grew up down there. As I understand, you were first awakened by the sound of a loud argument coming from Mary's home at approximately ten-fifteen. You told Scott of hearing two voices, that of a man and another you were sure was Mary's. Did you have any thought as to who the man was that was arguing with her?"

"Well, I did, but I didn't want to say at the time. I thought it sounded like my neighbor, Sean O'Hara. But that didn't really make sense. I know he and Mary had been friends for many years. In fact, I always suspected that at one time they were more than just friends. I just could not imagine them arguing like that."

"I never knew Mary Anderson and Sean O'Hara dated!"

"I always assumed they had, but I never had the courage to ask either one of them if my suspicions were correct. I wasn't going to say anything to Scott about that when I talked to him. I was concerned about protecting Sean's privacy, especially now with all that he's going through."

"What is it he's been going through?"

"The poor man has some terrible cancer. I can't begin to pronounce it, but I know it's very serious. There are some awful diseases out there. Some cancers are easily treatable nowadays; others are just as confounding now as they were decades ago. I should know, my husband had a two-year fight with cancer before I lost him. It was a terrible ordeal!"

"Later that night, after the slide happened and the power had been lost, did you notice if Sean was out on the street trying to see what happened to Mary?"

"I just assumed he was spending the night out."

"Why is that?"

"Because I briefly went out on the deck with my flashlight. As I told Scott when we spoke, I wasn't going to go out with all the mud, rocks, and branches scattered all over the street. I thought that would be very foolish of me. Not to mention the first fire and rescue truck came down the block just a few minutes after I went out on my deck."

"So, you didn't see Sean out there?"

"No. But before I went to bed, I noticed Sean's car wasn't parked in front of his garage."

"He always parked his car outside and not in his garage?"

"Sean has done that for years. Sean is a hoarder. He can't bear to part with all the silly things he had in his garage."

"What kind of things?" Eddie asked with a half-laugh, finding it hard to picture his serious-minded sailing instructor filling a garage with "silly things."

"Oh my, it was quite a collection. A pinball machine, a couple of old arcade games. There was one of those exercise rowing machines. Not to mention things he bought for the love of his life."

"Sean remarried?"

"Heavens, no! I'm talking about that yacht of his. I remember being happy for him because when I awoke after the slide had happened, Sean's car still wasn't on the deck so I knew he must have spent the night out. He didn't need to be out there trying to play the hero. Sean's a good neighbor, but when he's had too much to drink, he's been known to do some foolish things. The night of the slide was not a good time for anyone untrained in rescue work to play the hero. One misstep and he could have gone tumbling down that hillside as well. Then I wouldn't have lost one old neighbor, but two! How sad is that?"

"When do you remember next seeing Sean?"

"The following afternoon. He came over, rang my bell and asked if I was alright and wondered if any of the rocks and trees coming down the hillside had done any damage to the back of my house. The emergency workers were still every-where—up here and down below where most of Mary's house had come to rest. I told him what a terrible night that was, starting with the fact that I heard Mary arguing with someone who actually sounded like him."

"How did he react?"

"Amused, I would say. He told me he had spent the night out with friends."

"Anything else?"

"Yes, Eddie. I remember telling Sean about the sound of screeching tires at ten forty-five."

"How did he react when you told him that?"

"All I remember him saying was, 'Sounds like an awful night.' And then he told me he was glad to have missed it all."

"Had he mentioned anything about where he had been?"

"He just said the weather was so bad he decided to spend the night with a friend he was visiting up in San Rafael. I told him it was a good thing he had. It was a terrible night to be driving."

CHAPTER TWENTY-SEVEN

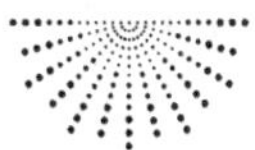

Eddie went to the leasing office for Madden harbor and quickly obtained the exact location of Sean O'Hara's boat. If it had been someone other than Sean as his prime suspect, Eddie would have requested that a deputy accompany him to take Sean in for questioning, but that just seemed overly dramatic. Additionally, he'd rather walk back to his car with Sean uncuffed, which would not be possible if he had requested backup. If anything had gone wrong, including Sean making a break for it and a civilian being injured in the ensuing chase, everyone from his superior officers up to Sheriff Canning would have come down hard on Eddie. But when he had spoken briefly with O'Hara, an hour earlier, Sean looked tired and not in any shape to wrestle with a man half his age, and time and half his weight.

"Twice in one day," Sean said happily when Eddie walked up the gang plank onto his 40-foot motor cruiser. "More questions about that dark and stormy night I suppose," he said with his usual casual demeanor.

"You and I have to talk, Sean."

"About what?"

"The night Mary Anderson died."

"Sure, what can I tell you, pal?"

"Let's start with why you told me that you were home that night and heard a car come screeching off her deck at ten-forty-five, when according to your neighbor you were out the entire night."

"Eddie, you can't believe everything someone as old as Kayla Fox tells you."

"At this point I'm not as worried about her vision or recall as I am about you not being straight with me. Sean, it's time you told me the rest of the story."

Holly and Rob did their best to stay focused until their last edition of the week was completed and transmitted to the printer for its Saturday release.

Shortly before four o'clock, Rob's cellphone started to chirp. On his phone's display was one word, "Eddie."

"Having a good day?" Rob asked.

"Fantastic! You?" Eddie replied.

"If I had to describe my day in one word, I think I'd go with, 'Amazing!'"

"Sounds like the perfect day for the three of us to celebrate! Are you and Holly up for having Friday cocktails at our old hang?"

"Smitty's?" Rob asked while Holly shook her head vigorously in agreement. "You think it's safe to go back there without being overheard?"

"Several hours ago, I found the missing pieces to our little puzzle. And after your last two lead articles in *The Standard* about Mary Anderson's financial shenanigans, the cat's out of the bag regarding her as well. Anyway, I'm ready to celebrate. How about the two of you?"

"You're right about Mary Anderson losing her halo. And it sounds like you've got some big news of your own?"

"That I do, pal!"

"Good! Five o'clock at Smitty's?"

"Absolutely," Eddie replied happily.

"See you there!"

The three of them were unsurprised to see that during the weeks they had stayed away, nothing at the old bar appeared different.

"This place hasn't changed since the three of us were kids and used to peek in here to see what all the excitement was about on Friday and Saturday nights," Rob laughed.

"What we didn't know then is the excitement was about shaking off a long week's work and letting go of any worries you might have. Just enjoying two or three hours with old friends and neighbors," Eddie added.

Smitty's staff was experiencing their usual quiet time. On both Fridays and Saturdays, the real party started after eight and went until closing. During that time, as the expression goes, the joint was jumping.

"It's good to be back," Holly said, lifting her favorite cocktail, a very dry martini with three oversized olives. Rob and Eddie clinked glasses filled to the top with their favorite beer, Guinness dark draught.

"Sounds like you two had a very good day," Eddie said.

"Amazing!" Holly and Rob answered in unison.

"So was mine."

"What made your day so wonderful, copper?" Holly asked.

"I made an arrest in the deaths of Anderson, Harriman, and Pollock."

"Wow! That's huge news," Rob said, putting his hand forward to shake Eddie's. "I'm sure you'll be happy to move that case to the closed file if you get a conviction."

"No need for that. The perpetrator indicated he wants to sign a confession for all three deaths."

"Harriman, Pollack, and Anderson?" Rob asked.

"Yep."

"Well, don't keep it a secret, copper. As they say in the mystery business: Whodunit?" Holly asked, inching closer to the edge of her seat.

"Sean O'Hara."

"O'Hara! Our old sailing instructor?" Rob barked, which was quickly followed by him choking on the Guinness he had been attempting to swallow at the moment he heard Eddie's news.

"Easy pal," Eddie slapped Rob's back. "Believe me, it took me by surprise as well."

"Good gosh! How did you arrive at that conclusion?" Holly asked, obviously more concerned with Eddie's news than Rob's chocking.

"When I realized it had to be Sean O'Hara, I wasn't in the

middle of drinking a beer. I was having tea and cookies with Kayla Fox."

"Fox?" Rob said, nearly chocking a second time."

"Yep! Fox. She's pretty sharp for someone older than Moses," Eddie added with a smile.

"Stop toying with us, Eddie. Details!" Holly demanded.

"Turns out Sean had two things that pushed him over the top. First, and most importantly, he's been stricken by a relatively rare form of cancer, and second, he had a seething resentment, which he kept to himself, of all three of his victims, Anderson, Harriman and Pollock. And in my opinion, not without good reason."

"Go on, Sherlock," Holly urged impatiently.

"Bloody Mary turned Sean down when he approached her for financial support to offset the cost of an experimental treatment in Zurich where they've made some impressive advances in stopping his particular form of cancer."

Holly winced, revealing her aversion to discussing any and all aspects of serious health issues. Particularly unnerving, the incurable kind!

"What kind of cancer is it?" Holly asked hesitantly.

"This is a tricky one, but I'll give it a try," Eddie reached for his notebook. "I'm not sure this is the correct pronunciation: Duodenal Adenocarcinoma. One of the many reasons I could have never gotten through medical school. I doubt I could learn to pronounce two thirds or more of the terrible illnesses that are out there, no less spell them!"

"Yikes!" Rob said. "That is a tongue twister. What the heck is it?"

"It's a form of cancer that grows in the small intestine, and it's a particularly nasty one. Typically, it goes undetected until it's reached a more advanced stage. Let's just say you have to be a class one warrior if you're going to beat the darn thing. And even then, there are no guarantees."

"Sean must have known that Anderson was collecting buckets of money from all over town if he approached her for financial support," Rob noted.

"Bingo! But it goes deeper than that, at least according to what O'Hara explained. He was largely responsible for creating Anderson's shakedown scheme! Apparently, it all began in the early years of her being a member of the city council. She was frustrated with the other four people serving alongside her. Hearing her disappointment with being repeatedly outvoted, O'Hara suggested a plan that would allow Anderson to control the council by selecting her own slate of candidates and most importantly…"

"…providing them with the financial backing needed to run a successful campaign," Rob interrupted, completing Eddie's explanation.

"How the heck did you know that?" Eddie asked.

"I'll tell you my story when you finish your story."

"Okay," Eddie said with a shrug, followed by a smile and a shake of his head. "According to Sean, Mary started small. Her initial targets were mostly restaurants, all of which kicked in one hundred bucks a month. It wasn't long before she had two allies on the council that she had both recruited and funded. That gave her a three-two majority on a five-member board. Once she cleared that hurdle, it was time to consolidate her power. After the following council election, she controlled all five seats: her own, and four other members whom she expected to vote as instructed. Inevitably, there were issues on most meeting agendas where she had no particular interest in the outcome. That, of course, was a good thing. Any council consistently voting five in favor, or five opposed, is going to attract unwanted attention."

"I'm guessing her control of the council was particularly important when it came to her holding onto the mayor's seat. Plus, having candidates she wanted in control of planning and design review," Holly added.

"Exactly. And as Sean explained, once she controlled the council, design review board, and the planning commission, the monthly contributions she expected from every restaurant owner, barkeep, retailer, and anyone else who needed the city's approval to operate unimpeded by a long list of regulations, went up in price. If you need city inspectors to look the other way over violations like incomplete conformance with health and safety regulations, or a dozen other issues, pay their price and you can set your concerns aside. Noise issues, city signage regulations, and so much more."

"Even something as simple as a sign at your entrance about a sale going on like Mike Banks' brother wanted," Rob added.

"Exactly, the bigger the rulebook, the more leverage you have over merchants and service operators, who would prefer that the city be far less strict in code enforcement," Holly added.

"She turned Sausalito into her own pay to play scheme, complete with her personal collectors," Rob grinned.

"Correct," Eddie nodded. "That doesn't mean any or every other municipality is going to play this type of game, but the opportunity to corrupt the system is always there. Put together an extensive rule book and a dishonest player like Sausalito's late mayor and the possibilities are limitless."

"And voters who are too busy with their own lives to pay attention to what games one or more elected officials might be playing is key to getting away with an operation like this year after year," Holly added.

Eddie paused to enjoy his Guinness as Rob encapsulated the day he and Holly had, beginning with Ethel Landau's remarkable disclosures.

"Sounds like all three of us had an unusually great day," Eddie smiled.

"Remarkable I'd say," Rob added. "I can't remember when, or if, I've ever received the kind of info-dump I got from Ethel Landau this morning."

"Why do you suppose she chose to share all those embarrassing details regarding Mary Anderson?" Eddie asked.

"Holly and I wondered about that as well. Our conclusion was she and her longtime bestie, Alma Samuels, preferred to rip the bandage off in one fast move rather than have us tear it off slowly with weeks of ongoing articles filled with increasingly embarrassing disclosures. I'm reasonably sure that Cora Jones clued in Ethel, and possibly others, regarding your visit and the court order you were carrying. They knew it was time to cut bait. Once you were into Anderson's accounts, the myth they had safeguarded of her being a dedicated public servant with clean hands was about to come crashing down."

"You're right, Rob. It says they admire what you do, even if they would prefer that one or more of their colossal missteps could have been buried and forgotten," Eddie observed as he gave a short laugh.

"Not to mention, the Ladies of Liberty's letter writing campaign on Mary Anderson's behalf was certain to continue if Alma and Ethel didn't short-circuit their praise of the dearly departed queen of Sausalito politics," Holly added.

"Despite closing in on one hundred, Alma is still one of the sharpest tools in the shed," Eddie shook his head, awed by that reality. "Here's to the old girl—and to keeping all our marbles as long as she has."

"So, Sean O'Hara needed some quick and significant financial help from what we suspect was the well-stocked vault of Mary Anderson, but she told him to take a hike. Correct?" Holly asked.

"Get that girl a second martini!" Eddie waved Gail over, quickly ordering a second martini and two more beers. "Sean took her for dinner in the city and pleaded his case for her help."

"They weren't lovers, were they?" Rob asked, giving a shudder over the very thought.

"Not according to Sean. They were neighbors and drinking buddies. As he put it, 'Mary apparently trolled different waters, having always had an eye for the ladies.'"

"Oh my God! That was my guess!" Holly said in a breathless rush.

"But he was the one who assaulted her on that dark and stormy night. Correct?" Rob asked.

"Mary not only told him she wasn't going to help, but added dismissively, 'I'm not a charity.' That, as Sean tells it, was what put him over the top. And just as Max imagined, in a moment of rage, Sean swung his right forearm into the left side of Anderson's jaw. POW! She goes down, banging her head on a step, unexpectedly ending her long reign as the wicked queen of Sausalito."

"Wasn't he concerned when she went down so hard?" Rob

asked.

"Not as concerned at that moment as he was outraged over the way she had treated him. As he said, 'She acted like I was a beggar walking in off the street, rather than someone who invented the scheme that brought her over two-decades of power along with a windfall of cash.'"

"What happened then?" Holly asked, sitting at the edge of her chair.

"Sean spent ten of the next fifteen minutes angrily walking around her home, looking in places he thought she might have stashed at least some of her cash."

"The poor guy was not only furious; he was desperate as well," Rob said.

"Did he find any of her cash?" Holly asked.

"He found one envelope with sixty-five hundred dollars in cash, which he kept."

"With the money she was bringing in, there was probably more cash stashed away at her place than that."

"I think you're right, Holly. But Sean, not your typical criminal by any stretch, was getting increasingly anxious to get far away from what he now felt certain was a crime scene.

"When he walked back past the house's entryway, Sean knelt down and saw that Anderson had stopped breathing. He froze for a minute. I don't think he experienced any regret that she was dead, but he definitely hated the thought that he might be caught up in her death. He spent his final minutes inside her home using a cloth napkin to wipe down all the places he could remember having touched and possibly leaving his fingerprints. At least he was aware enough to take that cloth napkin with him."

"O'Hara, of course, had no idea that a few hours later the

entire front part of her house would be destroyed," Rob shook his head in wonder. "No one was going to look for fingerprints in a pile of mud-soaked debris that had to be cleared using a bulldozer. And you said the back bedrooms all came out clean according to the forensics team that went through, correct?"

"Correct Rob, it was clean when our team did their sweep. As for the rest of the house, I cannot imagine a crime scene more completely destroyed than that one."

"So how did his car come to be on Anderson's parking deck? He only lived across the road and one house over."

"Simple! Sean drove up to her place because he was bringing her back from dinner in the city. As he explained, he was not going to do a big ask without inviting her out to dinner. And, he went all out, treating her to Gary Danko in San Francisco near Ghirardelli Square."

"Wow, that is going all out," Rob smiled. "Karin's parents treated us to that place for our anniversary last year. Michelin star and the whole bit. And they have the prices to prove that it's not just a meal, it's an 'experience,'" Rob noted with air quotes, showing his general disdain for restaurant tabs that were higher than the average monthly home mortgage payment.

"By the time they got back it was raining heavily," Eddie continued. "So, Sean drove onto her deck, getting them as close as possible to her front door. He planned on doing his big ask over cake and tea, which Anderson suggested they have back at her place."

"Well, *that* was certainly a lovely evening that ended badly," Holly said with a shake of her head.

"So old Kayla Fox was right when she heard a car bolting off of Anderson's deck later that night," Rob said.

"She was," Eddie smiled. "And I visited Kayla this afternoon. She not only heard that terrible screech at ten forty-five, but she told Sean about it late Sunday afternoon when he came by wanting to talk to her about the slide. He knew she was right about that screech of tires trying to catch traction on Anderson's deck because he noted ten forty-five on his car's dashboard display as he drove off from her place."

"Wow," Rob and Holly said in unison.

"Even though Sean never told Kayla that he had been out Saturday night, she knew he was gone because after the slide occurred, she looked up at his place with her flashlight wondering if he had suffered any damage. She saw that his car wasn't parked in front of his, as she described it, 'junk-filled garage.' In fact, if you remember, when you told me about Scott's conversation with Kayla after Anderson's service, she confirmed the same time that Sean himself told me when I interviewed him as part of my checking with the neighbors to see what they heard or saw that night."

"Wow!" Rob said with a shake of his head. "So, Sean told you ten forty-five in your interview thinking it likely one or more of his neighbors would report hearing that same awful screech that Kayla heard."

"Exactly," Eddie said with a nod. "If it wasn't for dear old Kayla sharing that time with Sean, he would not have known to share that little tidbit with the intention of impressing me that he had spent that rain-soaked night at home watching an old classic movie."

"Where did he go after leaving Anderson's place?" Rob asked.

"Sean drove down San Carlos and parked over near Campbell Hall at the Episcopal Church for a time and thought about his next move. He was so spooked by what had happened to Anderson, he told me, that he couldn't return home, so he drove up to Corte Madera and took a room at the Best Western. Kayla nailed it when she said Sean was out for the night."

"What brought you back up to Sausalito Boulevard to speak to Kayla earlier today?" Holly asked.

"When the three of us talked Wednesday afternoon, we all agreed that beside Anderson, Harriman, and Pollock, it was likely at least one other person was involved in this whole racket that the three of them had going."

"Yes," Holly jumped in. "The gravitational force of the hidden object, as you suggested. Either Harriman or Pollock could have argued with Anderson over their cash haul and struck that fatal blow, but that possibility seemed unlikely once both of them washed up at Dunphy Park."

"There was no guarantee that the boat they boarded went out of Sausalito. Even though the three of us all grew up here, none of us would venture a guess as to how many boats are docked at the piers along the Sausalito waterfront."

"Other than saying well over a hundred, I agree," Holly shrugged.

"I'm with Holly. I don't know either," Rob shrugged.

"The only place where an informal record is kept of boats coming and going is down at the Sausalito Yacht Club, so I went down there this morning to check their log for boats that went out last Sunday. It's not always complete, and not necessarily accurate in the exact time of departure and return, but I figured, nothing ventured, nothing gained," Eddie shrugged.

"And there you saw that Sean O'Hara took his boat out late Sunday afternoon?" Holly asked excitedly.

"Unfortunately, no. I came up empty. After I left there, I

decided to take a little walk to get some fresh air and think about how I could narrow a search from a huge number of boats to a handful of possibilities. One of those boats might have had trace evidence that Harriman or Pollock had been aboard. Finding which one, however, would be like searching for a needle in a haystack. I interviewed over a dozen friends and neighbors who knew Pollock, Harriman, or both. Not one was able to recall either of them talking about plans for a cruise on the bay Sunday afternoon. That would have fit the timeframe Max Brownstein estimated as to when Frick and Frack boarded their one-way cruise to the great beyond."

"Were you thinking about O'Hara as a possible suspect at the time?" Rob asked.

"He was certainly on my radar. After coming up empty at the yacht club, I needed a little fresh air and time to think about my next move. I was walking along the Madden docks and ran into Sean, who tells me that he had been busy cleaning his boat. I don't believe in ignoring a fortunate coincidence. So, after we chat for a bit, Sean hurries off and I head to my car to drive up to headquarters. I was sitting at the light on Bridgeway thinking I need to either strike O'Hara from my list of possibilities or find a reason to give him a much closer look. So, when the light flashed to green, rather than turning north, I turned south and drove up to Kayla's place."

"Were you concerned that O'Hara was on his boat attempting to obliterate any evidence that Harriman and Pollock had been onboard?" Holly asked.

"Not really. By now Sean had many days to do that. Still, when investigators use a chemical like luminol there's a reasonable chance you'll find prints, or a stray hair or two, that will confirm that one or both victims were aboard the vessel regardless of the great cleaning job Sean did. What nearly all of us think of as a thorough cleaning, is not. Of course, with O'Hara giving a full confession, that's now academic.

"I had heard from one of Anderson's other neighbors that Mary and Sean had been more than just good friends in the past. But if we had a twenty-dollar bill for every individual in Sausalito who is rumored to be having an affair with one of their neighbors, the three of us would be sitting on our own pile of cash right now. Plus, I have to hand it to Sean, he was relaxed and matter of fact when I first interviewed him about what he might have seen or heard in the hours before the slide."

"I think when you're reasonably sure that your chances of being around six months from now are slim at best," Rob said, "you're not as concerned as the average person about getting caught."

"Makes sense," Holly nodded.

"At some point you must have asked if he knew what happened to Pollock and Harriman?" Rob asked.

"I did. He just shrugged and said, 'I took them out on an early evening cruise,' and in his words, 'They decided to go for a swim.' He insists that he warned them not to go in the water that late where he would not be able to keep an eye on them if they drifted too far from the boat, but they wouldn't listen. He says he spent several hours looking for them, but had no luck finding them."

"Do you believe him?" Rob said with a half-smile and a raised eyebrow.

"Not for a second. But without toxicity tests back proving the presence of something like Ecstasy, it's academic at this point. He's clearly pessimistic about his chances of being around four to six months from now, particularly having not gotten financial support from Queen Mary for that experimental treatment in Switzerland. Bottom line, I don't think he's all that concerned about facing a long prison term."

"Wow, what a story," Holly shook her head. "What do you think will happen to Sean?"

"Regarding Anderson's death, this is clearly a case of manslaughter," Eddie replied. "Given the racket she was running and her interaction with Harriman, Pollock, and O'Hara, that would probably keep a jury deliberating for days."

Holly raised her glass. "At least one good thing came out of all this. Mary Anderson has earned her own spot in Sausalito's long history of shady characters."

"An honor she richly deserves." Eddie tapped Holly's glass, and then Rob's. "You two are going to have a few busy days getting Anderson's story ready for print."

"Not as busy as you might think, Eddie," Rob said with a smile. "Thanks to the three of us pulling back the curtain on all of Anderson's dirty little deals—along with the assist I got this morning from my new bestie, Ethel Landau—this story will mostly write itself. Pulling back the curtain on Mary Anderson's shady deals is a story I've waited a long time to write. But I have to admit it turned out to be a far bigger scandal than Holly and I imagined."

Just as they finished the last of their second, and final, round of drinks, a hand reached over from behind Rob and grasped his shoulder. Rob turned to find the smiling face of Smitty's managing partner, Pete Francis. "My two favorite reporters and my favorite cop enjoying the quiet in here before our Friday night rush. Hey Gail!" Pete waved her over.

"Yeah, boss?" Gail replied with a smile.

"Whenever these good people show-up, the first round is always on me."

"You don't have to do that," Rob protested.

"I know I don't have to, Rob, I just want to."

"I appreciate the offer, Pete," Eddie said. "But in my job, accepting free anything is frowned upon."

Gail looked at Pete, who shrugged. "No problem at all, Eddie. I completely understand. Gail, when Rob orders a Guinness, bring him two beers. If he wants to give one of those beers to a friend, who might happen to be with him at the time, that's none of my business."

Rob laughed. "Thanks, Pete."

"That story you guys put out on Wednesday was amazing," Pete said. "Got anything good for this coming week?"

"I think you'll be even more amazed with what comes next week," Rob said with a smile.

"I don't doubt I will, Rob," Pete said with a smile. "I don't doubt that in the least."

EPILOGUE

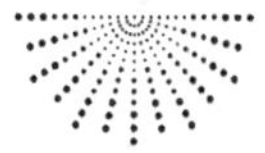

Sean O'Hara never made it to Zurich in search of a cure. He never made it to trial either. The week before he died, Eddie and Rob drove down to Palo Alto to see him at Stanford University Hospital.

O'Hara was pleased and grateful to see his former junior sailors.

"I sure screwed up, but there is one thing I'm glad about," he said while grasping Eddie's hand and showing the hint of a smile. "The fact that Mary died the way she did unraveled all her secrets. That's a lot better than my dying thinking that the town would erect a statue in memory of all her supposed good deeds. I certainly didn't plan on hitting her the way I did. And I didn't expect the result. I just went nuts and when she fell back and struck her head, that was absolutely unplanned. Still, it was well-deserved ending. As for dropping her two errand boys in the water—what did you call them, Rob?"

"Frick and Frack."

"Yeah, Itchy and Scratchy," Sean said, coughing and laughing simultaneously. "Spiking their drinks and suggesting that we all go for a swim was a terrible thing for me to do. I just couldn't stand the idea that they were benefiting from the plan I inspired Anderson to create. Worse still, the idea they would outlive me was intolerable. I can only take comfort in the certainty that I'm leaving the world a better place minus all three of them."

In Sausalito's long history of shocking revelations, from the Gossiping Gourmet to the tragic tale of the Terrifying Teacher, none shook the community like the disclosures surrounding their once powerful mayor.

"How could something like that happen here?" That was the question most commonly overheard in countless conversations in the weeks and months following the investigation's conclusion. There were, of course, many good answers. The majority of residents, new and old, had a hard time believing that with relatively little effort, Mary Anderson was able to take control of the city, and reshape it to serve her needs.

Rob and Holly's stories detailing how Anderson underwrote the campaign expenses of her chosen fellow city councilmembers was picked up by newspapers throughout California, which in turn led to a state-wide reassessment of how elections are monitored to produce honest results. That was reward enough for Rob and Holly's persistence in bringing the story to light.

In disgrace, all four of Anderson's hand-picked city councilmembers resigned. The political neophytes who were elected, three to two-year terms and two to four-year terms in keeping with the traditional city council election cycles, all pledged to work for the betterment of their community and not their personal interests. In turn the new council members requested and received the resignation letters of every member of the design review board and the planning commission. What the new council members lacked in experience they made up for in a shared determination to never again allow one individual to bend the mechanisms of good governance to their own purposes.

Mike Nelson and Andrew Dexter escaped prosecution by agreeing to provide investigators with information detailing their roles in the shakedown of new property owners, but both lost their licenses to practice their profession in California. Rather than leaving the state and re-starting their careers, they decided that early retirement was their best option. A decision some of the local wags dismissed as, "Take the money and run!"

Eddie was given a promotion to Detective Chief Inspector. Better still, he received a fifteen percent pay hike, which allowed him, Sharon, and little Aaron to take their first-ever family vacation to Disneyland. It was not Eddie or Sharon's first choice, but well worth the trip to see their son's wide-eyed wonder when he met several of his favorite Disney characters in person.

Eddie received a letter of congratulations from the dean of Marin County judges, Peter Botherton. Seeing Mary Anderson's legacy left in tatters delighted both Canning and Botherton. They frequently and happily spoke of her spectacular downfall as they marched up and down the fairways of the Presidio Golf Course.

Alma Samuels died in her sleep one week shy of her one hundred and first birthday. She had resigned her post as president of the Ladies of Liberty just two months earlier. Alma never recovered from the stain of Mary Anderson's transgressions. "Let us hope," she said softy into the ear of her successor, Ethel Landau, "Sausalito and its citizens remain vigilant. We must never again succumb to the wicked ways of a malicious mayor."

THE END

NEXT UP!

THE JADED JOURNALIST
(Book 7)

Rob Timmons and Eddie Austin grew up in the small bayside town of Sausalito, California. From their early childhood as sworn enemies to the roots of an enduring relationship that began when they were placed on the same eighth-grade basketball team, Rob and Eddie were destined to be the closest of friends as they grew from teens to college graduates to young married men.

Not long after completing their college studies, Rob became the owner of the *Sausalito Standard* and Eddie joined the Marin County Sheriff's Department. When Holly Cross quits her job as a local restaurant manager, she quickly becomes an indispensable part of Rob's expanding newspaper group, where she discovers her passion for crime-fighting journalism.

All three join forces for the first time to solve the mysterious death of James Armstrong, Rob's former boss and the wealthy publisher of Marin county's only daily newspaper, *The Independent*. Armstrong is driven by the powerful combination of shady investments and misleading journalism. The mystery Rob, Holly, and Eddie need to solve is how and why Armstrong's life as a jaded journalist came to an unexpectedly violent end.